For Sale,
The Serious
Reader in
The Family.

All
Love
From

6/11/77

By Nicholas Delbanco

POSSESSION

William Morrow and Company, Inc.
New York / 1977

Copyright © 1977 by Nicholas Delbanco

All rights reserved. No part of this book may be reproduced or utilized in any form or by any means, electronic or mechanical, including photocopying, recording or by any information storage and retrieval system, without permission in writing from the Publisher. Inquiries should be addressed to William Morrow and Company, Inc., 105 Madison Ave., New York, N. Y. 10016.

Printed in the United States of America.

1   2   3   4   5   6   7   8   9   10

Library of Congress Cataloging in Publication Data

Delbanco, Nicholas.
   Possession.

    I. Title.
PZ4.D34Po   [PS3554.E442]   813'.5'4   76-27834
ISBN 0-688-03146-3

BOOK DESIGN   CARL WEISS

IN

LOVING REMEMBRANCE

OF MY MOTHER

THE AUTHOR wishes to thank John G. McCullough for his generosity in making available the files of the Park-McCullough House. The location of this novel more or less accurately describes the locus of that house—but I wish to make it clear that the characters within it are wholly invented, not real. It would be a poor return for kindness indeed if any reader were to confuse my imaginary Sherbrooke tribe with the residents of the Governor McCullough Mansion, present or past.

BOOK

1

I

IT IS COLD WHERE HE SITS. THE BIG HOUSE TOO IS COLD, BUT THERE at least they can set fires. He has laid in forty cords, just having the fence-lines trimmed and thinning the pines from the hardwood lot by Bailey's. What with fourteen fireplaces, he figures on a cord a week. It has taken better than that—but not a bad winter for snow, not as high as the window where he sits. Still, it has been continual and wet, with a March that set Harriet muttering: why not California, she cried at him, why not Carolina; why not anyplace but this place; what keeps us here this winter?—answer me that.

He made no answer, of course. She never in her life had left and would never leave. You can lie here, Hattie said, all right, I'll grant you that; you can be buried here, we'll all of us be buried here, but what's the matter with a trip to Carolina in the winter? Or maybe New Orleans; you said you loved New Orleans; remember how you said that once?

The cords line the front of the cow barn. He had had them stacked there in October, starting on the north wall, to keep at least that much wind back. It took ten cords to front the wall, and then they'd gone eighty feet east and eighty feet south and west. "Biggest log cabin around," Judah joked. "Now all's we need's the roof."

Still, it is a charmed enclosure, four foot high and four foot wide and trim. They took the deadwood first, from the south. He had walked in November through the space the ash logs left and stood in the center of his heat fort. "Lord, give me one more winter," he would pray. "Lord, grant me one more spring." Early on, he had had the habit of prayer and then, as he grew older, the habit of blasphemy. Now he mixed the two and wasn't sure of the proportion. "God, let the sap in me run."

"You've got no earthly reason," his sister would say, "not to waste this time. Not to visit New Orleans instead of just lying up here."

But lie there he would, or sit, or stand in his diminishing fort. From the window where he sits now, in April, the wood is a single squat line. There is sugar maple left to burn, and locust, and hickory wood. He'd not permitted sugaring this year. He'd lost his sweet tooth anyhow, and the profit wasn't worth the trouble, and he wanted sap in the trees. There'd been bloodletting and leeching enough in his time.

So he cut a hole in the pond ice and took the thousand sugaring taps and funneled them down through the hole. Then he took an awl and pierced the thousand buckets three times through each bucket base. It had been slow work. The buckets stood in the sugarhouse, piled ten high and in one hundred piles. Judah worked the best part of an afternoon each afternoon for a week. He'd take a bucket and upend it and drive the awl through in irregular patterns, working it around so just a drop of solder wouldn't fix the leak. Then, when he'd finished with a pile, he'd set it back in place; his right arm tired easily, even in methodical destruction, and he took his time.

The sugarhouse was empty but for the buckets and vats. The rafters were charred. There were raccoon leavings at his feet. There was wood by the north wall, though not from this year's cutting, and Judah remembered, fifteen years back, working with the men. The vats would bubble, boiling, and they cut the syrup down with fat. They'd string lard across the pans, maybe four inches over, and he never tired of watching how the froth would bubble and accumulate and mount to the fatback, then fall. He tired of nothing, those years. He never tired from the heat or the twenty-four-hour work shifts or the taste of Scotch with syrup. "It sweetens the whiskey," he said. "And it sours the sugar water. Best of both possible worlds."

The sun shines through the twelve-pane window to his left. He turns his face. He shuts one eye, then the other. With one eye shut, his nose appears, and he concentrates on his nose and shifts eyes and watches his nose line shift. Harriet would want him in for drinks.

"You mix," she'd say. "I'll have what you're having."

"I'll have a whiskey," he'd say.

"Not that again," she'd complain. "How about a whiskey sour? Or a sloe gin, maybe. Or a Manhattan; why don't you offer me that?"

"I'm having whiskey," he'd say. "You have whatever you want."

"Make me a Manhattan, please," she'd say. "I can't abide whiskey straight. And one single maraschino cherry, for the taste."

He would have started already, since he knew the game. He would select the bottles and glasses from the sideboard, measuring her measures with deliberation.

"Your health," he'd offer.

"Your health."

There would be ice in the ice bucket, and maraschino cherries on the silver tray. Judah watches his nose, in the sun's light, go incorporeal; he rearranges his scarf. It is cold at noon in the Toy House where he sits, and he has been attending to details since dawn. He fills the house. It isn't over-windy, but he's brought his sheep rug and has some deciding to do. He thinks himself a hunter; his first quarry is his wife. His sister can wait on her maraschino cherries, and he can wait on scotch.

There are ways and ways, Judah says to himself. *All kinds of ways. There's fifteen ways to skin a cat, and the whole town's studying. I got to bait them with the prettiest. There's lawcourts, come to that. I got to know what I'm about before I get untracked on it; I got to bait my traps.*

This satisfies him, seemingly; he puts his hand on his belly, then thigh. The chair he rises from is a child's settee. His grandfather had built the Toy House for his children, and his children's children and their friends. It is a replica of the Big House, scaled one to ten or so, but without the fireplaces. His grandfather had caused equivalent gables and the clock tower to be erected; the Toy House, in faithful imitation, is built of white clapboard and slate. Since it is four stories high, the Toy House is tall enough for Judah to stand at his ease. He measures six foot two in socks; now he has boots on, and stretches. His right hand touches the upstairs landing, outside of what was Maggie's room; he puts his middle finger on the place where she would sleep.

Past seventy, Judah Porteous Sherbrooke started counting. Numbers were a code he'd cracked when young. But six is consistently six, and six times six is thirty-six even if you have to multiply it, in 1976, by six again before you get what six could buy when he, Judah, had been born. He'd lived through the nation's lean times. But there'd been good enough to eat, and more than enough to go round, and they'd shipped apples and eggs and beef down in the club car to his cousins in New York. He wondered if his Wall Street cousins sold the apples on Wall Street. And though he's joked for years that what this country needs is a good five-cent cigar, it isn't such a joke by now; it makes him sad to think that nothing worth the buying costs a nickel now. They've wiped the silver, he would say, off of that buffalo's ass.

Still, eighteen times eighteen is six times three times six times three; he can verify that. And a square has equal sides, though the sides can be eighty feet or eighteen inches, and the sides enclose equivalent angles, each of them ninety degrees. He remembers license plate numbers long past his memory for cars, or who was driving them, or why. He remembers telephone numbers long past the time when friends or his son or mistresses relinquished the numbers and left. He dials the numbers sometimes, just to keep his hand in, and because there is direct dialing now. He has social security numbers and license plates and bank account numbers, and he knows them all by heart—they are the ciphers of integrity. He ranks and musters digits with the certainty things fit.

Elvirah Hayes had been the daytime operator, and Lucy Gregory had been the nighttime operator. In the town's small switchboard, they needed no one else. He knew that they had apple trees, so Judah sent them pears. Sometimes he'd asked Lucy to call Elvirah up for him and inquire how she was feeling that night.

"Who wants to know?" she would ask.

"Your devoted admirer," Judah would say, courteous. "J. P. Sherbrooke calling."

"Why, Mr. Sherbrooke," she would say. "How very kind of you to ask. I might have known it was you. You and your consideration that would call."

"Considerateness, Ellie."

Her voice would flute and twitter, scaling octaves when not on the job. He imagined that the earphones kept her orderly; she was white-haired and raised Dalmatian dogs.

"Yes. I'm fine. It's a lovely summer breeze this evening. It's kind of you to ask."

But the operators now are long-distance operators, or information operators out of Burlington, and their voices are not voices he can trust. He sometimes calls to verify his memory of numbers, and then they are rude.

"If you knew the number, why'd you ask it?" one of them complained. "We don't have all that much time."

He remembers the confirmation of Maggie's legs by the lilt of her four final numbers; six-eight-two-three was the rhythm she assumed, somehow, when walking. Numbers segment the visible world—and he knows each fraction of his thousand acres, the way the fields and woodlots edge. Once, at the Rutland State Fair, he had guessed the quantity of pickles in a pickle barrel to the nearest five; once, at a Bulova Watch Display, he guessed the grains of sand in an hourglass to the nearest hundred and won the Bulova Watch. "Them that's got shall get," he said. "And them that's not shall lose"—and handed the trinket to Maggie and told her to hoard time.

Harriet sounds the gong. The gong is electric but she can set the frequency of beats; there is a bronze fist that beats on the gong shield. The gong hangs on the porch in summer, and Judah remembers hearing it from the far pastures, summoning him. "The sun is past the yardarm," his father would say. "It's time to wet the decks." His father had booked passage on the *Titanic*'s maiden voyage, but had had to cancel three days previous. He talked about his brush with death; he had, his wife complained, a sailor's tongue.

They say a baby whale's six foot by fourteen foot. And when it feeds it swallows waves entirely, then spits the salt part back. The pasture where he lay would swarm with bees, there would be timothy grass and butterflies above him, and the gong's call would sound, in the windy distance, like the call of mourning doves. Sometimes he packed a picnic lunch (his first horse was an Appaloosa and stood fourteen hands; he remembers that, and the Morgan's height, but not the horses' names) and rode to Shaftsbury Hollow or followed the Walloomsack six miles down to Eagle's Bridge. *The whole damn town's a salt lick,* he pronounces to himself. *An edifying sight, my Lord, all those tongues in that one groove. The central declivity, yes my Lord, and envy up the shaft. They've salted down the crops and laid the region waste and are proud of it into the bargain; they plant mothballs now and concrete. They print brochures.*

He shuffles to the Toy House door. It opens out; he opens it and finds the April noontime warm; he locks and padlocks the door. There are lilac bushes to his right, and a tamarack tree; the tamarack is starting to bud. He crosses the gravel driveway and starts for the Big House porch, stepping on the flagstones, sidestepping mud. He brings both feet together on a single stone, gathering himself. He uses his left foot first. His boots are Dunham boots, with enough tread on them still to pick up all the mud he'd need to bank a ditch, and enough mud anyway to set Harriet screaming. They are eyelet boots and trouble to unlace, and he hopes to keep them on and therefore takes care with the path. His familiar chorus starts on the seventh step; he rests and waits it out.

All things begin again, young woman. Maggie. Except this one thing, since it never stops. Judah, her heart's on her sleeve. She's coming back to you. Then Ian. There's venality abounding on your chosen plot.

He holds his hand up, imperious. There is wind in the lilac branches, and the gong has worked itself to equanimity. He mounts the Big House porch.

"Finney"—he had used the garage phone—"I need advice."

"Shoot. What can I do you for, Jude?"

"Advice," he said. "The sort that takes some thinking out. Not just off the top of your head."

"I'm with you," Lawyer Finney said. "I'm listening."

He leaned against the pony cart. There were swallow's nests above him; the floor was cement.

"Let's say about snowing," he said. "Let's say it doesn't snow by night and there's no snow on the ground. Then you wake up in the morning and it still ain't snowing but there's snow two inches deep. Well," he rested his left hand on the black telephone. He coiled the cord. "It's circumstantial, ain't it, that it snowed? I mean that's circumstantial evidence, correct?"

"Correct," Finney said. "That's a valid inference."

"How valid?" Judah asked.

"About as good," said Finney, "as the one that says the sun will rise. No law to prove it, I suppose, but nothing likely to disprove it, and the inference is sound enough to argue on."

"In front of any judge?" he asked.

Finney ruminated. "In front of any I know."

"So no one's got to see the snow to prove that it's been snowing?"

"They got to see the *ground* snow," Finney said. "They don't have to witness the act."

"And what if they was in another county when it snowed?"

There was noise on the line.

"You're losing me, Jude. I don't follow."

The cord was split. He saw the wires through the rubber casing. He put his finger on the rubber's oval separation.

"What if they arrive too late, I mean, to witness it? What if the ground's gone muddy again, and there's no snow left excepting only that I tell them it's been snowing?"

"Hearsay evidence," said Finney. "Inadmissible in court."

"I thank you," Judah finished. "For your trouble."

"No trouble," Finney said. "That'll be a triple Scotch and one ham sandwich, thank you."

"Sold," he said. "Don't be a stranger"—and hung up as he always did, without saying good-bye. He needed no permission now, nor to define his action before acting; he knew Finney's license-plate number, but not the make and model of that blue sedan. They called cars after Indians who never got to drive.

He had kept Maggie's car washed. It would gleam, awaiting her, and Judah made certain the chrome was polished and the insides always scrubbed and swept. The Packard sat like some gray chariot with dark blue trim in the first of the four garages; they had been stables once. There was the pony cart she called a carriage and, at the farther bay, his truck. She left him messages. She would write CLEAN ME on his fender, in the dust and grime that settled there daily, or "Darling, don't forget. At eight o'clock the Clarks are coming" and leave it on the seat. When she left him, the first time—taking Ian to New York, saying that their son required adequate companions— Maggie drew a heart around the handle of his door. He found it two days later: her farewell.

Judah had been drinking. He clattered off the porch, into sun that made him squint. His mouth felt like the bottom of a birdcage, and by the time he reached the truck he was sweating; by the time he backed it out he had the shakes. It was July. The maples had a sleeve of dirt; the bottom of their leaves were brown with his raised dust. So he got out and pumped up some water and drank that. He soaked his red bandana, rolled it tight and tied it to his neck. He turned back to the truck and raised his hand to the door handle and saw it shaped an arrow in the center of a heart she'd drawn. He bent his head. He blinked and cleared it, but her fingered message remained. He could not rub it out. When he sold the truck the next day on a trade-in for a Ford it was there still: fading, smudged, a Valentine with the rust-pitted chrome latch to prove where his heart cracked.

Names stick. You name a thing and that's the shape it takes. His grandfather's father, writing from California (where he had gone to practice law and ended up railway-rich, crony to Frémont and Stanford, sporting fur and silver in the oil portrait Judah possessed), had named it the "Big House." "I have always maintained and will maintain," he had written, in his copious left-handed scrawl, "that Vermont is where you find it. It being the true repose of the soul, whereas this Western paradise delights the flesh exceedingly. . . ." (Judah has the letters. He has every laundry slip or bill his ancestors received. They were pack rats, all of them, and assiduous in accumulation and transaction-proud, and he sometimes thinks he and Hattie keep the mansion just for storage space.) "Yet we return from Babylon, though these be not waters to weep near but praise, and in our private coach. I wish the latest architect arrived from London to be retained, and on a seemly retainer, and set to building us a Big House against our soon retirement. I dream in these long nights of family and friends from school-time clustered to the several hearths, of faces flushed with God's exertion, not the demon rum. I wish the house to be of a pleasing façade, yet modest and particular in shape. The fashion of the time is ornament, a glass to grandeur. We shall be fashionable only in restraint."

Nothing Judah knows of Daniel Sherbrooke accorded with restraint; his Vermont kin called him "Peacock" and were by turns awed and outraged. The construction process took six years. Sherbrooke was meticulous, in his transcontinental planning, with that attention to detail that others might call foppery but he called the key to success. He had the final edict—from problems of the siting to patterns on the parquet floors—but never traveled east.

An architect was hired and brought from New York. "I wish him godly yet mondial," the magnate wrote, "and with some comprehension of our local stuffs." The architect built scale models of country houses in the Cotswolds and shipped them, according to Sherbrooke's instructions, west. "Peacock's" answering letters were hortatory in praise, but each would mention some new wing that "might be an addition of some slight extent. The House needs be a meeting house; I must have space wherein to meditate upon the narrow final confine we each of us inhabit. How but by contrast might the shelter prove exemplary, or give the wearied Spirit its adequate reach?" Therefore porticos were added, and capes and trellised walkways and even, at Sherbrooke's insistence, a widow's walk.

"Though two-hundred miles from the ocean," he wrote, "and sheltered from its ceaseless surge nor yet an intimate of watr'y Storm, I wish continual reminder of the souls gone screaming down in shipswrack, and their proper attendants on shore. These are Pleasing Protuberances, with grillwork that testifies to the vigilance of watchers in God's sight. I wish the widow's walk to circumnavigate the cupola and gables and be of ornamental iron painted black."

His pious architectural injunctions, over time, produced the largest and most lavish house in the region. It looks, Maggie said, like that prose style of his; it's crazy and ornate and out of date. Neighbors dubbed it "Peacock's Palace" or "Sherbrooke's Showplace" or "Pride's Peak." But the first name became the final name and it was always now, only, the Big House. There are stained-glass windows in the tower, and a ballroom on the second floor, and a central staircase that is foot for foot the equal of the central staircase in Mark Hopkins's house. It was a Victorian extravaganza, with four flights of servants' quarters that Judah's father leveled, raising a greenhouse instead. Maggie had tended the greenhouse in winter, loving the luxuriant heat and the blossom profusion where she stood—except for that one width of glass—waist-deep in the wet snow.

The magnate, Peacock Sherbrooke—for that name also stuck— journeyed east in 1869 to die in his ancestral town and newly finished house. His voyage had been arduous, even with a private railway car, and a retinue that filled it of servants and daughters and his son-in-law.

"He suffered from a wasting fever," the daughter, Anne-Maria, later wrote, "but was upright and upstanding to the last. What wrack it was I dare not think nor scarcely venture to recall that caused the sweat to form upon his noble brow. That brow that frowned at each Malignity but lightened at the footfall of some loving tread. So pity us that watched him and could prove no comfort save the Book we read from and provided him to touch and kiss continually, which is of course Sufficing comfort & abundant recompense. We brought him from the station on a kind of litter, bundled as an infant 'gainst the Weathers importuning, and the rude shocks I myself was sensible of administered by these towpaths and oxtrails they call roads. My father as you amply know was a man of Sunny Countenance & also Determination & Will, but I who witnessed saw the Sun bedimmed by Rain clouds that started from his staring Eyes, as Will & Can may sometimes war, the latter in ascendance. We attained the gate at four forty-seven o'clock; I remember he queried the Time.

"There were Workmen standing, caps in hand, on either side of the Approach drive, nor did he stint to thank them with the hand that shook with palsy but was firm in Christ's close Grip. We made a grim

Processional, that had thought to be a glad. For when the Big House rose before us, starting from the Maple trees that garlanded it greenly, and in the gathring dusk that was the Dark he voyaged through before —I do profess it—entering Eternal & Absolute Light, then did he raise himself upon an elbow and commend His works. I thought for an instant my father intended the architect's accomplishment, not Christ's, and turned to make some slight rejoinder, adding praise to praise, but saw his dear Orbs sightless and His Head cast back. His last words were—as sevrally attested—'I pronounce myself content.'"

II

AT NINE O'CLOCK THAT MORNING, HE'D LEFT THE TOY HOUSE FOR a haircut—and it was a question-ordeal.
"Long time no see, Mr. Sherbrooke." The barber welcomed him.
"A pleasure to see you again."
"Yes. Well. I've been busy," Judah said. He took the middle chair.
"At what, if you don't mind my asking?"
"I don't mind," Judah said—but did: minded the habit of gossip, minded the ease of the flourish and that oversize napkin he had in his collar, minded the man's name even, Vito. There was a *Playboy* calendar tucked in the mirror's edge and not even registering April but only a girl on a picnic blanket, serving up herself instead of food.
"Nice weather we've been having," Vito said.
He held to his silence.
"They say it'll snow later on."
"Yes."
"We've had too much snow already," Vito said.
The room was empty. There were three chairs.
"Well, what'll it be?" Vito asked. He snapped his scissors like a soldier coming to attention, and his left hand brandished the comb.
"Just trim," said Judah and leaned back and shut his eyes. He remembered the shave and manicure jobs of his youth. When they took you in the back room there it meant you bought whatever they were selling, and there was whiskey in the lotion bottles and those *Playboy* calendars had been the actual thing.
"A head of hair like this," said Vito. "Makes you look like nobody's been caring for you. Not enough, Mr. Sherbrooke."
He opened his right eye. The white shocks about his ears were on his shoulders now. The thatch had been reduced. Vito bustled behind him, snipping. He hoped the family was well; he had seen Miss Harriet inside the Stitches Shoppe. He hoped the town would vote against the trailer ordinance and vote for one with teeth; there were so many regulations it was a wonder you could spit in your own driveway now, not to mention what he had to do with towels to keep his license, so why not rules for trailers, Vito asked. Would you believe the wetting down and washing down and mopping up he had to go through; would you care for hair spray, sir?

"I would not," Judah said.

Next he walked to Morrisey's and ordered ten pounds of sirloin from the startled grocer.

"What's that, Jude?" Morrisey asked.

"Ten pounds," he said. "And wrap it in one chunk."

"You've got a party?"

"I got a black eye, Alex, from walking in that door. I'm told that sirloin steak is just the thing."

"All right." Morrisey busied himself with his apron. "Ten pounds. Ain't sure I got that much in sirloin."

"You used to," Judah said.

"Not in one slice. Never."

"Well, cut it up then. And get me some camembert cheese."

"Yes, *sir.*" Morrisey was mock-deferential to cover his true deference. "Yes sir. Coming right up."

"And have them send it,"—Judah turned. "But not before lunchtime, hear? Not till three o'clock."

So he who had been geared for some brave battle never got to fight. He'd donned his manhood's armor at fifteen. It had been imperceptible—that lengthening, that deepening, that equality with field hands who came to hay or pick. Judah had been slow to learn but slower at forgetting what he learned. He had been, he decided, witless then—a giant of a rich boy who would rather be a farmer because lock, stock, and barrel it had been his father's farm. So he selected that. He filled out. And once the line was crossed you couldn't backtrack or beg for delay; you didn't notice, passing it, that there'd been a rite of passage but the world about you noticed and the upstairs maid would giggle and the field hands tell a different sort of joke.

And because it had been owned outright he was able to keep what he owned. "I'm a gentleman farmer," he'd say. "But not much of a gentleman and nothing of a farmer." He'd fought a holding battle and held on. And there has been some work to that—what with supermarkets and tax laws changing and roads going up on the land's perimeter, and his neighbors selling out to make motels. He's held on sixty years. He'd bought machinery on time. But he'd mortgaged nothing else and had outlasted every payment anyway and everything was his. So his life's work was play. It was offhand work for him, as banking had been offhand work the years he'd joined the bank. And the wars went on without him, and the stock-market fortunes won or lost were not his fortunes, really, and the cities prospered or went bankrupt somewhere else. It has been sentry play. He's stood and watched while men went out with bayonets or wire clippers and came back triumphant or dead. They come back on their comrade's shoulders or in their comrade's arms or sometimes slung in a fireman's carry, already a carcass and stiffened to that boomerang position. And he, who was weaker than no man and stronger than most that he'd fought, stayed home to mind the store. He minded the storekeeper's wives. He fought holding actions only, while the world was in that flux about him that they called progress-advance. Then (sudden as the one before, he crossed a second line that said: this far, no farther, boy, take off your chain-mail suit) it had been retreat. Then his manhood fled him, and sentry play was too much work for one winded codger with a heart condition. Then he laid his armor by and shriveled into winter clothes and shivered cutting wood and stacking it and shivered feeling it burn.

He hears a plane. He hunts it, squinting, and sees it off by Woodford Valley, catching the light. He'd been in a small plane once that Will Carr owned, and they flew to Brattleboro and circled back above his land and he recognized it all, has aereal maps, knows which way the drainage ran and where the sumac needed clearing, knew all of it in March because the leaves were down and nothing green or growing yet, but Will insists come August he'd be baffled. Can't tell the Green Mountains from the Alps or Burma, he says, and Judah wonders why he doesn't say the Allegheny Mountains or the Adirondacks, come to that. "You've been there, I suppose," he asks, "flown over them?" and Will says no, not really; it's imagination really; I can see them clear as that set of foothills, and points—imagination, Judah thinks, is like that hand, shaking in the plane's clatter, what looks like a Boy Scout ring on Will's fourth finger where the wedding band would be, and some vague comparison tricked up as truth that lies: imagination was his ruin when he dreamed he'd found success.

Forgetfulness: he covets it, has lived the life most men would live, has kept some standards up with what—depending on the mood of it—he'd call stubbornness or mulishness or fierce determination; which standards has he kept, he asks himself, and comes up with a wash of words all meaning *loyal,* all meaning *live with what they call fidelity or die;* he's sidestepped less than most. The record players now boast high fidelity; there's a marching band that marches right across the living room. And when the violin comes at you it comes from a speaker where you don't hear flutes; he'd even swear he tells the left hand from the right hand when the radio plays piano music, when he goes to shut it off. He uses his right hand. In Arab countries, he's heard, you use one hand for eating and one for wiping shit, and it's a mortal insult to offer the wrong hand to a stranger; he thinks *fidelity is eating-hand, and high-fidelity is shit.*

His sister stands in the hall. She is wearing a thick-ribbed red sweater and the shawl he gave her; she has been preparing, she announces, to wind the gong again.
"Shut that door," Harriet says. "It's cold."
"It ain't that bad," Judah says.
"The radio says snow," she says.
"Yes. Well."
"It's almost May. It's cold."
"April seventh," he tells her. "We've got the mud-thaw this morning."
"You had a haircut," she says. "Is that the reason why you didn't hear the gong?"
"I heard it," Judah says.
"Where were you then? There's owls in the chimney. There's some sort of bird, and I don't dare to light the fire; there's feathers all over the logs."
"Just put a piece of bread down there to catch the drippings," he jokes. "What are you having to drink?"
They are in the study, and Judah pours his own. Swirling her Manhattan, he reflects he's made it past the front parlor with boots on. He has left his blanket by the door.
"You don't believe me? About the birds?"
"I believe you. But there's wire on that chimney, sister. Here's to your health."
"*Your* health. Where were you at this morning you didn't hear the gong?"
"I heard it," Judah says. "I didn't mean to worry you. I'll have them look at the chimneys. You'll want a second cherry."

"To sweeten my disposition"—Harriet makes their old joke.
"Sweets to the sweet," he says, and spoons the cherry for her. Its stem stains his fingernail pink.
"I thank you, brother," Harriet says. She is eighty-one, five years his senior, and accepts such gallantry as due her age, not her sex.
"What did *you* do this morning?" he asks. He is anxious to appease her because of his plan; he has intended to announce their supper's surprise at lunch.
She lists telephone calls. She tells him, again, of her trouble with the owls. She embarks upon the history of Ida Simmons's health, and who was right with regard to sciatica, and which shots helped and for how long; she, Harriet, knows there is no remedy for sciatica, but doesn't want to tell poor Ida or be the bearer of discouraging news, since Lord knows Ida's discouraged enough, considering her boy's arrest and the way they're building the highway right past her pantry door.
Trailblaze. That was it, Judah thinks. That was the name of his horse. Fourteen hands high and not a hand that wasn't dappled musculature, fat with proper feeding and curried till he shone. The two of them would take the day and spend it on the land's far reaches, hunting or mending fence or just on the say-so, asleep. The herd was Ayreshire then. Now the herd, or what is left of it, is Holstein and nowhere as particular to keep. He would wander off on Trailblaze and dream dreams of glory, of clearing out the German trenches with his hunting knife between his teeth and fists full of dynamite. Calvin Coolidge came to supper and Judah dreamed of Washington, of catching Walter Johnson or catching Cobb at the plate. He brought trout back in abundance from the river's shallows, and the smell of trout in his tote bag—mingled with the sweet pine air, and Trailblaze, and his saddle's wet leather—is a smell he still can smell.
"Maggie called," Harriet says.
"What?"
"She called."
"Who? When?"
"Margaret Coburn," Harriet says, redeeming her error by blushing. "At eleven o'clock. She wants to ask you not to just join the Library committee, but to be its honorary chairman. That's what she said."
"Tell her no," Judah says.
"She wanted to ask you herself."

"Tell her no. Tell her not ever to call."

It's a kind of blasphemy, he tells himself, *this naming. One time it sings on your tongue. One time it's the loveliest name that ever was invented, and for the loveliest woman, and now it's for some blue-haired bitch who's drumming up attendance for her rummage sale. Take that name in your mouths again,* he threatened the men at the bar, *and I'll take all your teeth out and the tongues that do the licking: I'll split you back to front and leave you for the crows to clean. They're used to filth in their beaks*—he finished, his excitement spent—*and then this chemic crap.* The men looked down at their drinks. They bent their heads, suppliant.

"She meant no harm," Harriet says.

"And she'll accomplish none."

"I meant no harm by it either."

"No. Likely not. But her name is Mrs. Coburn. You remember that."

He shod his horse himself. He said I put my own shoes on, and Trailblaze does a sight more walking. The pines were antler-stripped; he marked them where he fished.

Coincidence, he tells himself. *There's nothing coincident now. She reads my mail. She washes out the toilet bowl and found the letter-scraps and because the ink ran wants to provoke me to telling. Hattie's a cat and the cat's got her tongue and we're none of us telling catty Hattie what's-a-mattie,"* he jingles, vengeful, remembering. *Wife, you should be here.*

Ten days before, he had had Finney come to see him in the Toy House. Hattie had been at the village Library. The two men jostled, fitting in the children's space.

"Well, what did she say?" Judah asked.

"It's cold in here. You ought to have a heater, Jude."

"You think so?"

"Yes. I'm freezing."

"What did you tell Margaret?" he asked.

Finney rubbed his hands together. His breath steamed. "She said she'll come."

Judah sat. His legs gave out.

"She said she'll write you that it's her idea to come."

He sat on his hands. There was a rising motion in his chest. He heaved and breathed and his stomach plummeted the way it did in a high-speed elevator.

"I told her what you told me to," the lawyer said. "That you're dying anytime now and she'd better come up soon."

"When?"

"Soon. That's all I can tell you."

"How soon?"

Finney rolled his shoulders, anxious. He adjusted his coat. There was mucus hanging from one nostril; he inhaled it back.

"How did she sound?" Judah asked.

The drop descended. "The same. She sounded like she always does. I'm freezing, Jude."

"You've said that."

Finney sniffed.

"Well this is what I want," said Judah. "Tear up everything you've got. I want three wills." His chest had cleared. He felt Finney's heat too palpable beside him and spoke quickly: "Hattie's got her portion and she'll keep it like before. The same with the charity leavings. But everything else. One will says it's Margaret's; one will says it's Ian's, and one will says fifty-fifty—got that? Otherwise I'll die without and they can fight over it."

"Judah?" Finney said.

"What?"

"I've got to ask this. You might call me legally bound."

"It's nothing illegal. Now is it?"

"No. Not till you've got witnesses and signed. But morally I'm bound . . ."

"Ask away, then."

"It's not a simple question to . . ."

Judah interrupted him. "Being of sound mind and body," he said. "It's my decision. Mine."

"When I said that you were dying, was it true?"

"What?"

"That you were dying," Finney repeated.

"Yes, but"—Judah considered this, shifting where he'd settled, and he released his hands.

"But what?"

"But nothing. But not"—and he lowered his lid ponderously and winked—"right away."

"So it's a lie," Finney said.

"You knew that."

"Not for certain."

"We none of us can know for mortal certain . . ."

"You made me make a fool of . . ."

But Judah brushed this aside. He raised his hand to his ear, palm out. "I want three testaments. That's what I want from your office. And make each of them binding," he warned. "Come to supper when she comes and bring them with you. I'll sign one."

"You could save us all some trouble," Finney began.

"No. Being of sound mind and body, that's what I hereby declare."

"And Ian?"

"Write him. Say the same."

"I don't have an address."

"Use the last one you've got," Judah said. "Just write him. Just don't call."

He stood and loomed above his friend but hireling, and extracted a linen handkerchief. It was red, and folded into eighths. "Here," Judah said. "Don't say I didn't give you proper compensation. Wipe your nose."

There is a pianola by the wall. There are music rolls that feature John Philip Sousa, and music from New Orleans. Maggie played the piano, and there had been a Steinway grand where the pianola stands. She schooled him to love music then. He would sit at her stool's edge, behind her and a little to the left, watching how she tucked her lip in at the louder parts, astonished at her foot's thumping agility. He marveled how she knew the notes, or when to turn the page. She played with a rapt stillness and the hands of earthly angels but, to hear her tell it, out of time. He complimented her. "Rachmaninoff," he said, "himself couldn't play that piece better. Artur Schnabel's no more musical than you."

"Oh, Jude," she said. "You're sweet. You're a dear to say so. But you've got a tin ear, darling, and don't think I don't know. Or you're lying to make me feel proud. Or taking the intention for the deed.' "

"No," he protested. "Not so. I love to watch you play."

"But not to *listen,* darling, and that's the point of it."
"All right," he said. "To listen, then."
"That was Chopin," Maggie said. She touched his sleeve. "This is a mazurka."
She'd smile and choose another sheet and play some other melody that set his heart delighting. When she left him, the last time, he had had the piano hauled out to the far woods. He'd learned Rachmaninoff's name and Artur Schnabel's name to please her, and had taken her to concerts in Boston and New York (with Maggie on his right-hand side, in silk, freshened and excited by the trip, her gloved hands emulating the prodigious maestro's hands; they'd have box seats always, and she'd press her elbows in with pleasure, clapping, while he watched her breasts expand) and maybe she was right and maybe he did have wax in his ear and maybe couldn't change. She'd said so, at the end. He'd change, he told her—not begging, but announcing change. "You simply can't do it," she said.
So he doused the sounding board with kerosene and filled the works with paper and wrapped the legs in soaked rags. It had made a pleasing conflagration, and the strings snapped, jangling; then he bought a pianola and played that instead.

There is the portrait of Daniel Sherbrooke and a portrait, done from memory, of Peacock's wife. Most of the Big House paintings, Judah knows, had been ordered in bulk lot from a supplier in London; the supplier had charged less for the paintings than frames. "Send us suitable emoluments," Peacock wrote, "of scenes both lively and Inspiring. Also I require Floral arrangements and Pictures of apples and two or three scenes from the Hunt. Like unto the fox is man when pursued by conscience-demons in the guise of that goodly baying Pack. We must sniff out Iniquity, e'en to Reynard's lair."
What friends they have are gone from them, are dead or estranged or fled south. There was a time the Big House seemed continually lit, and he'd find strangers sleeping in the corridor, or come back from the river to find dinner set for twenty and the cook in a desperate bustle; they'd kept cooks then, and maids, and he wondered whether Ian thought the world was mostly peopled with guests and maids and drunks.
There are cameos above the mantel, and scrimshaw cornucopias;

there is a wooden sailor with a carved ivory leg. "Who says we can't change?" Judah complains now to Harriet. "Who said so; answer me that?"

He had been avid of instruction, wanting to learn the mazurka and how it differed from the waltz or valse polonaise. He had turned the pages for her, not reading the notes really, but reading the toss of her head. Her teeth would bite her lower lip and he would chew his, hard.

He had been to see the doctor three weeks before. There he got his plan. Dr. Wiggins's face was grave; he listened routinely to Judah but was listening to some heart-speech the stethoscope would translate, attentive only to that.

"Fred, let me ask you something," Judah said.

"Yes."

"We've been friends for thirty years."

"Mm-m."

"Thirty-five years, nearly."

"I came here," Dr. Wiggins said, "in 1945. After the Pacific."

But Judah was not tempted into reminiscence; he watched the man across from him unblinkingly.

"Fred, what are my chances?"

"We're none of us gambling men, Jude."

"Let's put it bluntly. Am I sick?"

The doctor looked down at his charts. He tapped a ruler on his desk; he snapped a tongue depressor. "Bluntly, no."

"But could I be?"

"Of course. You've got that heart of yours."

"Could I say I was dying?"

"You could. In that respect. But not because your doctor says so."

"I wouldn't quote you," Judah said.

"In that respect," said Wiggins, "none of us can win this gamble. Specially with angina. We're every human being bound to lose this bet."

"I wasn't asking *if* I'll die. I'm asking when."

Dr. Wiggins looked at his hands. They were pink from scrubbing and his nails had perfect crescent moons.

"Jude, I can't tell you. It's a guessing game. You might go on five years, fifteen; you might go on till they haul you out kicking and it would take a freight train even then; you might, with that heart of yours, wake up anytime now and . . ."

He spread his hands. They were expressive. They told Judah everything he needed to tell Hattie, and what to tell his lawyer to notify his wife. Leaving the office, later, he had practiced the gesture—he spread his hands and fingers and then let the fingers contract.

His sister had been handsome once. Or so he can remember thinking, and so Macallister had thought, and Jamie Pearson and the widower Powers from Manchester. Judah hopes she's taken pleasure when it had been available to take. For now she sits behind the lamp, a raw-boned woman, fretting. She'd never married—though Jamie Pearson had proposed, and maybe the widower Powers; she'd called Jamie Pearson's proposal more a proposition than an offer.

"What's the difference," Judah asked. "What kind of distinction is that?"

"It's a business proposal," she said. "That's what's the difference. He wants to marry the family, not me."

And she was right, he'd thought; Pearson drank too much and couldn't hold his drink and therefore couldn't hold his bank job without some influence. But half a catch is better than none, he had said, even if the catch is half-baked—or, like Jamie, boiled.

"Brother, you insult me," she had said.

"That's not my intention."

"And the family," Harriet said. "You insult them too."

So she married history and took an uncle or grandfather to bed each night. She'd wedded herself to their letters and daybooks and bills. She kept file boxes in her room with all the clippings she could find, right down to Daniel Sherbrooke's second cousin, Augustus Cobb. There was a great-great-uncle lost at sea. He'd gone down with a clipper ship off Hatteras, "cut off untimly," a survivor wrote, "in his manhood's beauteous prime." Judah knew she mourned him, and he joked she got more heat from Tommy Sherbrooke drowned at sea than from her hot-water bottle. He wished her joy of ancestors, he said. He wished her joy and consolation in the watches of the night.

"You misunderstand me," she said.

"I don't. Not at all."

"You're doing it a'purpose. You're being a tease, like you always were."

She said the same of Samuel Powers, who had lineage to equal theirs and therefore wasn't in it for that kind of gain. His mother was a Colonial Dame; his father's forefathers fought with Ethan Allen in Bennington and then at Saratoga Springs. But he scarcely knew their names and didn't care when she told him, and didn't read the articles she left for him to read.

"They were probably bastards," he said. "Thirteen percent of all the children born then were born out of wedlock. That's something to think about, when you get to thinking."

Judah agreed. "The man's got sense," he said to Harriet. "And knows how to laugh besides."

"It's no laughing matter," she said. She disdained, she said, that easy-earned disdain. There were certain things worth taking seriously, if you took them on at all, and why should she trust Powers to take her on as family—with his sham family sense? What kind of proof could he give her that he honored what she stood for if he didn't also honor where she stood?

"You're talking circles," Judah said. "You just don't want to leave my house for his."

"Why should I?" She had smiled at him, coquettish. "It's a losing trade."

So Harriet aged and solidified, her flesh gone gray. She used the word "spinster" first. "I'm your spinster sister," she would say—deflecting the pain of it, lifting her hands—"I'm the one who's here to mind the store."

Jamie Pearson drank until his liver quit. Samuel Powers married a redhead from Connecticut, who was divorced and had two children. They flew to Nassau for their honeymoon, and the plane went down. Doc Macallister was long since dead, and Harriet, surviving, put their obituary notices in her Miscellany file.

Now he completes his drink. He opens the dining room door; his sister precedes him, bustling. He pulls her chair for her, then pushes it forward to the table with her slight added burden. Harriet has been thin then plump then fleshy then corpulent and now is thin again. She ate bonbons and maraschino cherries in quantity, but gained no further weight. She would have candied apples and chocolate and peanut brittle in abundance when the children of the village trooped by for Hallowe'en. Still, she is fond of children and had done her part in raising his. "Oh my," Harriet exclaimed—as each child shuffled in, sack at the ready, big-eyed behind masks—"oh my, but we look marvelous tonight. Tell me what you want to do for trick or treat."

Then the cowboys would yodel or brandish their capguns, and Cinderellas curtsied and twirled. Pocahontas war-whooped while she filled her sack, and the princes bowed. The Big House porch would be lamplit—Judah had rigged jack-o'-lanterns—and they played movie tiptoe-music on the pianola. In the rare lulls, when no one was there or could be heard coming, Harriet would clasp her hands and bow her head and say, "My, my, brother, but they do exhaust me so."

"It's worth it," he said.

"I'm sure. I do know that. The girl with all the crinolines—the Scarlett O'Hara, I think she said she was—is Maisie Petersen. Isn't it *astonishing?*"

"This is her last year in that kind of outfit," he said.

"How much she's grown," Harriet marveled. "How quickly she'll be beautiful."

"It happens," Judah said.

None, no single one of them would ever equal Margaret. She was and always will be his definition of grace. She had hair the color of wheat and cornflower eyes and legs that made him think of jumping deer. He knew these images were cheap but prized them nonetheless, and he would not call her simply blond and blue-eyed and long-legged. Nor does she wither and age in his recollection; she is always twenty-three, running flat-out from the house to meet him, arms pumping, feet raising dust. He would have trouble focusing, from all those hours in the sun, and she would be a doubled, jerky vision, wearing a white dress. He cracked two ribs from squeezing her, but there was no fragility in her athlete's stride. Or thirty-three, her long hair longer but not one whit altered in its coloration (though later he'd suspected and accused her of hair dye and she'd said so what, so what if I just touch it up?) nor five pounds fatter to mark the decade, standing at the staircase, dressed, lifting her dress to come down. His sons had kicked her belly out, and he saw her nine months pregnant, a moon. An arm or leg would shove at her, and he'd watch her bunch and ripple; she'd smooth her skin and rearrange herself on the three extra pillows in bed.

"My goodness, we're near out of chocolate," Harriet said. The children scratched at the door. He fed them peanut brittle. She returned from the kitchen with a basket full of chocolate kisses, and packs of Hershey bars.

"You'll like this," she told Davy Crockett. "Only don't murder raccoons."

"I didn't do it, ma'am," he said.

"But would you? Would you do it if you had the chance?"

"I got three woodchucks," he announced. "With just my .22."

"You'd do it," she lamented. "All those dear creatures slaughtered for the sake of coonskin caps."

"I got it for my birthday," Davy Crockett said. "It was give me. Trick or treat."

Judah found the Toy House windows soaped on mischief night. Once someone stuck a toothpick in the doorbell, and he had to pull the wiring apart. Maggie, their last Hallowe'en, had dressed herself up as a witch and climbed the maple by the porch and lowered buckets of cooked but cold spaghetti on a rope. She cackled it was worms and raised and lowered the bucket, intoning: "Take, take, take." He himself had worn a beard. He had strapped on the sword that belonged to Ulysses Grant. He had watched her in the tree's fork, luminescent, ghostly, and known she'd go for good the next time gone.

III

"If you please," Harriet says, "I could use a touch more Sanka."
"What?" She has startled him. "What?"
"If you please," she repeats, and slides her cup toward him.
"I'm sleepy," Judah says. "I must have been about asleep."
"You've not been all too talkative," she says. "I can guarantee that."
"How much?" he asks. He lifts the pot and poises it.
"Half a cup," Harriet says. "Not even."
"Say when," Judah says.
"When."
There is liquid on her saucer. He sloshes her saucer's leavings into his own empty cup.
"Sugar?" he asks.
"Yes."
He measures out one teaspoon of sugar. She does the serving if they meet for breakfast, and he does the serving for midday meals, and she serves at night.
"I thank you."
"Yes. I must have been sleeping," he says.
They drank from goblets once, and chalices. Judah called it drinking glass, but Margaret insisted they were goblets: chalices replete with her love draught for him, and her desire's potion. That had been early on. They had clicked their drinking glasses, no matter from what distance and every time they drank.
His sister's voice is shrill. "You missed the gong," she said. "You took ever so long with the whiskey. You dawdled with the servings and shouldn't wonder it's late."
He clears his head. He shakes it.
"Sanka doesn't trouble me," she says. "You know that, I expect. I could have a third cup if I wanted and still not have it worry me. I could drink the pot."
"You know what I've been thinking?" Judah asked.
"No. What?"
"Been thinking that I'll take her back."
He had not known how to say it till he said it, had not known how it sounded but knows it for the truth.
"Her. Who?"

"My wife. Margaret Sherbrooke," he says. He looks at Harriet. She colors.

"That's a name," she says, "I thought we'd agreed not to use."

"Yes."

"Well?"

"It's over." Judah stands. "The agreement. I'll take her back when she comes."

"What makes you think she's coming? What makes you so certain?" she asks.

"She'll come," he pronounces. "She'll be here by suppertime. She's making the four-forty bus."

Hattie slides her spoon along the cup rim. "I mention Maggie Coburn and you just about bite my head off."

"That's different. It isn't the same." He edges his chair to the table again. "I got to get some rest."

Jude, he tells himself. *Keep on. You've done it up properly now. Seven lean years and sixty-nine fat.* He shuts the dining room door behind him and makes for the hall, performing his familiar calculus. *There's a monkey,* he says to himself, *that hangs from a branch by both hands. It drops and you have to shoot it, and it's ten feet from the ground. Where do you take aim to be sure of hitting; you ask the doctor that.*

The wind carries snow. It slaps at the Big House shutters and he hears it in the chimney, humming. He would wet his finger, sometimes, and circle a glass rim till it sang; the wet wind rimes the chimney now with that low single note. There had been omens enough. He'd known when Lawyer Finney said, "It's five years since you seen her, Jude. And seven since she left. You want to change the will?" He'd known when he opened the Toy House again and sat where she had sat. She was an invading presence—not five years lost or seven gone but only absent—and he acquiesced.

So when the letter came two mornings back, he had not been surprised. He'd recognized her script at once, and the mocking deference with which she'd written, "J. P. Sherbrooke, Esq." There'd not been a return address, though the postmark was Grand Central Station, New York. She'd used a three-cent and a ten-cent stamp that said: "It all depends on ZIP code," and showed planes and mail trucks and trains. The stamp was multicolored and, Judah decided, expensive to print. The plane and parcels were yellow, and the train was two shades of red, and there was green earth and a rainbow and blue-fringed clouds and stars. She'd used no zip code on her letter, nor even his post office box, but only "The Big House."

He imagines her in Grand Central Station. He, Judah, has been there once. There were waiting rooms and information booths and so many shops he'd figured you could stay there for a year and not need anything you couldn't find on one of the two levels. You could get your hair cut and buy clothes and food and records and magazines and jewelry, and anytime you wanted you could take a train to anywhere you wanted, getting out.

He had sliced the letter open, using his right hand. It was folded twice. He smoothed and held the letter, waiting for his breath to quiet. She had used blue ink. Her hand had been the last hand on this paper, he reflected, and she'd tongued the envelope flap. (He knows the sequence, has watched her at it often: she'd tear the stamp from the stamp roll, not abiding by the perforation and tearing half a head off presidents, then licking the stamp and placing it at the envelope's middle or edge—"The glue won't work," she'd say. "And it's probably toxic besides.")

"*Jude*"—he peered at the inscription. "*I've been away. I'll keep this letter short because I'm not even certain you'll read it.*" He switched on the light. He'd burned her early letters, or flushed them down the toilet, torn into eighths, unread. He'd refused the ones with postage due or written on them: Return to Sender. Addressee Unknown. "*But there are things I have to tell you and things I have to ask. You'd do me a kindness to let me visit soon. As you know, I'm not one to beg. I'll be at the Bus Station Wednesday, arriving at 4:40 from New York. If you meet the Greyhound Bus, I'll be happy to get off; if not, I'll understand. Or try to. But try to meet the bus, for auld sake's sake if nothing else; it's more than auld acquaintance surely, and we owe each other that. I'll not ask again. I'll travel on to Rutland and not bother you ever again. But I come in hopes the love I bear you and you said you bore me once will alter your opinion of the proper way to act. I hope this finds you well. Meg.*"

He takes her signature for omen, and the tense of "bear." He takes her memory of his catchphrase, "For auld acquaintance sake," and the fact she's used blue ink. It had been Monday. Monday was the day they married, and Wednesday the day they first met. He took the letter to the Toy House and held it to the light—his plan's first fruition—repeatedly, rereading. He can tell it off now by heart. *"I'm not, as you know, one to beg."* There are flurries. The wind turns southerly—so he takes the snow's measure and knows that it won't amount.

Ian was a breech birth and had been difficult. Maggie had contractions Friday night, and they pulled Ian out of her Sunday at dawn. She had been able to sleep the first night, but neither of them slept on Saturday, and she had pinched and staked and bound up tomatoes all that morning. He had admired her. She was his stork who had swallowed the bundle, his half-moon waxing, his sweet sugar beet.

"Don't overdo it," Judah warned.

"I'm not overdoing it. I'm doing it, that's all."

"There are others to do it," he said. "You're in pain."

"I *want* to do it." She was flushed with bending and had a sweat moustache.

"Well, do what you want," Judah said.

"Yes."

"I worry about it, that's all."

"You mustn't worry, darling. I need some distraction. I'll stop when it's time to stop. Promise."

He wondered what would signal her that it was time to stop. He put his hand on her stomach and felt the muscle band.

"It's the world's biggest girdle," she said.

"The tightest, leastways," he acknowledged.

"Oh, darling," she sucked down breath. "Jude. Judah P. It hurts me so much when it hurts."

He took the green twine from her, and the scissors. She exhaled. There were tears at her eyes' edges. Later, eating or staking tomatoes, assaulted by their pungency, he would remember her nest-building bravado and the way she'd distributed weight. She smiled at him, hands on her hips.

"It's better now. It doesn't hurt."

"It's kicking up a storm in there," Judah said.

"Mm-mn. He's got an elephant kick."
"A football player," Judah said.
"A whole team really. Quadruplets."
"He's got the hiccoughs," she said. "He's doing a double-flip back dive, complete with a half gainer. He loves the swimming pool."
"I'd just as soon he swam on out," Judah said. "Into this visible world."

When he came he came out kicking. There were forceps creases on his head. Judah heard her (down the hall, he could swear to it, and one flight up and behind every door, bellowing for him, her husband, telling the doctors there'd been some mistake, some impossible mistake, and she could go home now, go quickly, he, Judah, was waiting and besides they'd put in for adoption, she wasn't up to delivery at this particular moment, at any moment in particular, he'd endow a hospital, and where was the promise they'd made her, where the nurses' estimate that it'd be over by noon, then three, then seven, then eleven, and where was the gas they'd sworn to give, where the injections, where was relief since she'd rather be shot) screaming: "Please! Please stop it. Please."

They'd stopped it at dawn. There was silence. Ian Daniel Sherbrooke weighed eight pounds. He was a solemn baby and lay and mused for hours, wide awake. He cried without rage, dutifully, flailing his arms and legs as if he knew that's how an infant cried—but out of choice, not instinct, and not out of need. His mouth distended later in what was more a rictus than a grin. Judah, watching, crooning, knew that things were serious and life no laughing matter—no matter how much Maggie laughed. She had had true levity scooped out of her with that first wailing son—as if all body blitheness was ejected with the afterbirth. Sheep eat the afterbirth. Sows eat their farrow, given the chance. There are nutrients a mother needs—and loses when she loses the fetal food sack. He'd have taken that placenta gladly, had they thought to offer it. He'd have separated out the waste lines from the veins for humor and for body blitheness, and made Maggie swallow them back.

Judah ascends. There is an elevator, but he avoids that. His father had had the elevator shaft constructed as a courtesy for his, Judah's, mother when she was bedridden with phlebitis. The machinery is in the attic, underneath the cupola. The oak cube fits four. His mother would wheel herself in and close the door, heaving it to. He, Judah, went with her. It was a moving closet and it rose and fell interminably, and the oak took on her illness-stench. When she was sick with more than phlebitis and too weak to manage the doors—too weak, even, for the buttons, though he put her hand on the buttons and helped push—she nonetheless insisted on a ride each morning. She had had nurses, of course. But she depended on him—"Only Judah's strong enough," she'd say. "He'll help. He'll lift me out of this forsaken place."

So he would wheel her on the tour. The halls were long and broad, and he grew adept at maneuvering through rooms. She'd point to bedspreads or curtains that needed cleaning and say: "You must note that. Inform Maria. It's outrageous what has happened to the house. She'll sweep that carpet by tomorrow or you must have her dismissed."

"Yes, mother," he would say.

"Don't *yes* me like that, Judah, or take me for a fool. I know what's happening here. There's laxness and corruption and I know what made that bedspread dirty. Just don't take me for an idiot. Maria cleans that carpet or hey-presto out she goes."

Maria swept the carpet. She had been engaged to Harry Jackson who left his job in the lumber mill and died in the ditches of France. She used that expression "died in the ditches of France" to amplify her grief, and Judah would watch wide-eyed while she bent to unlace herself, sobbing. He had been seventeen. His mother, the next morning, accepted the guest room carpet and curtains but pointed to the hanging lamp; the lamp needed polish, she said.

So he manipulated her through storage closets and in bathrooms and along the upstairs landing. "Oh, Judah," she would say. "Don't suffer this indignity. I wouldn't wish indignity like this on my worst enemy. They take me for an idiot, forgetting I have eyes. Forgetting I know what I know."

He held his breath in the oak box. The front and back were doors. The doors alternated on each floor, so he could wheel his mother in and stand behind her, hands on the chair rim, and then continue pushing in the same direction. She hated to be pulled. When she had made the full inspection and he had consigned her again to her room ("Don't leave me, Judah," she would say. "Don't forget your mother.

And don't take me for an idiot or think I don't have eyes."), he'd jump the steps three at a time and run to the stables and saddle up and drop his head to the horse's flank and breathe deeply, cinching the girth. He would inhale the smell of oats and animal expectancy, and swing himself up and be at a canter by the time he'd cleared the barn.

So when his mother died he closed the elevator up. They inspect the hoist rig every six months and keep the wires oiled. Margaret had made him love her in the elevator once. "I want to screw," she whispered, "in every single nook and cranny of this whole huge house. In each individual bed. In every place you've ever been, my darling, or anyone has ever been. There. Here." She'd rubbed against the dust-dulled walls and brought them to a sheen.

His son is his principal rival, he knows now. Ian slept with Maggie when he had scarlet fever and again when he had mumps. Judah watched the two mirroring heads. His son's hair had been lank with sweat, and Maggie'd tied her hair back tightly, so they seemed twin skulls. Ian was the reason Maggie left. He was her final lover, Judah thought—calling daily maybe, meeting in secret, sharing her apartment if he traveled through New York.

"I'll not abandon him," she'd said.
"Sooner or later you've got to."
"No. It's hard enough . . ." Her voice trailed off.
"What?"
"Nothing."
"Finish what you started," Judah said.
"It's nothing to talk about."
"Maybe."
"Ian is my only son," she said. "I think of the other one always. That's as it should be and I'm not complaining but I won't lose Ian also; he's worth the world to me and you'd better know it, Jude."
"I do."
"Not really. Not deep down."
"He's my son too."
"Then how could you imagine that I'd let him live here, hating it? There's a world outside. There's high school to finish and college

to go to and maybe law school and medical school and all sorts of people to meet. Musicians. Women. Politicians."

"Whoever," he said.

"And the point is Ian's young and needs to get outside these walls. He's a prisoner here, Jude. You can't invite the world."

"If he's lonely . . ."

"I know: let's invite some friends up for the weekend. That's not it. He's got to learn that town means more than Rockefeller Center and a boat trip on the Hudson and the Empire State Building. He wants to go and I'm taking him with me since it's what you'd call abandonment to stay."

Judah'd tried to warn her she should leave Ian alone. He'd tried to make it clear: the Sherbrooke place was world enough for father and it ought to hold their son. Go and you take yourself with you, he'd said; that's the problem with departure; leave but don't ever come back.

"It is important," Peacock wrote, "that the stair-crest be sufficing Broad. I wish it an Adequate Perch for the announcement of Arrivals, and jollity to be surveyed by the Provider thereof. But let there be currents of air. Else the pestilential vapors will foregather and Accumulate, as unwelcome guests at such festivity, and rioting in secret in that lecherous Enclosure soon make their noxious Presence known, infecting the Host unawares. There shall be Crimson Carpeting in the center of each stair-tread, which Carpet is to be secured by a Brass Rail."

He takes his time on the steps. He leads with his right foot, then brings his left up even, then leads again. He stays on the right of the stair treads, on the wood not carpet, and keeps his hand on the banister. He had bounded up them once. He hadn't counted then, and his energy was boundless, and the muscles of his calf had been coiled steel. That was Maggie's phrase for them: coiled steel.

"Good afternoon," he calls to Harriet.

"Good afternoon." She is at the elevator, watching.

"Sleep well."

"Yes. Thank you."

She too takes an afternoon nap. "Give Tommy Sherbrooke my best," he says.

"I'll rest," she says. "I've had two cups of Sanka but it doesn't trouble me."

"That's good," he says. "You've got a clear conscience. That's good."

"I hope I'm not the only one." She squints up at him, meaningful. "I hope *your* conscience is clear."

"As mud," he says. "As always. Happy dreams."

"I'm not reproachful, brother. I wouldn't want you to think that."

"Then don't reproach me, Hattie." He takes the seventh step.

"I can see," she calls to him, "that the subject is closed."

"What subject?"

"You know very well. The one you raised."

"No. Which?"

"The subject of your wife," she ventures. "Margaret."

"I raised so many subjects," Judah turns again. "You're right. Yes. The subject's closed, and she'll be here on the four-forty bus. Yes, my conscience is clear."

"Good afternoon. Happy dreams."

"And when the subject opens it's her and me who'll open it. All right?"

"I'm not reproachful. Don't think that."

"I don't," he concludes. "I don't think about it at all."

But that's not true, he tells himself, ascending. *Reproachfulness is all we think of. And recrimination. There's nothing openhanded in the house.*

He turns at the crest of the stairs. His plan is ready, his traps set. He will call them together about him and announce: he'd little time left, the doctor had warned, and could wake up any morning dead and he wants to settle accounts. Let no one say he left them owing, or that he's been ungenerous. His room is the fourth on the right. The door is ajar, and the bedside reading lamp switched on. Their room had been the fourth on the left, at the hall's opposite extension, facing south. There is one leather chair in his room, an oil lamp, a water pitcher and a drinking glass. There are gilt-framed standing photographs of Ian on the bedside table, but nothing on the walls. The walls are green. The floor is parquet squares. There are no rugs or curtains nor any ornamentation beyond the ornamental moldings and the single sleigh bed. The bed is gray, its tracery is green. He shucks his clothes laboriously and pulls his bedclothes from the closet and sits on the bed, facing out. He is winded. He sets the alarm for three-thirty, in case. Snow eddies past, so lightly that he thinks (what with the lamp's reflected glare, and the day's chill reckoning, and whiskey) it is his eyes.

He shuts his eyes. The snow continues. He puts his right hand out and touches the window and, opening his eyes again, tracks the pane's frost filigree. His fingertips stick to the glass. He has forsaken creature comforts, embracing this severance. He runs his index finger across his gums and teeth. When she forsook their plush sunlit room, he thinks now, leaning back, she had perhaps relinquished comfort also. She was in Grand Central Station, maybe, with only the price of a stamp.

There is the afternoon to get through. There had been the night before and Monday night and this Wednesday's dawn and morning and noon since her letter arrived. There have been the ten days since Finney told him she'd come. Judah summons control. He has till four-forty and he can change his mind. He thinks of not meeting the bus but driving to Rutland instead. She would look out the window and scan the station and wait two minutes and maybe get out and ask at the desk if there were any messages for her, Mrs. Margaret Sherbrooke, and the attendant would say no, and she would ask if he were certain, and he'd riffle through his note pad and check the board again. "No ma'am, nothing," he'd say and she'd turn and exit and climb back to the bus (it would be raining, maybe, or the snow would still be there, and just a single taxi and pickup truck that she'd know at a glance wasn't his. Still she'd check, irresolute, because he might have bought a pickup truck again, because he might have taken a taxi—but knowing all the time, knowing from the instant of arrival, and while the driver cut the motor and opened the doors, he, Judah, wouldn't dream of showing and what had she been dreaming of, and why?)

The tarmac was wet. There would be slush on her window. The air would have that bone chill that passes for spring in Vermont. ("You know what they say," he'd said. "About the weather here. Nine months of winter and three months of poor sledding." She, Margaret, had laughed but later insisted he take her to New Orleans . . .) She'd inhale the bus exhaust and shiver and sit down again. The bus would shudder, starting. "Next express stop, Rutland," the attendant would announce. "Arriving at 5:52. All aboard for Rutland, please. Next stop."

So there she'd be, abandoned, who had abandoned him once. She'd watch the roadside markers and the motels and restaurants in town. Some of them were familiar and some were unfamiliar, and she'd note them with disconsolate intensity, not ever expecting to see them again. There would be half-glimpses of a car or face she thought she knew, but soon the bus would gain momentum in the gathering half-dark. It would run through the gearbox and clatter out onto 7 and she'd settle back. She was marked "Return to Sender" and had been unclaimed.

Judah smiles. He feels himself smile. There would be tinted windows and the bus would have its lights on as it bowled its way through Manchester, then north. His wife, Mrs. Margaret Sherbrooke, would put dark glasses on—and maybe her neighbor would notice and think it strange since it was more than half dark now, though the weather would be clearing, though the storm clouds had got trapped and emptied somewhere short of Equinox, and there, to the west, was the moon, a sliver only but luminescent, scudding through the sky beside them—and bend to the window, throat working, shoulders hunched. "Are you all right?" her neighbor would ask—would think of asking, rather, since the woman brooked no interference, even in discomfiture, and was forbidding now as she had been forbidding the whole trip from New York. "Yes, quite all right I thank you," would be the answer surely, glacial and inviolate and false.

So Margaret, his second wife, would be delivered to the Rutland bus depot. She would deposit herself on the tarmac again, this time with her canvas bag. She would be flotsam on the traffic tide and turn to make her way back south. She'd tighten her cloth coat. She'd breathe and blink and find him, Judah, there before her, grinning at the game he'd played and won. There would be explanations but no need of explanation, and she'd be in his arms again, unstrung.

"Jude, how could you do it, Jude?"

"Do what?" he asked.

"Do *this*." She sobbed but would not let him see her sob and inclined her face away from him, down.

"Do unto others," he said.

"That's not the golden rule," she said. "It's cruelty, pure cruelty."

"I wanted to surprise you."

"Nothing you do now surprises me."

The conversation is wrong. He had had advantage and she takes advantage from him, pressing where he yielded and compliant when he pressed. They have had this talk before; he hunts the memory.

"I meant no harm," he said.

"You did. You do," and she was racked with tears now and on his shoulder, trembling.

"There." He stroked her. "There. I'm sorry."

"Judah. You'll never change."

"It's cold out here," he said. "You must be cold."

"Yes."

"Come into the house," he urged.

"Yes."

"Megan. Maggie. Whatever you call yourself."

"Meg. Mrs. Judah P. Sherbrooke," she smiled.

"Welcome, whatever your name is. Welcome what the cat dragged in. Margaret. Welcome home."

Pleased with his imaginings, he climbs into the bed. The ceiling pattern is familiar; there are plaster cracks the shape of a spring-tooth harrow. He courts sleep. Tonight, he tells himself, he will have most need of it. He has several techniques. He puts his arms behind his head and presses his elbows back as far as they will go and lies there breathing, stretching, remembering the license plate numbers of every car he's owned. He chops the second willow down—the one by the pond that is dying anyhow, and killing the tamaracks to boot—and sees, in his mind's eye, how he will get at it and in which direction he intends it to fall. Then he chops the limbs off and segments the trunk and then chops the trunk into log lengths and splits and stacks the wood. Willow wood is stove wood, no good for burning by itself but useful as a mix. He turns to his right side. "Which of the senses," Maggie had asked him, "if you had to lose a sense would you find it the most difficult to lose?"

"Sight," Judah said. "That's the worst."

"Think about it," she had urged him. "What about sound?"

"I'd miss that too," he considered. "I'd miss them all. I might not miss smell all that much."

"For me it's touch," she said. "I'd hate to lose it most of any. Imagine, Jude."

"Yes." He put his hand on her.

"That too. But imagine not even knowing what you stood on when you stood. Imagine hot things on your arm and not even knowing— not until you smelled or saw it—that you burned your arm."

So he imagines now, in bed, that he has lost the sense of touch and that his body lies in some sheet-shroud. He wills his toes insensate and then his ankles and his calves and knees and thighs and wills his manhood unresponsive, and his belly and chest cavity and neck. His hands are difficult. He wills oblivion upon his hands but cannot quiet them. He reconstructs her letter. *"I come in hopes the love I bear you and you said you bore me once will alter your opinion of the proper way to act . . ."* He, Judah, had no opinion to alter; he is, he tells himself, indifferent to propriety.

He occupies himself; he sings "Begin the Beguine." The word "beguiled" sticks to him like a burr. He would beguile the time until the bus arrived, as she had been beguiling and he had been beguiled. There were guileful people and there was the town of Guilford and there were wiles and guiles. Giles Cavendish had lost his arm in Normandy on D-Day, and he thinks how close that qualifies to "dead in the ditches of France." He, Judah, by the accident of age has never been to war. He was ready for the First World War just when the war was over, and the Second came too late. He could have joined up somehow, he supposed. But the lumber mills were useful, and he expanded their output five-fold. They'd have put him on some desk job in Washington, D.C., and if he couldn't fly or man a tank he'd rather, he decided, shuffle lumber mills and farms around than some stack of papers. He had taken catnaps standing, though Maggie called them "horsenaps." She had complained he wasn't horizontal ten minutes, ever, before she heard him snore. She would lie reading, or brushing her hair with the silver-handled brushes that had belonged to his mother, and he would look at her and shut his eyes and take her beauty-pattern as the imprint; he had coveted wakefulness, once, as now he covets sleep.

He reconstitutes touch. He lets his hands release and know the texture of the blankets and their position on the blankets. His right hand is, he calculates, at sixty degrees to the line of his forearm. His mind is a noise riot; he listens to the furnace hum and hears cacophany.

"Jude," she whispers at him. "Judah P."

He makes no answer.

"Judah. Jude, I say."
He turns.
"Come a little closer. Just this close."
There are rocks. She sits on the forward rock. She is combing out her hair. It cascades.
"I'll tell you a secret, J.P. I'll tell you something that I've never told to anyone."
"Not anyone?" He finds his voice.
"Not anyone. And I'll never tell it ever again. Not to anyone but you."
She employs an amber comb. He has presented it to her. Her hair is amber also, and has teeth.
"Come closer, Jude. Come here till I tell you."
He advances. There is water. He swims.
"It's not the sort of thing," she says, "one ought to beg to say."
He flails his arms and flutters his legs and is advancing.
"Not to a gentleman . . ."
He rises.
"Judah. Darling." She exhorts him. "Jude. Judah P."
She bends and holds her hand out and her hand is at sixty degrees. He reaches for it but she is receding.
"Try," she sings. "Try harder. Husband."
There is water in his mouth. There is water in his nose and eyes and, catastrophically, water in his ears.
"Lover," she calls to him. "Love." But he is unable to hear.

"I wish a cupola to Crown the house," Peacock wrote, "and be its Glittry Diadem werewith to catch the Morning Sun and honor Him who made it, as He created light and every living Creature. There must be variegated glass, and of as many colors as was Joseph's Coat. I see a Signal Beacon to the footsore traveller or pilgrim Pelerinating with his eyes cast up at dusk to catch the fading warmth and certify Direction. He shall see our constant Rainbow and take his bearings thusly and know, I do devoutly think, heart's ease. It is no small consolation to see the Steeple rising at the forest's rim. Often have I lingered at the Path's fell turning, with such the final sight. It affords no little Comfort to hear the mellifluous church-chime breast the Tempest's howling like some Sturdy Swimmer with consistent stroke. And surely Mariner must say a Thankful prayer when he spy the lighthouse winking in the Blackamoor and minstrel face of Night. What tho the dawn will scrub the nigger Visage clean, and each Ship prove its goodly Harbour and traveller attain his wonted Resting-place, yet would I have our Cupola be th'unchanging Watchman, a *twelve-sided* sentry of the Soul. . . ."

BOOK

2

I

HE IS AT THE DEPOT, IN THE INCREASING DARK. HE STANDS BY THE porch bench, in front of the soft-drink machine. Descending, she sees him and misses the last step; her ankle twists in. So she limps toward him on her two-inch heels, transferring the bag to her left hand for balance; she had expected Finney, or a taxi sent to fetch and bring her to his bed.

"Judah," she asks, "should you be here?"

"Who else?" He takes a step toward her. "Let me help you with that."

And reaches and takes the bag and hefts it with a strength that could not be a dying man's, and she who has prepared for shock is shocked that there is nothing changed, is suddenly back from a weekend's excursion and not seven years.

"Well," Judah says. "You made it."

"Yes."

"It's been raining," he gestures. "First snow. It can't make up its mind what weather we're having tonight."

"You're here," she says.

"As you see me."

"I can't believe my eyes."

"Believe them," he tells her—slipping into his protective condescension, shepherding her to the car. "I'm here."

(Her father thrives. He has his cronies, he tells her; he plays canasta every Wednesday and bridge every Saturday night. He's doing just about what the good Lord intends him to do. There are oysters here, he says; you come on up for Decoration Day and I'll feed you so many Wellfleet oysters you'll never want to look at a bluepoint again. There are ways to cook up oysters you've just never dreamed of, he says. She calls him every Thursday and he always answers, "Hiya. How's my girl?")

In the car she quizzes Judah, but he is laconic. "When you got my letter," Maggie asks, "were you surprised?"

He drives with both hands on the wheel, and the attentive caution of the aged.

"Were you expecting it?" she asks. "Or was it a shock to you?"

He makes a left turn, heavily.

"Power steering," Judah says. "It helps. But get a breakdown in the power steering unit, and it's harder than all hell to fix; it's like hauling a Mack truck with pulleys; might as well walk."

She settles back. Things are familiar, not strange.

"How's Finney?" Maggie asks.

"Fine. The same. He'll be there for dinner," he says.

"And Ian? Have you heard from him?"

"Not likely."

"Hattie?" Maggie asks.

"The same."

So this is it, she tells herself, this squalid litany; how's the grocer's nephew with the harelip; how's Elvirah—she marvels at her memory for all of this inconsequence—Elvirah Hayes?

"And you?" Judah asks.

"I'm as you see me."

Remembrance is a trick time plays; the world is déjà vu and everything incarnate and nothing new under the sun; she has seen it all already, known everything before. Elvirah Hayes and Lucy Gregory live in that brick cottage to her right, behind the picket fence.

"Pretty."

"We're none of us immortal," Maggie says.

"Pretty always."

"Flatterer," she says.

"Why did you come?"

"Why not? What else is one to do on Saturday?"

"It's Wednesday," Judah says.

Embarrassed, she looks out the window—seeing sleet and the huddled houses. They relax, she thinks, with summer—they sprout awnings and porch furniture and the accoutrements of easy weather.

"Don't laugh at me," he says.

"I'm not. I wasn't laughing."

"Maggie," her husband articulates. "Is that what they call you these days?"

"You call me what you've always called me, Jude."

He has loved her for her love of liberty, while she loved him for refusing to offer free rein. He had the possessor's vanity; her vanity has been to do without all ownership. His love was exclusive, she knows, but likes to think her own inclusive—that all of god's chillun got wings.

54

So Maggie can oppose him term for term—could insist that jealousy was shopworn, marriage a convenience and the slave yoke lifted from the "second sex."

"I called you many things," he says. "In my time."

"Maggie will do. Mrs. Sherbrooke."

"You're being nice," he says. "You'd never been this well behaved before you took that bus."

"It's just I'm surprised to see you."

"Don't be," Judah says.

So they circle each other, cautious; he signals for a left turn at the Library.

"We're taking the long way around," he says. "That way we'll miss the hill."

"It's slippery."

"I wouldn't want to lose you now you're here."

He says this with such force she takes it for the first true note of all his praise and banter; she raises her hand and rubs it on his cheek. "Feel Daddy's scratchy face," she says. "That's from *Pat the Bunny*. I remember Ian used to raise that fist of his before we even turned the page, before we'd get to Peekaboo."

"Hide-and-seek," he says. "Seems like every game you name is one we tried to play."

"Succeeded in playing," she says. He tries to kiss her hand—still staring forward, still driving, and misses and smacks his lips at air while she sees his neck-flesh roil and fold.

There had been purple martins by the pond. Judah wanted purple martins to keep mosquitoes back. They rarely settled this far north, he told her, and had to be lured and enticed. So he coaxed them with houses set up on poles, the proper distance from the pond and built to Amos's satisfaction; Amos said they liked their houses just so. And he kept the entrance stuffed so grackles wouldn't settle while the martin scouts were out, but put the houses up early enough so they'd weather. He tried lure feed and had waited for three seasons, with no luck. Then Maggie settled in and with her came the purple martin families; they settled that fourth season and returned. They skimmed and flitted across the pond, and she took them—the first evenings, so swift was their flight—for bats. Maggie joined him in the evenings on the Big House porch, and they watched the birds and heard them in the near shade trees.

"An owl," she said. "A wise old owl."

"A mourning dove," he said.

"This time of night?" she asked him. "Wouldn't it likely be owls?"

"It's not the time of day," he said. "It's the sound that decides it."

"I thought they sounded off early," she said.

The mourning doves signaled each other.

"It isn't that kind of morning. It's sorrow mourning, not the time till noon."

Maggie felt herself color. "I never knew that," she said. "I thought it was morning A.M."

"They're nothing like you think them"—Judah was expansive. "They're fierce birds. Put two turtle doves in a cage and they'll make fighting cocks look tame."

> Oh don't you see yon turtle dove
> Who flies from pine to pine;
> He's mourning for his own true love,
> As I will mourn for mine—

She sang to him, and her voice was gentle, he said, and he fed on the melody's feast.

"Or for that matter," Judah said, "I wouldn't especially care to stay in one cage with an owl. Especially if I was a rabbit, say, or a mouse. Keep at it; that song. It's fine."

He praised her with that condescending kindliness she'd heard in Hattie often when a servant choice reflected well upon her own astuteness in the choosing. They praised her, Maggie knew, behind her back; Judah said a man who's spoken well of when his back is turned has spent too much preceding time upon his back or knees.

> As I will mourn for mine—she sang
> Believe me what I say.
> You are the darling of my heart,
> Until my dying day.

He believed her, he said; he had taken the fraud-song for truth. He considered promises were made to keep, not break. He figured purple martins were as good a sign as any that his luck would change, but would not change again.

* * *

Maggie feels herself a juggler and despairs of true juggling dexterity —trying to keep things aloft. People practice with oranges or tennis balls or Indian clubs; she has had to practice with people. They present themselves to her as props. She has juggled relatives and friends and lovers and opponents like some agile but gigantic clown—never quite collapsing, always on collapse's verge until the whole heap dropped.

There are those, she knows, who can drop one orange or Indian club yet not falter or break juggling rhythm. There are those who train with horseshoes and can throw and nail the horseshoes as part of their performance. Some jugglers can stack cups on saucers, even, without shattering the cups—but she, Maggie, would get flustered and mournful and everything would break. She is more agile than most. She keeps a close inventory of relatives and lovers and loves the patterned arc they make, from throwing hand to catching hand, suspended. Yet when one died they all died to her; when one left they each of them departed, and she broke and mourned them all at once. "Don't go," she wanted to warn them. "Don't break; don't rot; don't die."

Things lost their animation. Men would intrigue her, or some cousin returned from Melanesia with tales of tribal rites, and how they drink the broth of turtle sex glands there. Politics intrigued her, and she joined committees and worked with animation for her chosen candidates or in support of abortion reform. She has had hobbies. The piano was more than a hobby, but needlepoint and gardening and yoga were what Judah called woman's work.

"That's nice," she said. "That's complimentary."

"It's how I meant it," he said.

"Men do yoga too," she said. "The world's best athlete is a ballet dancer."

"Who says?"

"*Time* magazine says," she said. "And they must be right."

"I didn't call it sissy work," he said. "Just hobby stuff. Just woman's."

So, to spite him, she kept at it. She taught Ian to sit in the lotus position. She took things up like oranges that would soon drop or rot. And intrigue could animate her—looks exchanged in public that were private looks. She juggled her allegiance, lovers claimed. She swore to leave but did not leave, or promised to arrive and postponed her arrival. It is suspension's welter that she fears—the moment (known so quickly, unmistakable) when the grasp and reach go fuzzy, when her fingers are too fat or weak to catch what she herself has thrown, when all of it goes tumbling down like some card house in wind.

There are those who keep their life an open book, and those who keep it closed. There are some, she knows, who preach pure honesty and some who preach restraint. Her preachment had been reticence, and then she grew dissatisfied with reticence—"A thing that's worth the doing," Judah said, "is worth admitting you've done it."

"What if nobody asks?" Maggie said.

"Then nobody's any the wiser," he said. "And that's all right too."

"Yes," she pressed him. "But what about things sworn to silence?"

"There's some things we don't talk about," he grinned at her. "And some we talk about doing and some we only just do."

So she kept *doing* and *talking* aloft, not shifting her eyes from the arc. Things hung there suspended an instant, her throw's force in perfect opposition to the force of gravity—only rotating, not rising or falling or disrupting her influence-reach. There, for that perfected instant, she could keep three men convinced they were her only man, or aunts persuaded that they were her favorite aunt. At such times, also, Maggie could persuade a Catholic with seven children to embrace abortion laws, or to vote for George McGovern since he'd bring the boys back home.

Still, Judah maintained, any honest renegade wants to set up his own sort of town. Any liar dreams he'll be caught out and pardoned; any faithless person reasons faithlessness is faith. There's something in a clown, he said, that needs to get egg on his face.

Maggie assesses herself. She loves to sing in choral groups. She likes motets particularly, and belonged once to a motet choir. There are harmonies that make her quiver—making of her backbone a sounding board, making her whole body resonate. She is familiar with dissonance, that squeak of chalk on blackboards that sets her teeth on edge, or Ian's habit of cleaning his teeth on his fork tines. She, Margaret, shivered each time her son clamped his teeth on the fork's metallic edges and raked his mouth in; her nerve ends would jangle and clamor as surely as when she'd swallowed sand.

Meg taught herself to walk as Ingrid Bergman walked. She strode directly ahead—with just a hint of sashay-languor and the promise of abandon when she stopped. Judah moves. He looks at her. She might have been a journalist, or in the foreign service even, or done welfare work. Nostalgia washed each might-have-been with colors of the rainbow, making dim things roseate and every path seem primrose strewn. It makes good sense, looking back. It all seems foreordained. Of course she'd model and hate it of course; certainly come to the Big House hunting (as she'd told her analyst long since, but been bored with the pat equation even in the telling) some father surrogate, some memory of titans who would dandle and comfort and change her. Of course he, Judah, fit that bill in every particular: titanic and comfortable both. She could explain it all.

Maggie loves her father, wanly, still. He lives alone in his retirement home in Cape Cod, and she would spend stray weekends there, dutiful, admiring his seashell collection. He is full of sea lore but has never been to sea. He'd pace the wharf of the trails to Great Island for all the world like a retired admiral, jaunty, sheltering his pipe. He'd discourse to her of wrecks and scallops and altering tides and the time that there were taverns on that sandbar, there. He limps and somehow manages to convey that it is a sailor's roll, that his parquet flooring is a pitching deck. He sports yachtsmens' caps. She waits for him to acquire tattoos. She hears him out but hears within the babble only, "Help. Megan, not the man I was. Megan, have some sort of patience, it's the holiday season; it's the way we all were, remember, in a southwest gale off Hatteras, the tuna sinking everything in sight. . . ."

She walked with him where fishing boats weathered the winter—swept up to the wharf as though by an outlandish tide and stranded there on cinder blocks and jacks. She lagged behind. The prows were huge, rotting, barnacle-streaked. Boats with names like *Mudlark* and *Norman Scott* and *Li-Burt-E* towered above her, their cabins painted jaunty colors and their decks piled high with nets. Her father spoke of basking sharks the size of whales and how the whales would dance around the boats. There was ice on the dock. She leaned toward him with a familiar yearning—that he find an audience in coffee shops and at the post office; that he be not consigned to muttering his tales alone, aloud. She took his arm. She leaned her head on his shoulder, but was too tall to make it more than mawkish, embarrassing them both. She straightened. "I've been to New Orleans," she said. "I've been to San Francisco since I saw you last."

He smiled at her vaguely, obsessed. "But when a whale is sickly," he continued, "and the herd knows it's a goner—this is true for dolphins too, mind you, and seals, and anything with the slightest spark of compassion or instinct for decency, mind you—then they shove it in to shore. That way it can go in peace; that way the sharks won't get at it; that's the fish equivalent for burial at sea."

And suddenly she knew she'd go to Judah if he called. Suddenly she made a covenant with some moral second self: The Golden Rule. Do unto others. If someone watches over father, anyone, she told herself, I'll watch over husband forever and ever, amen. A Dodge appeared. She noticed its ancient shape in the far distance, noted its wavering arrival. She heard it the length of the dock away, and with the wind at their back. It made for them; she made out a man at the wheel. He sat erect, using both hands to steer down this wide and empty avenue; his car was of a burnished blackness; he brought it to a halt. Gulls wheeled above them, dropping and shattering clams. He rolled down the window, rolling it all the way, using his entire arm to crank. He was polite; he doffed his cap. There was rheum at his eyes' pouches and a red waxed moustache. "Hey, Harry," he said. "You fortunate man. We've been watching you with this young lovely."

"Not so young," she said. "But I thank you just the same."

"It has to be your daughter, Harry. Good afternoon, miss."

The chromium was pitted; she put her hand on the headlight's abrasion. They "geezerized" for minutes—it was her father's word for conversation—in the wet wind. She would go to Judah when he called.

She thinks that women have a harder time of it these years than men. Not only do they have the housework and child-work and beautywork to keep up with, but they also have to feel dishonored if they honor it as work. She thinks of what she might have done and whom she might have done it to, and all of it is trading off of sex. When a man has a profession they call him a professional; when a woman takes up a career, they call her a "careerist." "It's a brutal world out there," they say, and if you take the world on then they call you brutalized. Hattie tried. She loved the boys. In her own way, Maggie thinks, the eighty-year-old had been game. She'd kept to what she stood for, standing fast. Sometimes it had seemed more standing pat than fast, and then there was change all around her so that standing still was change. So Ian left, and Seth was taken from them, and she turned to her huge brother, making him a boy. It could not work; it was not a sufficient career.

Maggie had spied on him once. She had been in Providence but came back unexpectedly, and it was dark. She told the taxi driver to let her off at the gate. He did, and she took her single suitcase in her right hand. The mountain ash trees had bloomed in the brief interval; she had been thirty-two years old. There were stars, but clouds obliterated what she guessed was a half-crescent moon. She believed in psychic age. Men were born a certain age and stayed that way till death; Judah, for example, was always forty-five. Women, too, had psychic age—though she thought her own age shifted and might shift, as would her name, again. But thirty-two was how she felt and had been feeling since thirty, and would till thirty-nine.

Dogs barked at her, then quieted. She walked on the driveway's grass rim. She wanted to look at her husband—to see him unseen. It was not spying exactly, she told herself as she stepped out of her shoes. It was looking at the life he lived without her, thinking her gone. It was hunting some new access to his charmed enclosure.

"How long will you be off?" he had asked.

"A week," she said. "Maybe less."

"And maybe more?" he asked.

"Maybe. I doubt it. Ten days at the most."

"He needs your help," Judah said. It was a question really, but she took it as his answer.

"Yes. There's so much furniture," she'd said. "There's so much we've got to decide."

"Don't bring it here," Hattie warned her. "We don't need anything else."

"Some mementos only," Maggie said. "The things I want to keep on remembering with."

"Yes," Judah said. "Sure. You have it shipped. Your uncle's rolltop desk."

"And his ladderback chair," she'd said. "I feel like having that."

"Have what you like," he said.

She stepped, therefore, secretively onto the porch. The watchdogs wagged their tails. Later she would tell him how the cousins had divided up house spoils. She needed nothing and had taken nothing but her uncle's ladderback chair. Timmy claimed he needed the walnut rolltop desk. Later she would tell him how she missed him there in Providence, walking in the chill bay wind and seeing the house lamps light up. The living room lamps, here, were lit. She craned to see her husband where he sat. Judah sprawled in the green leather chair. His sleeves were rolled to his elbows, and she saw the white hairs riffle on his arm. He bent to eat a sandwich, leaning forward, mouth making anticipatory shapes, and something about that gesture—a weary domesticity, the time he'd taken to make and arrange his setting, the hurried way he turned to what had clearly been a hurried preparation— touched her, moved her as none of his elaborate courtesy could, nor any of the regal meals she had imagined him sharing.

He was six feet from her, maybe, with glass and gauze intervening, but she saw his head in profile as if he slept beside her on the second pillow. He sucked on his cheek. He had had the habit of chewing tobacco, he told her, and it felt like flesh was his tobacco plug. From twenty years of chewing, Judah said, it didn't make much difference what he chewed. He wore his brown corduroy pants. She had mended them more times than she would care to count, and offered to buy him a new pair, but he said not until I wear it through, but thanks, but what about this button, do you think you'd manage that?

Later she would tell him that she hated Providence. They were crows over carrion, she'd say. They'd argued over furniture and even stamp collections, like a flock of crows. It was good, she'd say, to be back home where nothing was in question or out of its accustomed place or on some sort of auction block, with legatees bidding. Providence, she said, was full of boys on motorbikes, wearing beanies, stealing books.

She yearned for him. She was, she told herself, in love. It wasn't a term she much liked. It was attended by guitars. It had meant *crush* —some hero's sock stolen from the basketball court, and treasured, rolled into a totem in her top right drawer. Later it meant four-leaf clovers proffered as they walked through fields, and later the wine bottles shared. So love became a pawing intensity—and the terms were making out, then making it, then making him, then making love. Later still it meant submission. It meant Billie Holiday singing "Hush Now, Don't Explain"—the whiskey seams in her voice come unstuck, a fiddler using nerve and hair ends for her strings.

Maggie had admired Billie Holiday. The melody had not been counterfeit. When some song's bubble burst, it was truth that would burst through, not lies. There was naked need as she slid off her note, and she reached back toward it with a lover's reach. So Maggie thought that love meant grief, and urgency, and a multitude of phone calls from some iced-in phone booth, crying how could you, and why. . . .

Judah moved. He looked at her. He craned his head to the left and was staring at her, she could swear, was staring through her at the willow trees. She flattened herself. "I'm crazy about you," she whispered—having learned that, lately, as a substitution for simple four-letter "love." "I'm crazy insane for you, Judah. Crazy mad."

Hattie comes to the door. They greet each other, constrained. Her voice is high-pitched, querulous. "What brings you to these parts?"

And Maggie says, "I wanted to see you. Both. You know that."

"Well, look your fill," says Hattie. *"We're* not leaving, him and I."

"I didn't expect so," she says.

Maggie takes her bearings. There is nothing changed that she can see.

"It's just the way it always was," her sister-in-law says. "I'll vouch for that."

"And Judah?"

"He'd say so too," Hattie said. "If he ever noticed. But he'd notice, you can bet, the minute there was something different in the house."

They are conspirators again, cackling about "menfolks." That had been Hattie's word for masculine assertion and mistakes. "Judah's absentminded," she says. He follows them into the house. "He won't eat the food on his plate and if you tell him to he'll likely as not ask for seconds; it's inertia," Hattie says, "it's what he starts he won't stop."

"Yes, well," says Judah, entering. "We'll stop this now. We'll let her alone just a little bit, sister. Just long enough to wash."

"I don't mind," Hattie says.

"I didn't guess you would," he says. "We'll see you in a while."

"How long?"

"Just long enough," he says again. "We'll start up in a bit."

They turn from her, together.

"I'll be in my room," Hattie says.

(Hair in the flanges of his nose, hair in his ears; a nose like an Indian's, where rain could practice skiing, Maggie said. Eyes that were blue in daylight, gray at night, and green in the pine woods or when he looked at grass—the only changeable thing in him, Maggie said, an absence of color really, not a hue to name. Big ears to hear her where she walked, a mouth like Cupid's crossbow, with the skin so often cracked and healed it seemed scarified. That was how his whole skin moved, independent of the bone struts beneath, so that when he squinted his cheeks would fall, not rise; that was how he used his hands, wrapping them like swaddling around the fork he held. There was stubble on his chin that seemed as if he had rubbed his wet cheeks in white sand; she has been robbed, she tells herself, of his resplendent youth. She has the photographs. He stands there pole-trim, erect. His white hair had been yellow then, as everything was yellow in the print. He is, she hears herself telling Mary, just the most beautiful man. He's everything I dreamed of, he's the strongest man in the whole wide world, just dreamy, just too nice for words. He's rich, her city friend says. Yes, he's very rich. He's old, she says, not all that old, just graying at the temples. But—and Mary drops her voice, sybilline, insistent—do you love him? Love him, Maggie answers, oh my, yes. I'm mad about the boy. He has this team of horses that he broke himself. He has a carriage—you know, the old-fashioned kind, with plush seats, all the trimmings and a place to put your parasol—and he takes me in it sometimes and we ride for hours and don't ever leave his land. It's a one-horse carriage actually, it's for the Belgian workhorse that he got in Canada. But Mary says it's boring; it isn't boring now but will be twenty years from now, she'd rather shop at Bendel's. And twenty years from now is eight years ago, and everything they'd argued on or prophesied had come to pass, is past.) Judah stands there, her sizeable beast, her leonine husband who is twice the size of that dead emperor they called the Lion of Judah. And his eyes are yellow now, and the pouches of his flesh reek of the dying animal that he, the container, contains.

II

ACROSS THE HALL, SHE HATES THEM. SHE HATES HIS OFFHAND dismissal. She had said, "I'm not reproachful," but he had reproached her nonetheless. He hasn't, Hattie knows, the right. She'd done some things in mind and deed that merited reproach—as which of us hasn't, she asks herself now. She'd done some things to anger him that merited his righteous anger. She'd not deny that. She never denied it, in thought or in deed, and no matter what it cost her in his teasing disrespect. He doles her maraschino cherries out like alms. She knows he will provide them, in common courtesy. She can afford to buy all the maraschino cherries in the state of Vermont, and in all of New England if pushed to it. She could have hoarded or have swallowed them in clumps. She could drink cherry pop or cherry brandy or Cherry Heering, come to that. But she prefers to ration her pleasures and not to be discourteous and to await his toast. "Your health," he'd say, and she'd answer, "Your health," noting how the sweetness bobbled and spread out and sank. There was little enough, otherwise, to sweeten up the bitter draught he made her drink.

She imagines, sometimes, a maraschino cherry tree. She has heard that somewhere they tie bottles on the fruit bud and let fruit grow in the bottle and then pour liquor in. That way you get a pear or peach too big for the bottleneck but in the bottle anyhow and saturated, growing. The maraschino cherry trees would line the streets of Washington and the banks of the Potomac, and springtime there would be completely bliss. George Washington had chopped down a chokecherry tree. She is certain of that. She is certain that our nation's father spared the proper cherry tree and cleared the nuisance—the chokecherry—out. He never lied and tossed a silver dollar straight across the wide Potomac and could have cut the chokecherry down with three mighty strokes.

There are other misconceptions. There is the misconception that he had silver teeth. In fact his teeth were wooden, and he spent the night of Valley Forge inspiring the troops. He proved his gay insouciance and his scorn of prideful Redcoats by whittling at his lower teeth with his bayonet blade. She, Harriet, had no problem with her teeth. She is blessed with every single one of them, and they do not corrode. Her brother said that cherry acid was as good a paint remover as any, and better than most, and that he'd filled a bathtub with it once and worn out the enamel.

He was always teasing her. He'd teased her since she first remembered and is at it still. She supposed his teasing was a surrogate for courtesy, his way of saying: "Harriet. I'm glad you're with me. Sister. It makes it easy you're here."

"Thanksgiving's not a harvest feast," he'd say instead.

"Of course it is."

"You're wrong. I'll prove it," Judah said.

"Prove it then," she challenged him.

"It happens in November, right? The final Thursday of the month."

"That's Roosevelt's doing," she said. "That's when he regulated holidays, remember?"

"I remember. But it was somewhere around then anyhow. Well, give or take a week."

"All right."

"And it started in New England."

"Yes."

"And they're bringing in pumpkins and corn from the fields."

"Of course."

"It's not 'of course' "—he triumphed. "There's nothing growing then. There's not a pumpkin left to harvest, or even Indian corn."

It was a misconception, and she'd set him straight. Samoset had brought in corn from the storehouse, not off the stalk. But Judah pointed to her picture books and showed the pilgrim-settlers coming laden from the fields. Samoset walked down to meet them, grinning, arms filled full.

"It's the artist's fault," she said. "That's not how it happened at all."

"You don't know, Hattie. You weren't there either. It must have been slim pickings is my point."

"All right," she said. "All right."

"Admit I proved it," Judah said.

"You didn't."

"Admit it. I did."

So they would fall to bickering and squabble as they'd squabbled seventy years before. He'd bested her at checkers, though she had taught him the game. He'd bested her at chinese checkers and, when he was losing, overturned the board. He said he did it by mistake, but she knew that he'd done it a-purpose, and the marbles collected underneath the couch. There was a dip in the floor. He'd bested her at riding, and in their mother's heart of hearts. He'd bested her by the involuntary arrogance of size. But there was voluntary arrogance also, and she had curbed that in him. She'd made alliance with Maggie, and they'd bridled him for years. Then the alliance was broken, and everything in the Big House was broken, shattered by Judah gone wild. He'd been obedient and docile and honored common courtesy. He had been all she asked for as the Sherbrooke heir. He teased her about the family tree, calling it scrub oak only, or like the poison sumac that was display, not roots. He teased her that the doctor said one bottle of maraschino cherries can cause insulin shock. He teased her that she never married and wasn't the marrying kind. "Love 'em and leave 'em," he'd say. "That's my sister Hattie. Got a string of broken hearts there knotted around her finger. Only none of us knows just exactly what she needs to be reminded of. Or who. She keeps her own counsel on that."

She kept her own counsel continually. He could not reproach her. She could have told him things. She could have told him, for instance, how they fashioned their woman alliance. Maggie had been making quiche lorraine. She called it "quiche lorraine," but it was really only pastry crust and eggs and onions and bacon. She, Harriet, was in the kitchen (watching the wreckage, thinking Maggie cooked as if she'd all her life had someone who would clean up after, scrubbing up the pots and mixing bowls as if it were a privilege to rinse what Maggie dirtied; thinking how her sister-in-law was prodigal, wasteful with eggs . . .)

"I hope you like it," Maggie had said. "I hope the recipe pleases you."

"Of course."

"I mean it," Maggie said. There was a pastry smear beneath her eye.

"Why do they call it quiche?" she'd asked.

"It's a peasant dish," she'd said—and Harriet wondered, was that the answer? "It comes from Lorraine."

"Lorraine who?" Harriet asked.

"That's a place, not person." Her sister-in-law straightened, smiling. "It's an area in France."

She wasn't ignorant; she just wasn't thinking, she wanted to say. She knew that Joan of Arc had once been called Joan of Lorraine. There were more people called Lorraine than places called Lorraine, and who knew for a certainty which one was named after which?

"You're making it for Judah"—she let resentment surface. "You're making it for him and for his guests."

"For you too, Harriet." Maggie wiped the pastry smear but managed only to enlarge it. There was flour on her hand.

"No."

"For all of us."

"For me least of all," she had said.

Her sister-in-law looked at her, speculative. There was evening sunlight on her cheek. The cheek was smudged.

"You don't care a, a"—Harriet ventured—"a twopenny damn. You're just being polite."

Then Maggie made their alliance. She laid the mixing spoon and the eggbeater on the table (not on the bowl, Harriet saw, not in the tray set aside so the drippings wouldn't puddle or trail to the floor) and put out her hand. "Don't despise me," Maggie said.

"Despise you? Why should I despise you? How could I?" she had asked.

"You've got your reasons, I don't doubt. Don't despise me. Please."

Nobody on God's bounden earth could have resisted; she, Harriet, couldn't resist.

"I don't hold you responsible"—she staked one final claim. "I don't think you intended harm."

"Don't think that I'm despicable," Maggie said. "I married your brother for love."

And money, she would have said. *And position. And the house. And for his salt lusts.* She would have said that earlier—five minutes previous she'd been watchful and suspicious, been the sentry of the Sherbrooke clan. *And for the name. And to lord it over us. And to eat up his substance with whorishness. Who knows?*

"I did,"—Maggie joggled her hand, palm out. "I love Judah Porteous. And his sister therefore is someone I shall come to love—if she'll permit it. Will she? You?"

So they were domestic angels, plighted and banded and with their wing tips clipped. They clucked and bustled in the kitchen, Judah later said, like a pair of broody hens. She had followed Maggie, chattering—from kitchen sink to countertop to stove to chopping block to sink—picking up her droppings, setting things straight. He said they'd got a pecking order, and that made him (teasing, kneading Maggie underneath her apron) the roost's cock. His wife had slapped at his hands. She told him to behave himself, but laughed. She was, Harriet knew, no hen but an eagle at rest—and her arms were mighty wingspans and her hands sheathed claws. She was domestic only on her own willed sufferance—and the avenging angel's wing tips would grow back.

But that was her wan, private knowledge, and she forgot it for years. Judah called his wife a hen and dove and stork. She had taken Maggie for a true ally—but had been taken in, mistaken. They had bridled Judah with conspiratorial efficiency—making him take off his shoes when on the ballroom carpets, making sure he came on time to meals. He had been docile, gentled, as her sister-in-law had been docile—and Harriet had thought for years she witnessed family love. She had partaken of it even, partaking of their bed and board and knowing there was room enough to spare. It had been a mistake.

Yet Maggie, in those first years, never made mistakes. She wronged them all repeatedly but seemed to do no wrong. Nothing Maggie ate or drank made any beauty difference; she could guzzle all night long and gorge herself on cakes and bread but not accumulate one pound. Her skirts would billow about her like sails in a mild breeze. Harriet baked cakes, despairing, and then baked rhubarb and pecan pies and fudge brownies and presented them topped off with homemade ice cream and shared it all and felt herself bloat and go greasy while Maggie ate, delighted, licking her fingers in the kitchen and licking the spatula clean. She had the complexion of a Camay model, and it would not mar.

"How do you do it?" Harriet asked.

"Do what?"

They were allies now, aligned—but Harriet still baked the cakes and pies and brownies, letting Judah have a tuck-in on plain New England food.

"I've burned the crust," she said.

"Don't be silly, Hattie. It's perfection."

"You think so?" she'd ask, shy.

"Yes. *Perfect.*"—and Maggie'd pare the drippings off the pie pan and swallow and make a perfection sign, curling her index finger to her thumb. She'd raise her other fingers and squint past her hand's circle, appreciative, nodding.

"Well, how do you do it?" she asked.

"A pinch of this," Harriet said, modest. "A dab of that. You know."

"Sugar and spice and everything nice"—Judah smacked his lips.

"This ain't half bad, Hattie. I'll have more."

"Tell her 'if you please,'" said Maggie.

"I do please," Judah said.

"You don't—you discourteous man." They were allies in this also—in making him say "Please" and keep his elbows off the table and wipe his mouth off every time he drank.

"OK, ladies. Hattie. I'll have more, please."

"Why, certainly," she said.

"Why, thank you," Judah said.

"You're welcome, I'm sure."

"Pretty please," he pronounced, "with sugar on top"—and she knew he had bested her and heard Jamie Powers crackling through the underbrush, whistling, laughing, and felt her face flame and threw the cake knife down.

"Now look"—Maggie scolded him—"look what you've done."

"I'll take a second piece," he said. "I'll have more."

"Not while I'm sitting here," her ally said—who would not, would never be bested, who was beauty without blemish and had perfect cheeks.

"Thank you," Judah said. "It's been a lovely meal."

"You've spoiled it. You're the one who spoiled it, Jude."

"I said pretty please," he said.

"You didn't mean it. You meant something else."

"I'm studying manners."

"You're not learning them," his wife pronounced. "You're a slow study, then."

"And you,"—he said, his face suffusing equally. "You're such an excellent teacher."

"It's your fault," Harriet echoed. "You're the one who spoils it"—and he overturned his plate and coffee cup and shoved his chair back and stalked out of the room.

"Now look what you've done," she asked.
"We've"—Maggie corrected her. "We both did it."
"Not me," Hattie said. "Never me."

They had had a second son, Seth, who came two years after Ian, with Judah fifty-three. He was a sickly baby, but patient and pleased with the world. He died at six months old, of what Wiggins called a crib death. "What's that?" Judah had asked. "What sort of sickness is that?"

The doctor said it was a name for no name, for something they hadn't figured out as yet but maybe was a sudden fever in the night. "He had no fever when we put him to sleep," Judah said. Seth lay there, extinguished, in blankets that doubled his weight. "I'm sorry," Wiggins had said. "We just don't know enough about it." Hattie feared it was God's judgment, that He who giveth taketh, and for reasons that we know not of.

"What reasons," Maggie said. "What are you implying?"

"Nothing," Hattie said. "Only that He passeth understanding."

They talked of it often, then rarely, then avoided talking till avoidance was a habit and Seth became mere memory, a bit of breath and trustfulness and bone. But the two of them who had been tamed were neither of them broken—and now when they fought it was as if wild beasts were fighting, savagely. They savaged at each other and she, Harriet, ran from the house. She ran with her hands to her ears. She ran out of earshot and screwed up her eyes, but Judah bellowed like Joshua's judgment—and she feared the whole house tumbling down.

"Hattie, I need you," her sister-in-law said.

"Yes."

"I need you for my friend still," Maggie urged. She had been under assault.

"Yes."

"What do you mean by that? 'Yes.' "

"Just yes," she concurred. "You need me for your friend."

But it was a *yes* of concurrence and not of agreement; it was a *yes* that recognized the rightness of the statement, but not the statement's case. She made no acquiescence with that "yes," nor any sort of pledge.

"Hattie, help. You offered me your help once. Hattie. He's insane."

"Excitable," she said. "Judah was always excitable."

"Hattie, he's *insane*," she said. "Your brother is stark raving mad."

"That's not true and you know it." She was being loyal but the loyalty was fair. "He just gets fighting riled."

Yet Judah was rampaging. The veins in his temples were blue. He stood, feet spread for balance, on the hearth. He had a work shirt on, and the muscles in his arms were knotted cords. His skin seemed flayed. He had coal lumps in either hand, and he clenched and broke and pulverized the coal. That was, she knew, a feat of strength. No ordinary man could do it, nor could Judah in his ordinary mood. He stood there grinding the black rock together, with coal dust streaming from his hands as though he'd picked up coal dust to begin with. His hands were black; his forearms blackened and caked. He sprayed small bits and shatter-fragments of the coal from his fist's vice—and stood in a black semicircle, back to the mantelpiece, silent. It was the silence, Hattie knew, that meant his true rampaging. Nothing of him moved except his hands and arms. His arms were working only from the elbows in; he kept his elbows splayed. She did not fear his trumpet bellow by comparison, nor his wall-tumbling word frenzy; *this* was the leveling rage. He held them all, she told herself (and all their perquisites and ancestry and expectation of a decent life, and why was that too much to ask for her who'd never done much asking, always satisfied or saying so at least, and her allotted portion an adequate allotment) in those closed clamped hands.

"Brother," she had ventured.

He looked at her, looked through.

"Won't you tell me what's the matter. Please."

There were foam flecks and spittle on his lips.

"You've been provoked. All right. Something was done to provoke you."

She watched his sinews working. He moved his fingers and his forearms indented and swelled.

"Brother, it's frightening. Please. You're frightening me. Us."

He smiled his rampage smile. It had no teeth.

"Judah," she had pleaded with him. "Please."

But nothing would avail until the seizure itself had availed, and he would stand there empty-handed, shivering. He would have crushed the scuttle load of coal.

"I told you," Maggie had hissed in the kitchen. "I told you he's impossible. I told you you'd not get a word."

"No."

"Not a single word from him. Why not?"

"It isn't me he's mad at," Harriet said. "It isn't me he's crushing out there."

Judah drove a wedge between them, therefore, and split their alliance apart. He'd split her off from Maggie—she recognized it now —like some skillful herdsman herding sheep. Maggie waited isolate, while her ally bolted and was driven and penned off.

"Well, what's he mad at?" Maggie asked. "What did he tell you I'd done?"

"He didn't tell," she said.

"I never gave him cause. There wasn't any reason, Hattie. Believe it."

She had made no answer. The coal was compressed trees.

"Why not? Why won't you believe?"

"He's mightily provoked," she said.

"And you're mightily frightened, I see." Maggie raised her long white arms and took her hairpins out. She shook her head and freed her hair and that meant no more kitchen work. "I see that much," Maggie said.

"You see it. Yes."

There were volcanic shiftings. The earth crust wrinkled like elephant skin, and the seas enlarged or shrank. The mammoth and the tiger shrank, and the horse enlarged. What had been the surface was no longer the surface but depth. There were mines.

"Oh, Hattie," Judah's wife said. "You shouldn't let him cow you so. It's insane."

"I'm not"—she stacked the dishes. "Not letting him cow me, I mean."

"Of course you are."

"I'm not."

The huge trees burned and toppled and their remnants coalesced. Judah stomped out through the parlor, and his boot prints were black.

"Those schoolboy antics," Maggie scoffed. "That show-off strong stuff." She gathered conviction. "Me heap big he-man. You Jane."

Harriet laughed. She could not laugh. She hoped Maggie would take her mouth-stretching rictus for laughter.

"The Johnny Weismuller," her sister-in-law said, "of the northern counties. Another county heard from. But it's ballot-stuffing, Hattie,

don't you see? It's a rigged election. It's one he has to win."
Harriet poured Ivory soap in the sink. She let the hot tap run.
"You don't even know," Maggie said, "what it was we argued on. You don't even want to know, seems like. You didn't ask him, and you won't ask me."
"It's not my business," she said.
"It is. It is, it has to be. Or it isn't, oh, your business to quake in front of that huge bully. He's your brother, Hattie, think of that."
"I do," she said. "That's what I think of. That's all I've been thinking of while you let him stand there. You and your fancy charities that don't begin at home . . ."
"It's my home too," Maggie said.
"It wasn't always and it won't be always, maybe."
So what was enmity then friendship turned to enmity again. Push come to shove, she told herself, she was with her brother and the born Sherbrookes, not wed. She was a born Sherbrooke, and not above announcing it or taking her pride-pleasure in hearing it announced.
"What do you mean by that?" Maggie had straightened.
"Just what I said," she said.
"You mean it?"
Straightening, she came to Maggie's chin, and breathed, and watched her breathing.
"I do," she said. "I mean it. Yes."
It meant she stood for something, where she stood. It meant the time-tried values of decency and loyalty and truthfulness were in the room—or ought to be. Then Maggie left and was not heard from or, when Judah heard from her, he kept his silent counsel. She, Harriet, never had heard. They had no further commerce. Her sister-in-law was an unsheathed eagle, not a broody hen or stork; she was a demon, not an angel, and a lamb outside the fold. Harriet thought of Maggie always like that, in the years that she thought of her often: the face, the figure went inexact, yielding to the image of an eagle or avenging angel or arms like the neck of a swan.

III

"SO I'VE COME BACK," SHE THINKS. "SO NOTHING MUCH MATTERS but that. A nice enough place to return to." Andrew's apartment was nice enough too, on East Sixty-third Street and with the cutest little balcony with green outdoor carpeting that simulated grass. From the next floor, she was certain, or from across the courtyard anyone looking would think the carpet was actual lawn. They had to vacuum, not cut it; that gave it away, she supposed. But she found the whole thing comical and pleasing and kept a telescope inside the balcony door. Andrew putted, and the automatic putting green spat shots back at him. She did her yoga there. Whenever she caught the binocular's telltale flash from 14D (that white-haired man in undershirts who was, inexplicably, her father looking down at her from the hill's height in Wellfleet, and not some sex-tormented dotard in a service apartment) she stepped inside and fetched the telescope and trained it ostentatiously along the sightline of the watcher watched.

The apartment walls were gloss white. Andrew said there was little enough light in New York, and he needed what light he could get. So, leaving, she had emptied the shoe-polish box and used his shirts for rags and smeared black and brown polish on the bedroom and living room ceilings and walls. She stood on the sofa to get at the ceiling and tied a black rag to the broomstick—but it was more trouble, somehow, than it was worth, so she concentrated on the walls and accomplished intricate designs. She rubbed Kilroys and toxin signs and crosses on the walls, then rubbed them over and wrote ViVA, then wrote NIXoN LIvES!!!

She knows he is dying, of course. She has known it, in some part of her, for years. She knows he would require her at his death's bed, to give and get his final blessing. She acknowledges she owes him that much. There are battlefield sites where they live. Their farm has been a theater of the Revolutionary War. Maggie laughed at the phrase. She asked Harriet to tell her what about war was good theater, and how many actors took how many curtain calls.

"Who buys ringside tickets?" she had asked. "Who wants to watch that spectacle? What's so theatrical?"

"That's not what the expression means," Harriet said.

"What does it mean then?"

"Theater of war. It's an expression, that's all—it's a way of saying Seth Warner billeted troops."

"Who's Seth Warner?" Maggie asked.

"You're joking. You have to be joking. Seth Warner and the Green Mountain Boys—they made all the difference hereabouts."

"Not to me," said Maggie. "All right. Washington slept in this bed. No wonder the man was universally loved. I mean, father of his country—he must have fathered thousands, sleeping in all of those beds."

"You're not being funny," Harriet said.

"Well, neither is it funny to prink about theaters of war. I wouldn't be boastful," she finished. "Not about that."

"Seth Warner was a decent man," her sister-in-law said. "And committed no atrocity and defended in an upright fashion what was his beholden township and his duty to defend."

So they took picnics to the battlefield and drove where the Green Mountain Boys had shinnied up hills and down gullies. Judah said, "It's always a shock. I mean, to see this acre and to think how many men were dead in it once."

"I thought Vermonters never died," she said.

"They died that evening."

"With their boots on," Maggie declaimed. "In rightful conflict and with noble mien."

"Something like that," Judah said.

"With thistle in their face," she continued. "And burdock. And probably cow patties."

"What is it?" he asked her.

"What is *what?*"

"The problem." Judah turned to face her. "Tell me."

A hawk spiraled past them, rising. She wanted to warn every sparrow.

"Nothing," she said.

"That's not true."

"Well, something," she admitted. "You know that I'm pregnant."

"I guess so," he smiled down at her. "I was in on it."

"And it'll be a boy maybe. And he'll be a Sherbrooke and proud of his rifle and end up on a field somewhere with his face in cow crap and someone saying, 'Wonderful. You died for your country. Good boy.'"

"He isn't born yet," Judah said. "You don't have to worry he'll die."

"Christ," she said. "I hate these proud memorials. I hate each marble slab. I hate what they did to them and what we're doing here and everyone who comes to glory in the memory of war."

"We came for a picnic," he said.

"I know," she told him. "I'm sorry. I know."

"We can go now."

"I didn't mean to spoil it."

"We can go," he said.

"Yes. Please."

So he became solicitous and watchful, and he would have kept her on the sofa bed the last ten weeks. She hadn't meant it that way, she explained. She'd been upset that once, and war was still a topic she'd be happy to avoid, but that didn't mean she couldn't climb stairs or fetch her food or go to the bathroom alone. Judah thought all women were helpless, of course. He'd wheeled his mother around too long and too considerately to consider any woman other than an invalid—who needed help with washing and needed her pillows plumped up. It hadn't been that way at first. At first he admired her seat on a horse, and the ease with which she ran or swam, but it was like some armor suit he had to find the chink in, or an attitude he had to prove was posed. He had to find the way she cracked, the place where she was joined together and would tear along the seam. He probed and tore at her for years. He had been clumsy-fingered and she could evade him, and he admired her evasive grace more than an easy yielding. Maggie knew that. She knew her fear for Ian's life would be a seam that showed. She had been fearless for herself, and hadn't thought to lock the door, but now each open door was risky and each crowd carried polio, even with the Salk vaccine, and every drinking fountain was a place she drank from, first.

"You'll make a sissy of him," Judah said. That was his probe point, her seam.

"I'll make a survivor," she said.

"A lot of people drink from fountains," Judah said, "without contracting polio."

"What does that prove?" she had asked.

"He'll drink from streams," her husband said. "He'll swallow a lot worse than water."

"In his own good time," she said. "And not until he wants."

Therefore Judah fastened on her fear of guns. He taught Ian how to hunt, though he knew she hated guns and visioned them shooting each other in some bizarre concatenation while they hunted deer. There would be a clearing; it would be rimmed with spruce. The newspapers would call it a "freak accident," she knew. Her son would face her husband and both would be wearing russet, having taken off their red hunting jackets because it got too hot.

"Be careful," she would warn them.

"Yes. Yes, ma," Ian would say—with that impatient knowingness she herself had mustered once.

"I mean it. Judah. Ian."

"Yes."

"Yes you'll be careful?" she asked.

"Yes we know you mean it."

So then she held her tongue; she delivered tongue-lashings enough. They would sling their rifles and walk through the darkening woods. Riding, she startled deer often, and knew the hills were full. They lifted their white tails and leaped incredibly; she could not think her son would shoot at such light loveliness and hated to think it, hated the smell of powder and stock oil.

Largely, however, she feared for his weakness, not strength. She felt herself protective of the boy-man who needed protection—and that she was inured to what she feared would injure him. So she wavered, hovering, between the notion of herself as a lady lion watching over cubs, and that of a cub being buffeted—"Feeding time at the zoo," she had called lunch, laughing. "Come and get it. Nice raw meat. Nice bloody cutlets, boys." Yet it wasn't always funny and she sometimes saw the great swatch of muscle and sinew, hacked back from the bone with a needle-bright blade, the animal bellowing not with sensate grief or pain but only amazement, only how could they do this to me, only what fair-weather friends have turned foul. That's what Ian said they said; that's what cows were good for if they weren't good for milk. "Hey mom, what's for lunch?" he'd ask.

"What's always for lunch?" Maggie asked.

"Food."

"Drink," Judah concurred. They washed their hands. She made them wash hands even with the Salk vaccine.

"It's Wednesday," Maggie said. "It's always spaghetti for Wednesday."

"Psketti," Ian lisped. He mispronounced on purpose then what had eluded him before.

"And dessert?" they chorused. "What's for dessert?"

"Your just deserts," she joked. That too was a Wednesday tradition—angel food cake. Her stripling coarsened while she and Harriet fed him and observed it, and she watched even-handed, balancing scorn and relief.

Still, she could have refused. Maggie might have ignored Lawyer Finney's summoning call. "Margaret," Finney had said ten days ago. "Or do I call you Mrs. Sherbrooke?"

"Whatever," she said. "How are you, Samson?"

"Tolerable," he said. There was static on the line. His voice approached. "I'm better than Judah is, Margaret."

"You always were"—she teased him. "You were, what's the word, exemplary."

"It's not a joking matter. I'm calling to tell you he's sick."

Voices intervened. She heard the operator ask if this was Akron, then asking for the routing code to Akron.

"How sick?" she asked. She lit a cigarette. "Did he tell you to call?"

"No," Finney said. "Can you hear me?"

"Yes. I hear you."

"Good," he said. His voice was higher-pitched than she remembered it. She thought, perhaps so big a man impressed her with flesh resonance, so that at a distance one forgot his speeches' squeak. "Good," he said again, and paused.

"Go on."

"What was the question?" Finney temporized.

"How sick?" she repeated. "And did he tell you to call?"

He paused, considering. "I'm calling on my own say-so; he wouldn't want you to know."

"Then why did you tell me?" she asked.

"I'd better correct that," he said. "He'd want you to know, but not want to know that I told you."

"Samson," she said. "Samson Finney. Don't play the lawyer, please."
"I'm sorry," he said quickly. "I didn't mean to joke with you. It's no joking matter"—he coughed.

She let his cough subside. She listened to it echo and wondered if it echoed all the way to Akron. She stubbed out her cigarette and watched the ash disperse. Death, she told herself, he's dying; why won't he dare use the word? "What word do lawyers use?" she asked. "What's the danger of decease?"

"Demise," he corrected her.

"Death. Death," she near-shouted. "Samson, how sick is he? Tell me what's wrong."

"I'm not a doctor," Finney said. "You needn't shout."

She lit a second cigarette. "I'm sorry. Thank you for calling."

"I wanted to tell you, that's all."

"Yes."

"I thought you should know. You're his wife."

"Yes. Thank you."

"I'm only his lawyer," he said. "I don't know the medical facts."

"The coroner's report," Maggie said. She was sleepy, suddenly. She wanted to lie back and sleep.

"What? How's that?"

"Can you hear me, Akron? Over and out," Maggie said.

"There's trouble with the lines. Bell Telephone," Finney said. "It's the second most mismanaged company. It's impossible . . ."

"Which is the first?" she asked.

"Con Edison. Consolidated Edison Electric. I'm not even a customer," he told her, "but it's famous for mismanagement. It'll bring the country down. It'll bring us to nuclear war."

Then she remembered his theories. He and Judah traded theories over coffee as to who brought the country down lowest, and in the service of which foreign power or infidel belief. General Motors, Judah claimed, was the country's curse. "What's good for GM is good for the nation," he said. "I believe that. I grant it for argument's sake. But also in reverse—and since those rattletraps they make are all tin and tinsel and glitter, why in hell should Americans be pleased?"

"Why not?" Finney asked. "We still make more cars."

"With—what do they call it—planned obsolescence? With a motor that won't take you fifty thousand miles and body work I'd kick in except it just might dent my shoe. Better do it barefoot," Judah said.

So they argued while she listened—first carefully then carelessly, then as to actors rehearsing. She had had water in her ear from diving. She heard the sea continually. It was as if she held a conch shell there, suspended, hearing always the sea's tide—but in her right ear, there where Finney theorized, she heard only babble, a small stream hauled over rock.

"So I wanted you to know," he said. "I think you have the right."

"Yes."

"It's up to you of course," he said.

"Yes," she exhaled. She had managed smoke spirals once.

"I wouldn't want to interfere."

"I'm coming," Margaret said. "I'll write him that it's my idea to come."

There was a Cole Porter song. It came from *Kiss Me Kate,* and that came in turn from *Taming of the Shrew.* Bianca—whose name rhymed with Sanka when her suitor chided her—sang a song explaining her flirtatiousness. "I'm always true to you," she sang, though her fashion of truth ran to lying. She sang about millionaire playboys and what they could offer her in exchange for what she offered. She whirled through stanzas, getting fortunes, driving her true love wild. He had fits of jealous haggling while she swore her faithless fidelity. The audience applauded. It pounded its approval night by night. The song was a showstopper, and even her stage lover had to smile and approve and applaud.

She made Judah take her, twice, to *Kiss Me Kate.* He was not happy in New York. Nothing cowed him, really, but the city could subdue him—could enclose his spreading dominance and limit his limbs' range. Other men might be impressed by the Empire State Building, or overawed or bored or busy calculating costs, but Judah, she knew, calculated only his chance for survival should the wind blow him off the tower. He would examine ledges for toeholds. He would gauge jumping distance and check the window joinings and be an animal at bay.

So his pleasure in the theater would be mixed. He could not forget himself. He gauged the strength of men beside him and in front of them; he thought the woman who handed them programs was lighting up the wrong row on purpose or making him shuffle thick-footed down the wrong aisle. "Darling, in my fashion," Bianca would sing—and he, Judah, would be watchful and grim. There was nothing humorous, for him, in all those Texas millionaires and Oklahoma tycoons she sang of, nor did he find it funny when she flounced away. In all those antic posturings, he saw only—as Harriet would see, and the chill northerners she'd come to make her home with—the set of the actress' hips. They argued betrayal; they argued pancake makeup as a substitute for flesh tint, and buttressed body garments as a substitute for flesh.

"Sit back and enjoy it," she said.

"I am." Judah was stiff-lipped. "I am."

"Oh, Jude," she said. "It's spectacle. It's a play."

"I am enjoying it," he said. "I just don't like our seats."

"When was the last time," she asked him, "you laughed out loud in public?"

"In aught-seven," he smiled at her. "At the hanging."

"You mustn't be threatened," she said. "There's nothing here to threaten you, except only people who laugh."

"I'm not feeling threatened," he said. "I just don't find it funny. That's all."

But *threat* was never far from him, she knew, nor the guises of challenge or menace. He walked into a room as if into enemy camp. She had thought him first a knight in an alien court—with ready gauntlet and stern countenance and a prickly sense of honor and prowess and rank. Then she thought of him as some sort of aging athlete—his body a battlefield and combat arena, but still the pride of hosts. Lastly she thought of him as punch-drunk—some fighting cock or dog that staked out dominion and would defend it fiercely, though the dominion be a thousand acres and huge house and family and wife. She threatened his possessiveness, she knew. She was the last best challenge to his habit of control. They locked in mortal combat that was nothing like the comic "battle of the sexes" that she saw in musicals and that ended, always, in bed. It was not a sexual striving —for their sexual strivings had been consonant, attuned—but rather a lust struggle that continued on past pleasure, past the fighting cock or dog's capacity for life. It was a question of dominion menaced and boundaries cut back—and he patrolled his habit-fences, making of their union a disunity.

* * *

She takes possession of the house. She walks its floors. The kitchen calendar shows deer in snow, standing alert to watch while Santa flies above them; the white-tail deer wear comical expressions. They stare from the lower left corner at the reindeer apparition that is harnessed and stepping in unison across the clouds like turf.

There is small light left outside, and Maggie moves from room to room without adjusting lamps. If there is a switch nearby she turns it on and leaves it on; if she cannot find the light, she does without. Often she cannot remember; though the rooms are familiar, she reaches for wall switches that do not exist. Her hand's assurance alters. She brushes at plaster and wood, certain that the room will come illumined instantly. It does not. It remains a shadowed enclave, her night nest. She traverses the rooms without haste. She has no purpose, walking, other than to walk the house entirely, from room to hall to stairwell to the cupola. She has been his bird in flight, he says. He worries if she feels he's clipped her wings. He fears she should be running, frisking, swift as any duck's trajectory. She'd waited for him, earlier, in the gathering half-dark, whispering *Jude,* darting from some thicket or barn's back when he walked home after work. And there would be fireflies and thick odor in the air, and she felt herself electric then to her very fingertips and toes. Then there was no question of juggling, or light; then she'd needed none to know her way around their world; then she'd been, he joked with her, his Eveready battery and charge. "Assault and Battery," she'd said, and taken his hand. "That's us." They'd walk home that way, or she'd lead him back past the barn. In those years she'd known stars. She could name the constellations and the times of night they'd show, and in which sector of the sky. Now Orion merged with Cassiopeia, and all she'd see for certain were the drinking gourds; now she'd identify satellites, or radio stations, or planes.

She knows the shape of silence; it is the room people die in. It is where you lay the body out. There the walls would meet in a ceiling more like an arch than rectangle, because the room was crowding and fallen together and it leaned on itself for support. The ceiling in a borning room would go the other way. The walls would crowd the floor and open out and only the ceiling would hold the space together; everything was stretched. There were cedar walk-in closets with sachets in the linen, and she felt herself organized in them and had a kind of orderly reserve.

Maggie consults her watch. It is nearly seven o'clock; she has dawdled in the halls. Dinner is to be at seven; she must wash. Descending, she feels light-headed nearly, as if a maiden once again and holding the hymnal, singing till she hyperventilates and thinks herself transcendant: *walks in beauty like the night,* bedecked with flowers and later with straw where her lover lay with her, *and all that's best of dark and bright,* the aspect and the eyes of it; he asked her if she's tired and she says she's short of breath.

The two women meet in the second floor hallway. Hattie masters herself. The one thing Sherbrookes sometimes fail in is politeness; she will do the proper thing and do it handsomely.

"You're welcome here," she says.
"I thank you," Maggie says.
"You're welcome."

There is silence between them. Hattie hunts for crows' feet at the corners of Margaret's eyes. She peers upward. "You've not changed," she offers.

"Oh, but I have," Maggie says. "Seven years."
"Not so you'd notice."
"Is that a compliment?"
"I meant it that way."
"Thank you then. You're looking well."
"Now that's a compliment," says Hattie. "But it isn't true. I look like something that could crack a mirror."

The women laugh.

"My goodness," Hattie finishes. "It's been a long time since there's laughter in this house."

"How is he?"
"Him?" She drops her voice, though there's no need to whisper.
"Yes."
"He doesn't change much, either. You travel light," she says. "You just brought that one bag?"

The hall ends in a west-facing bay; there is a sudden single lance of light. The sun is red, is going, and Maggie's hair goes roseate. Dust dances in the beam.

"So Jude's all right?" she asks.
"Or maybe you've luggage coming?"
"No," she says.

"Well, anyhow your things are here. They need a bit of airing."

"What do the doctors say about it?"

"Airing?" Hattie puzzles.

Her sister-in-law shakes her head. She is impatient but Hattie wants to tell her that the stuff of decency is patience, that the young must wait their turn and take their place in line. "Airing?" she repeats, but Maggie says, "His health."

"I don't follow," Hattie says.

The light is extinguished.

"Doctors"—Maggie prompts her. "How bad do they make it?"

"What? Judah's health?"

"Yes. Has it changed?"

"Not so you'd notice." She hears her voice crack. "Not except for what would happen to him anyway."

Maggie wears high two-inch heels. It makes her six feet tall, Hattie thinks, it's adding insult to injury.

"Would he tell you?"

"What?"

"If it's gotten worse, I mean. His heart. I don't mean would the doctors . . ."

This time Hattie interrupts. Now it's her turn to lose patience and to tell unvarnished truth. "He wouldn't need to. Not to me."

"Yes, but . . ."

"Some people, maybe. Some would have to get a phone call, I don't doubt. Or read about it in the papers till they'd come. Some would come on up with just one suitcase, thinking that's how long he'll last, that's all the time it takes. I'm eighty-one years old," she says, "and Judah's a sight stronger than *I* ever was. I never."

Maggie reaches out and takes her wrist. Her fingers seem a bracelet over bone. "Don't be offended," she says. "I didn't mean it that way."

"What way then?"

"Of course you'd know," she says. "You'd be the first."

"Yes."

"And they wouldn't have to tell you anything," says Maggie. "You could tell them all about it if they asked."

Therefore she is mollified. "What ails my brother," Hattie says, "is not for the doctors to fix."

They reach the stair's crest. Hattie returns to her room; "I'll just get set for dinner," she says and withdraws. Maggie gathers herself.

Her skirts fill as if they were sails. "Why, Jude," she cries, descending, "it's so very pleasant to be back."

Maggie hated the short days, hating to wake in the dark. The summer solstice, she maintains, means that the summer is over—and December twenty-first means winter is just about done. Andrew said that wasn't so, of course, and she said of course not, but anyway I think it. The year's shortest day is the worst. That's how I think about it anyway, it gets better by December twenty-second.

Lately her dreams have been troubling: she knows herself in woods but lost, but hurrying to get to where the game of hide-and-seek is played in less than this so deadly earnest. Men chitter at her from the tree forks like monkeys, and all the elms are blighted, are falling, and she stands beneath their rain of leaves as once she stood in a waterfall. She'd pressed back against the rock and breathed in the air the air pocket made with the water's white arch, was wet enough just from the spray but knew that she'd have to pass through the loud solidity and liquid pounding anyhow. ("Why?" she asked. "Why do I have to do it?" and the answer was "Because." She'd said that wasn't any sort of answer, that wasn't reason enough, and all they'd said was "Because . . .") Because, she knew, they'd laugh at her; because the water on the pool side was limpid and quiet and like, they said, a puddle; because the waterfall might shift its crescent arc, descending, or with a strong enough wind. Then she'd be a captive there, crushed against rock; because she would get cold at night; because her parents would miss her; because there never was a dare she hadn't dared to take; because Sammy Underhill was waiting, watching, and she'd jump through hoops for him if hoops were what he wanted—dreamed now the elm is slippery elm and excellent for chewing, what time she had to sweeten breath before he sucked it out of her, dreamed illustrations in the trees and that the hemp rope there is elm hair, dying, disconsolate, his trunk the elm's girth easily but yielding to disease.

IV

JUDAH MET HER FIRST IN 1938. HE REMEMBERED THE INFLUENZA scare of twenty years before. "You opened the window, and in fluenza" —that had been a chant of the time. Maggie flew into his window at thirteen. She knocked on the Big House side door. She was up for the summer, she said, and out riding her bicycle for the afternoon and would be late for supper and was lost. Judah had been balancing accounts. He liked the work: it had a neatness of notation and there had been that summer a deal more black than red, so he looked up not unkindly to set this girl stranger straight. She stood in his door like a stork. She was long-legged already and was rubbing her left leg with her right instep where it itched above the ankle. She was fighting back crying, he saw, and had grass stains and dirt and burdock down the side of her dress.

"You take a spill?" he asked.
"Yes." She pulled at her left side.
"Hurt much?"
"Yes," she said. "But not now."
"Well, where are you going to?" he asked.

She told him, and he knew the place and was impressed by her bicycling diligence; give or take a couple, she'd traveled twenty miles. Later, when he'd married her and they had children and the birth announcement was a picture of a stork, he remembered how she could have been his own child then, was more than young enough, her angularities just bone and raw-lunged stridency. She rounded off, in time. The stridency diminished and became contempt. The bone fleshed out, and the twenty-five-year difference between them was a quarter of a century, not years. He'd lived through "years," and first they were to his advantage and then his disadvantage, and "years" was a word they worried at like dogs disputing ownership of some cow's cooked rib. But "quarter of a century" had no age implication; it did not implicate him; you couldn't strip or splinter it or lie in the chair's shade, digesting. It was a time-lump, single, simple, and Maggie swallowed it whole.

Only then she was swallowing dust; he'd offered her something to drink.

"I'd like a glass of water, please," she'd said.

"We can do better than that. Have root beer. Have some cider."

"I'd like some water, please."

He went to the kitchen and let the cold tap run and drew a glass of water for her, seeing the glass bead. "You come on in," Judah said. "You can use the telephone if they've got a number to call."

He offered her the water, and she sniffed and swirled it, then drank. He watched her watching him. He saw her yellow bike propped against the fence. He was feeling generous (and knew the generosity not typical, knew even then it was compounded of the afternoon's accounts, and the honeysuckle smell in that soft air, the chill of his right hand's wet palm and the suspicion that she evidenced about the glass he gave —her city manners nicely according with this new country necessity— knew that he liked the bravura about her, not tears she had been fighting back, but not not-tears either, and the distance she'd traveled since breakfast; knew also he could circle back by Harry Nickerson's and settle up about the silo and visit with Harry and find out what was happening to Tim, knew suddenly the house had held him for too long and why not break a habit and accommodate this once, since she too was mistrustful and polite. . . .) and offered her a ride.

"I couldn't do that," the girl said.

"Why not?"

"It's too much trouble," she said.

"Going that way anyway . . ."

"I've got my bike."

"I got a truck," he told her. "We'll haul it."

"I couldn't," Maggie said. "Thanks anyway. And for the water."

"Put that glass down," Judah said.

He stepped around her and down off the porch and picked her bike up and slung it in the truck bed and tied it to the cross bar, then laid it on burlap so it wouldn't scratch. "Get in," he said. "We're going," and climbed into the cab.

She had obeyed him, of course. She edged the door shut, and he told her to slam it. She did. Yet there was something peremptory in her submission, a kind of acquiescence that made the favor conferred seem not his favor but hers. She accepted compliments as he'd seen some men take insults—as though it was the rightful portion, properly bestowed. Praise was her rightful portion, even then. Later she would enter rooms as though she knew he'd rise, expectant, and would walk to the room's door knowing some man would sweep it open. Beauty was conferred on her, he knew, and was its own authority (though at thirteen the conferral had been tentative, mawkish, a first rehearsing only of the spectacle to come—and she sat there stork-legged, voluble, pitching her voice high against the engine din.) He asked her name; she announced it. "Margaret Cutler."

"Where you from?" he asked.

"From New York City. Manhattan Island."

"Where in New York City?"

"Eighty-third Street," Maggie said. "In the just about exact middle of town. Between Park Avenue and Madison. Do you know where that is?"

"Close enough," he said.

"Well, I think it's the very nicest part of New York City. Because there's a museum there and I've a real bike, not like that one"—she tossed her head—"and I ride it to school if I'm late, or Mary doesn't feel like walking, or for any reason mostly, as long as I wait for the lights."

"And don't get lost?"

"You can't, really. Not in Manhattan. You'd know that if you knew it well. There's Central Park. There's the East River to the east and the Hudson to the west, and the even-numbered streets run east. . . ."

He cut across Route 7 and took the old East Road. She chattered while he watched her, idly, and he'd forgotten now (if indeed he had ever remembered, had then seen fit to remember or had listened even to her singsong litany of how to get to where you're going, and her game of naming trees) what else she had told him or asked. She asked though, he remembered, to be let off two miles from her house.

"My mother would be angry," she explained. "At me making you come all the way. I can make it back from here, really. Really and truly. I take the first left turning, and then it's just down that hill. Please."

He stopped the truck. The clutch was giving out; they settled, lurching. She smiled at him (the images coincident again, girl become woman, though practicing, and with her bite plate still) and pedaled off. He was not sorry. He started up and turned at the fork and made for Nickerson's. She'd known enough, he knew, not to bring some stranger back and maybe knew enough to work the sweat and dust up on her on her trip's last leg—arriving breathy, cheerful, just in time for supper and not admitting how she'd lost her way or found it, giving a fair imitation of hunger and hungry enough anyhow to do justice to the soup.

(He taxed her with that later. "Why me?" he'd ask. "Why me?" "You're fishing for compliments, darling."

"Maybe," he acknowledged. "What made you pick me then?"

"When?"

"The first time. Later. Whenever."

She smiled at him, showing her teeth. She had had a toothache in her right incisor, he knew, and touched it with her tongue.

"Why not?" she said. "No reason not to. It was such a lovely house.")

Now Judah knows, with bitterness, her talent for deceit. He wonders if he'd been a part of her sin-schooling then, and source to some white half-lie or omitted truth. He's watched her late arrivals often enough. He wonders how many doors she's knocked at, or been asked to enter, and how many times he's waited two miles from her drop-off point, consulting his watch. Her appetite was checked. She's reined it in too many years to give it its head now. So she'd arrive—not cheerful, not breathless to get at her plate—and ring for wine and have a cigarette. He hated cigarettes. They slaked her hunger, she said, as a glass of chill white wine would slake her thirst. She could puff out smoke rings and did so, coolly, while he watched. She was the only woman ever to dare smoke rings in his house. She crossed her legs and sat there smoking, drinking, in pure opposition. He knew she used the smoke stink to cover up her body's stench from love. He broke or hid the ashtrays, and she dropped her matches and ash on the floor. She was a woman, always, who landed on her two feet when she fell. It hadn't been an accident, he came to decide, that she knocked on the Big House door—and not at some farmhouse or barn.

Yet what he calls deception she had called tact. She was a reed bending before him, pliant, at first even obsequious in public, but she never broke. She took the Big House over like it was a toy house, something manageable. She charmed them all—just sitting there, crossing and uncrossing her legs, engaging in discussions as to Adlai Stevenson ("Christ," he had asked her. "Who's this Adlai Stevenson to get so worked up over? An egghead with egg on his face. A politician like the others, but a bit less expensive to buy. . . .") or practicing her scales. She read aloud. In the evenings she would read him Tennyson or John Greenleaf Whittier or Henry Wadsworth Longfellow, and often he thought there were messages in what she read, some selection code he couldn't quite crack. She read them with a deference that was kissing cousin to mockery. She read of babbling brooks in a voice that made him think of babbling brooks. She read of leafy copses and the azure empyrean in a way that made him see both woods and sky. Yet she did so—he hunted the term—holding back. She was always holding back. Even in her hurtling run, or the way she came at him headlong, or the ferocity she showed him when cornered at the last—there was something inside her inviolate, observing. It was like those Chinese boxes on the windowsill. There was Meg inside of Megan, and Megan inside Maggie, and all of them inside of Margaret. But inside Maggie —his final pet name—in the epicenter of her, impenetrable, there was a stranger that he could not touch or name. He had gone clumsy-fingered at the last. He could not pick that lock. Even penetrating his wife, with her pinioned beneath and Judah at his full extent, there was some final love veil that he could not lift. She stared at him, eyes hooded, and he never knew for certain what she, tilting, glazed, had seen.

Nor did he want to know. He was nearly, for the one time of his manhood, fearful. He had loved her, nearly, for the limitation of her love for him—he who had been limitless in love. It was that serpent glare he feared, her head thrown back, neck arched, and the veins in her neck working while he worked above her. He had power in reserve. He had wealth and women in reserve. He had had, for the first years, the advantage of years. So he pitted his battering strengths against her receptive inertia; he pitted his heat and her chill. It was a standoff mostly (though he sometimes thought he won, exulting in the warmth of her—then found it reflected, or fox fire, maybe heat she got in Providence those weeks she spent there with what she said was her cousin, maybe heat from a mazurka, or valse polonaise.)

Therefore he traded off his leverage and gave her cars, or the permission to smoke cigarettes, or not to visit with him when he visited their son at elementary school. He knew that he must look the clown. He knew what they said of him in the village, and what his sister must think. He guessed what "Cousin" Alexander said of him, in that pitch pine wainscoted third floor walk-up in Providence, on Benefit Street. He knew what the dairyhands said, even, and Margaret's mother—but they none of them would venture, in his impeding presence, one syllable aloud. It didn't matter anyhow; he shucked off gossip like flies. He had always done so, and would, and there had been envy and malice abounding. What mattered was her laughter at Alexander's jokes; what mattered was the way she had no eye hoods on when talking to the dairyhands, or watching Artur Schnabel—what mattered was decorum gone, the love veil and serpent glare dropped.

He saw her again that summer, at the summer's end. There was a carnival in town, and Judah went the third day. Samson Finney said the carnival strongman held the world's weight-lifting record for the two-handed curl and press. And maybe it was so and maybe wasn't so, but any man who'd lift that fat bearded lady was strong—and any man who'd do it more than once was, Finney joked, certainly a jerk.

Judah shot at sitting cardboard ducks. He studied the construction of the carousel. There were eleven horses on the outside ring, and seven on the inside ring—painted, in alternating patterns, brown and pink and white. The horses rose and dipped—he calculated by the pole's rubbed sheen—four feet. The carousel began. The music was the music of the Sheik of Araby. She clattered past him, wearing red. Her hair was in a cap, and plaited, and he knew her but not how he knew her. She swooped and circled, not sidesaddle, but riding as a man would ride, flourishing her cap. She was with friends, he decided, and playing Calamity Jane. He drifted to the ball toss where they tossed for kewpie dolls. His aim was inexact. He found—he told Lawyer Finney—this particular carnival dull. He'd lost his taste for carnivals, he said. There was a time the world seemed playful, and cause for celebration, and he'd down a bottle of applejack brandy on anybody's say-so to celebrate the world.

"Let's do it," Finney said. "Let's celebrate the world."

"It's going to hell in a handcart," Judah said.

"All the more reason. All the greater opportunity for this little drink."

"There's not any reason not to," Judah said.

He took a pull from Finney's flask. He was standing there, tasting it, feeling the heat course through him when she waved—he'd got her name now, Maggie, and the circumstance (though he hadn't been sure at the carousel's gate-edge and wasn't over-certain now—was thinking of that mad housepainter in Munich and his chances for wrecking the planet, was thinking of the sluiceway that his intestines made, how the applejack dispersed out even to his elbows, was calculating the profit at a nickel a ride, and eighteen people to the ride, assuming the carousel full, assuming the barker could fill it fifty times a night. . . .)

"Good evening," the girl said.

"Good evening. Maggie," he said.

"Mr. Judah Porteous Sherbrooke." She smiled. She shook back her plaits.

"You've got a memory," he said.

"I never thanked you properly. I inquired your name. You never told me 'Porteous'—I asked after that."

"You thanked me," Judah said.

"I'm going to New York," she said. "Tomorrow. I've had a lovely summer. I've got to go now, but thanks."

"You're welcome," Judah finished.

She bobbed and moved off, quickening. He knows the child is father to the man. The wish is father to the thought, and necessity the mother of invention. From that first spawning instant, the sex and size and wit of his sons was ordained. *The ordination of the chromosomes,* he thinks, *that's my true ministry. That's what I ought to preach. She was a demon always, so why not today?*

White clover, Judah knew, stays in the ground upwards of seventy years. Her propriety and laughter was a seed then, germinant. She planted something in him (though he would not know it, would forget her name once more, and this their second encounter until she reminded him, later, in their proper courtship, of how he'd rocked back on his heels and neglected to acknowledge how she'd grown, was growing, had won a picture of George Washington at bingo—would plow his bedfields under, repeatedly, and labor enough in his time to tire of it, nearly; would reconcile himself to widowhood, and bachelorhood, the two indeterminate, fusing, since his first wife had died early on) that took a decade to sprout.

Maggie had been twenty-three. She called herself, then, Megan. He met her at Morrisey's Grocery, selecting cheese. She was reading the label and price on camembert. He had taken camembert from the same counter two days before, and the cheese had been inedible. He had returned it, of course. He had complained to Morrisey that the stuff was so damn overripe the cow that produced it was ten years buried, and the cowhide wallet worn away with all those doctor bills. "Matter of fact," Judah said, "I shouldn't wonder if this was the milking that killed it."

Morrisey had laughed and credited him and produced a new camembert cheese. Judah told this story to the girl at the cheese counter, and she turned to face him and was familiar.

"I know you," Judah said.

"No."

"I've seen you before," he said.

"It's possible," she said.

"Yes. Not lately."

"No. I haven't been here"—she had calculated, lifting her right index finger—"since 1938."

"I knew you then," he said, recollecting. "You lost your way on that bike."

There was nothing timorous about her now, no trace of that thin supplicant. She was model-slim still (was indeed, she told him later, working as a model in New York—but hated it, hated the hair driers she sat beneath for hair drier ads, the vacuum cleaner parts she assembled and disassembled for vacuum cleaner catalogue ads, the people that she worked with sometimes, and their whole notion of chic—).

"Have dinner with me," Judah asked. "We'll have to fat you up."

"I can't," she said—but speculative, smiling. "Thanks anyway."

"Of course you can."

"You're kind to ask. . . ."

"For auld acquaintance sake," he said, and wondered why he pestered her and why he felt persistent.

"I'm with friends."

"Well, bring them," Judah said.

She replaced the camembert cheese. "My name"—she held her right hand out—"is Megan."

"And mine is Judah Sherbrooke, Megan. Maggie. Welcome back."

"I'm passing through," she said. "I'll tell the others."

"Yes."

"They're waiting outside. I'll be back. Mr. Judah *Porteous* Sherbrooke."

She turned, with her hair swirling, and he watched her out the door.

"Look at that," Morrisey said.

"I'll take ten pounds of sirloin," Judah said. "Now get behind that meat shelf and behave. You ought to be ashamed."

Morrisey wolf-whistled. "I am, lawsie mercy. I am." He listened to *Amos 'n' Andy* and was working on the accent. "Lawsie mercy," he repeated. "I'se gosh-all get-out ashamed."

Judah stood by the cereals shelf. He remembers wishing, for a moment, that she'd get back on her bike—or car, or motorcycle, whatever conveyance she used now, or some second stranger's pickup truck—and leave him to his evening's plan (a walk, a meal, a smoke, the solitude he broke from only in his aimless grazing, habit-penned.) She said to him later that week: "Three coincidences. That's once too often to take for granted."

"How else do people meet?" he'd asked.

"Through introductions," she said. "Through school friends or through family or work."

Her friends had come and stayed for drinks, then left (were never present really, were moustachioed absences between the bookcase and the standing lamp, were twittering there like magpies, wearing cameras, asking for Singapore Slings). He asked her to remain. She was his dream of welcome, with everything ajar. He barbecued ten pounds of sirloin and dropped the whole thing on her plate. It dwarfed the plate; it bled onto the cloth.

"You're joking," Margaret said.

"No."

"You'll spoil me with that kind of joke."

"Spoiled rotten"—he sat down. "If you haven't spoiled already. Like that cheese."

He leaned back, pleased with himself. He studied her gestures, engorging. She sliced and chewed with delicacy, and was theatrical. She would eat his life.

They stand there poised on the shore's brink, reflected, wavering, in an immobility that is motion arrested for the instant only. She is in the ocean, of it, turned three-quarters to Ireland, the sun in front of her so that he, squinting, sees the foam-nimbus smudge her body's edge—the outline of her indistinct in that spume halo, and all of it shifting, her feet hunting purchase, the sand floor accreting (so that he, Judah, no sooner puts his foot down than he finds it swallowed, is up to his ankle in silt), the tide continual and treacherous (though this too seems a code to crack; waves come in sequence, he's learned; there're maybe seven big waves, maybe nine, then nothing much—as if the trough and crest were components of a level whole, the subtraction of one water mass massed up against the next). Then there are riptides, she tells him, and crosscurrents and circle currents that they call a sea puss, lazily coiling, and though he's not afraid of it, can dominate what fear he has and enter the water behind her grinning, thumping, dominating the waves, he never thinks of it as better than an armed standoff or some sort of watchful truce: not his element, no, nor one in which he takes his ease, though the marble quarry up at Danby made a fine place for swimming, and he'd stand in some streambed for hours, snagging trout. But she has wished it and her wish, he jokes, is his command, and therefore they have driven to this coastal outcrop and she is in her element, disporting like some glad sea otter, though he's never seen an otter and doubts they wear pink two-piece suits; still, Megan loves lobster and oysters and clams, and he promises to have a seaplane bring them lobster. Still she laughs that he's like some forlorn stranded Neptune who's forgotten how to swim, standing there on that rock jetty, needing only a pitchfork for trident—huge, she teases him, and bedraggled and cranky as a soft-shelled crab.

"What kind of crab is that?" he asked.

"The kind that's good for eating," Maggie said. She licked her lips. "The kind that steams up pink and ain't as tough as it looks."

"A hermit crab," he said. "That's what."

"A god of the sea"—she touched him—"who's cranky and landlocked and loves his water sprite."

"Yes," Judah acknowledged. "Very much."

"And likes to watch her swim," she said.

"And loves to watch her swim."

"Considering the tasty morsel she herself might make."

"Yes."

"Yum yum." She put her fingers in his mouth. "Old Neptune's hungry again. Grr-r. Yum."

He's forty-eight years old, he tells her, and not the sort of person to joke with or make jokes about; she pulls her fingers from his mouth, salutes, and dives from the rock jetty cleanly, into the crest of the waves.

* * *

"Since we cannot take Material Substance with us," Peacock wrote, "I am persuaded that a Christian man must make display whilst still in the Possession of Appreciative Faculties, and health. The fireplaces shall be marble, not Parian marble nor the stuffs of Italy, Carara and suchlike, but from our neighbor quarries in Vermont."

He had traveled home via the Isthmus. The train across the Isthmus was a train he scorned. There were blockades in the Mexican Gulf, but they were under escort and out of danger's reach. They took a steamer up the Hudson and a train from Troy.

Peacock fulminated against imprecision in trains. His mine trains had a gauged wheel that could hold the track in snow or rain or ice. If he could keep, he argued, twenty tons of ore from falling off of mountain passes, why couldn't this rattletrap conveyance preserve itself on the track? "The camel finds the Needle's Eye," he wrote, "more readily than I find easement for what they call Pneumonia. Strait is the gate. . . ."

Through his law practice, Sherbrooke had acquired real estate and mining properties; he accepted notes in lieu of salary and was a paper millionaire by 1852. He bought Montgomery Street. He built brick office buildings that survived fire. He was, a letter writing wit observed in the *Alta California:* "*Golden* tongued. There be a stream of language issuing forth from Lawyer Sherbrooke's mouth with its proportionate amount of fool's gold, but by all accounts worth panning at sixteen dollars the ounce. His opponents would wish him *dried up.* His admirers say the *vein* is inexhaustible and will *run on* to the Supreme Court and dwarf the *Mother Lode.* Myself I do account him a *natural asset* to our fair state, babbling as the stream does babble or rumbling as the *mine-shaft* when it buries some unfortunate within. I propose a monument to Lawyer Sherbrooke's *weighty words* and will be thereof the first subscriber. I herewith pledge two *pounds* of *pebbles* for our Demosthenes' mouth. . . ."

"If the mote is in thy neighbor's eye," Peacock wrote, "pluck out the mote in thine own. Thus do we learn the gentleman's comportment—since I never yet knew scoundrel but could bandy reputations with the best. Truly to learn humility is, I think, the Christian's highest art—for many's the mock-humble man who thrives on Pomp and Praise. I pride myself on nothing half so much as this: that never have I claimed as due more than the bond's redeemable Value, nor ever left notes unredeemed."

* * *

There is Italian marble everywhere, and columns that his grandfather had ordered shipped from Greece. The house is what he labeled sizeable and others call huge. He moves through it with habit's ease, not noticing the glitter or the gimcrack elegance his mother had insisted on as *comme il faut*. He'd asked her what that meant, and she had said, "What it means is place. It's knowing your position in this town, and how to keep it up."

So the Big House is ornate in ways he only sees when seeing it as others do: Maggie, for instance, batting her eyes at him, staring at the mirror that had silver Cupids at the top. They married three months later, in the upstairs ballroom. They had a civil service, with a justice of the peace presiding, and only a handful of relatives and friends. Her parents motored north from New York. Her father was his, Judah's age, and none too pleased about it—but not, when he arrived and saw the farm and Judah took him drinking, any too displeased. They got along. They got through a bottle of sour-mash whiskey that first afternoon. He remembers Maggie's father with affection still—a dapper man wearing pinstripe suits and a moustache like Thomas E. Dewey's moustache.

"We could go the whole hog," Judah had offered his bride. "If you'd prefer."

"No. This is between us, not them."

So they'd stripped the guest list back and made no fuss about it, keeping private covenant and swearing private marriage vows and saving the parties for later. There would be parties enough.

Even across the continent's span, Peacock felt himself a native of Vermont. He sent ten thousand dollars home, as his subscription to the cost of levying troops. "We pay John Chinaman," he wrote, "so why should not the Slave receive like Wages and proud Liberty. All bondage—lest it be to Christ—is heinous in His sight."

V

"Hattie," James Pearson called. "Hey, Hattie."
"Yes," she'd said.
"Come on over here, hey, Hattie."
"Why?" she inquired.
"Why not?"
"Not till you ask politely, Mr. James Pearson, sir," she'd reprimanded him, smiling. "Not till you ask the way a gentleman would ask it."
"Please."
"That's better."
"Come on over here, hey, Hattie, please."
His face was red. His hair was red. He flamed at her from the room's dark corner.
"Well," she acquiesced. "Since you insist. *Parce que vous insistez.*"
"I do," he said. "I do."
She'd taken that as augury and walked toward him, blushing. He reached out his rough hand.
"Say please," she'd chided him.
"Please."
His hand was freckled, and the knuckles sprouted hairs.
"Say pretty please"—she took his hand—"with a cherry on top."
"Pretty please with a cherry on top."
"Say pretty please with a cherry on top, and marshmallow dressing and sugar."
He placed his left hand on her waist.
"Pretty please," he'd whispered. "With a cherry on top, and marshmallow dressing and sugar."
"No," Harriet pouted, withdrawing. "I don't like marshmallow dressing."
This completed their routine. She had learned it when learning skip rope. This was her posed, phrased resistance, and now she let him fondle her and gave herself up to his arms. He smelled of licorice. He pressed and mauled at her for minutes, for what seemed like hours though she kept close track of time. He disarrayed her clothing, and she let him paw the disarray. Then Harriet pulled back and kissed his freckled chin and said, "No, please. We mustn't."

"Yes."
"No. *Pretty* please."
The licorice transmuted; she smelled gin.
"Why not?" He had turned sullen.
"Mr. James Pearson"—she chaffed him—"you know the answer to that."
"Christ, Hattie . . ."
"Don't blaspheme."
And so they fenced and she parried his lunges and was the perfect foil. Only later, only when she met him by accident—Jamie, just come from propping up the Drop-Inn bar, whose nose had gone bulbous and stomach distended and red hair lost its wave and fullness and sheen—did she reconsider. She thanked her lucky stars. She watched him shuffle down Main Street, doffing his engineer's cap to women in comic obscene deference, doing a jig on streetcorners as he waited for the light to change—and she thanked her luck he did not see her nor doff his cap when she, Harriet, passed. Obscurely, she had been offended that Jamie stayed in town. He should have vanished from the streets and bars when he vanished from her last embrace. He had sworn to. "Hattie, I'm leaving," he said. "I can't stay around here like this."
"Don't go," she'd said.
"I'll go. I know when I'm not wanted."
"Please stay," she said, not meaning it and he knew she didn't mean it and, to spite her, stayed. He weaved and hiccoughed past her as an emblem of decorum lost; he lost his job at the bank. She noticed, when he did the hornpipe, he clicked his heels twice in the air. She wished on him, as retribution for her broken heart, that he would break his legs. He should, she thought, break his ankles at least and not prove so monkey-agile, capering.
"You'll break my heart," she had told him.
"There's nothing to break," Jamie said.
"You're cruel. You're being unfair."
"All right," he had leered at her, stinking of gin-sweetness. "Let's see your heart. Let's have a look."
So, breathless, not daring to breathe, not knowing why she did it but knowing that she had to, once, not knowing how she dared but knowing his juniper-nearness was a dare she had to take, she took her blouse off and then unlaced her chemise. She had been cold. There

were goose pimples on her arms. She dropped her chin because he might put his hands on her neck, and there was a chill wind blowing that made her naked neck contract. There were willow trees. They stood in a bower the willow branches made, and he reached out and twined his fingers in the long green willow strands.

"Keep going," Jamie said. "All I can see is ribs."

Her brassiere was white. It had lace eyelets and four hooks. She reached around and fumbled with the clasps and closed her eyes to concentrate so she would not be fumble-clumsy, and because the wind hurt her eyes. It was blowing at her from where Jamie stood, blowing his hair forward and hers back.

"Jamie?" she asked.

"A-yup."

"James Pearson-person," she said.

"Keep going."

"I've got a heart," she finished and dropped its final protection and stood there shivering. She screwed her lids tight shut. Her heart was in her throat. "Well, haven't I?" she asked.

"That's all you got," he said and laughed and turned on his two heels and left her in the willow's shadow and crashed across the stream still laughing, whistling, implacable. She hated him implacably. She wanted to put out his eyes.

Harriet closes the bathroom door. It squeaks; it requires oil. The door drinks oil, it seems, like Judah drinks whiskey; no matter how well lubricated, it soon enough dries up. That had been Maggie's joke. Most of the wit and levity within the household had been hers; she, Harriet, grants that. But there is such a thing as too much levity, as jokes in bad taste following the jokes in good. Their mother had had a saying: "There are six senses," she said.

"Which ones," Harriet would ask. "Which are the six?"

"How many do you know about?" her mother asked. "How high can you count?"

"Five. To five. One two three four five."

"And what are the five senses?"

"Sight and sound and smell and touch and taste," Harriet said.

"That's right. And then there's *good* taste, darling; that's the sixth proper sense."

So Harriet would chant while bouncing, "Sight and sound and smell and touch and taste and *good* taste" or skip rope to the rhythm of it, counting six. There was a sixth sense that she learned of later that meant you saw for distances you couldn't possibly see. It meant you heard things you had no chance to hear, and smelled smoke when there was something burning, though you couldn't smell the smoke. It happened to her, Harriet, sometimes; she walked into a room and looked at the clock on the mantelpiece and the clock started to chime. She shivered when she heard Fred Rowley's name and learned, the day after that, that Fred Rowley had died in a car crash just twenty-four hours before. She saw a painting on the Millers' wall (of the Connecticut River, with an Indian poised on the bank, wearing war paint and feathers and a loincloth, one foot in his canoe) and decided that she didn't like it and the painting fell.

That was coincidence, maybe; she grants that. But she had run from the Wittens' parlor screaming the day her mother died, and at the very minute—during a discussion of the Federalist papers. She still could not hear the phrase "Federalist papers" without going all over dizzy, and nauseous, and wanting to faint. She'd known (though in the Library, attending to the Periodical Shelves) when her nephew Seth had been born. It was her volunteer day, and Judah had said, "Go on, Hattie. We'll manage without you. We've managed before," and Maggie said, "If this one's half as long in coming as the last, why, then there'll be plenty of time." So she had been arranging the *National Geographics* and marking down the issues that they missed. They had a complete second set. There was no smoking in the Library, of course. She never smoked. But suddenly her lungs filled up, and there was the smell of Judah's cigar smoke all around her, and she had known beyond coincidence there was a baby born.

Harriet arranges herself now in the sheets. She uses an electric blanket, but also a hot-water bottle, since she does not trust the blanket while she sleeps. There could be short circuits or a defect in the wiring or faulty connections that she would not notice till the morning, till too late. Hilda Thornhill had suffered first-degree burns on her back. If the hot-water bottle broke, Harriet thought, all she would wake up was wet. She composes herself to pray for Judah's health.

"Lord," she murmurs. "Save my brother Judah from the ravages you visit on us all. Preserve my nephew Ian according to the love we bear him, and his just deserts. May Judah . . ."

She cannot continue. The prayer does not soothe her, nor is she composed. She is troubled by day-waking dreams, and turns to the file cabinet and pulls a letter out and smooths it and lies back to read. Let Maggie come, she prays, like an avenging angel to bring the whole house down. Let her beat her arm-wings and cause the rooftrees to crumble and the rafters to be powder and the walls and ceilings dust.

The junket had been excellent, she knows. It was just the right consistency, and neither too tart nor too wet. The Sanka did not trouble her—not even that second cup. She, Harriet, breathes with a sweet and inoffensive breath. Judah can tease or ignore her or flaunt her need for maraschino cherries, but her teeth are better than his, and her breath. She wonders what sort of wood George Washington had used for his incisors. She imagines Martha Washington held in the crook of her husband's right arm, face tilted back and breathing deeply, but breathing in the smell of cedar wood, not Crest.

"Hey, Missie Sherbrooke. You there! Hey, my maiden lady."

Her second suitor, Samuel Powers, was bluff about her chastity and found it a fine joke.

"Don't shout," she'd said to him. "I hear you."

"So you ain't deaf?"

"No."

"Not deaf to entreaty, neither?" He chuckled. "What about that?"

"You hush up, Mr. Sam," she said.

"Not deaf to my proposals? Not deaf to every argument?"—he winked at Judah hugely.

"No," she said. "Not all that deaf. You'd wake the sleeping dead with that bellow."

"OK,"—he slapped his sides, delighted. "All right then. OK."

"But hush your mouth and mind your manners, Mr. Sam." She was reading Southern novels then. She dropped a curtsy to him from her imagined carriage height but also dropped her handkerchief.

"Accidental a-purpose." He pounced. He gathered up her handkerchief and wiped his cheeks and kissed the handkerchief. "Hey, Judah," he bellowed. "Looky here. Look at this moo-chwower."

"*Mouchoir*," she interposed.

Her brother laughed, sardonic.

"It's mine, you unmannerly man. Give it back."

She stomped her foot in what she hoped was a heroine's fashion, pleading. He crumpled up her handkerchief and put it in his waistcoat pocket, covering the watchfob and the silver chain.

"Not likely," Vice-President Powers said. "I found it and I'll keep it. To console me, Missie Sherbrooke." He winked at her this time, and she checked for Judah's sightline—then saw him at the fireplace, back turned.

"Losers weepers," she smiled.

"Yes. You need consolation," he said.

"*Mean* man . . ."

"This memento," Powers said. "This fragrant memory, if I may so describe it"—his chest and belly shook with pleasure. "This, this, this *moo-chwower*."

She stuck her tongue out at him and bit the end of it. She had been impetuous and bit it over-hard. She turned from him to hide her tongue's true pain (like burning it on gravy or licking at the sharp edge of a piece of letter paper) and he resumed his chat with Judah as to railroad stocks. They were engrossed in some prospectus by the time she turned again, and he flung her compliments like bones.

"Hey, Missie Sherbrooke," Powers said. "Sashay this way, why don't you? Do a poor fellow a favor."

He and her brother swapped stories. They slapped each other's backs. They grimaced in the corner, huddling over balance sheets and toting up credits and debits. They bickered together the way old friends bicker, and drank. She was an accessory, she knew. Widower Powers solaced himself. He consoled himself, she knew, with whiskey and gin rummy and poker and cigars. There were other methods of consolation, no doubt—and he no doubt availed himself of them—to judge by his burbling smug whisper to Judah when he came back from Bridgeport, Connecticut.

"There's things"—he grew expansive—"things to *see* there. Yes."

"What sort of things?" she asked.

"I can't hardly begin to describe them." He smiled. "Don't know as it's proper in—saving your pardon—mixed company."

"Why, Sam,"—she fluttered, letting her voice break—"you've learned something after all. After all these weeks."

"A-yup," he chortled, nudging Judah. "You can say that again."

"Bridgeport, Connecticut," she continued. "It's on the water, correct?"
"Right. Leastways I think so."
"You didn't notice?" she had asked.
"Nope. Not me."
"I thought you said you saw things there."
"Hattie," Judah intervened, "he never got out of his room."
And she was tired suddenly, tired of their self-delighting schoolboy charade. She was weary of their glib obscene fraternity in lust. Powers would use the phrase "amorous lists." "I've joined in the amorous lists," he would say. "I've entered the fray. I've thrown my gauntlet down and plan to be a-jousting soon"—he winked—"in the time-honored amorous lists."

So when he married that redhead from Bridgeport, Connecticut, Harriet was not surprised. She had felt, perceptibly, relief. She was thereafter relieved of his importunings (smoothing his hair past the bald spot, crinkling up his eyes in heavy-handed laughter at some heavy-handed joke, clinking the silver together in his side pants pocket, fist working at the coinage, cloth-swaddled, huge) and relieved forever of courtship's importunity, at peace.

Nor did she feel embittered by Judah's teasing title "Spinster." She, Harriet, selected it. It was an honorable name—the spinning sister contracted—and her chosen fate. Time passed, and the passage was simple. She relinquished vanity. She relinquished her courtship wiles and stratagems with what she knew was relief. She had been young then youthful then a woman in her prime then middle-aged then past her prime then old. These were distinctions that had seemed all-important once but now seemed unimportant, indistinct. She had eaten sweets and then relinquished sweets in order to preserve her lines and now eats sweets again. She had tried, persistently, to battle time lines and age, but it was a losing battle and better not to fight. Time was, she joked, the perfect diet; time brought her weight at seventy-seven back down to the weight she'd had when seventeen. She'd thought her girth irrevocable—but it has been time-revoked.

Nor did she feel requital when Powers and his wife died on their way to the Bahamas in a charter plane. She had not wished him—as she certainly wished Jamie Pearson—dead. She bore no grievance that would demand requital in some coral reef off Nassau in the Bahamas. She, Harriet, had never been to Nassau in the Bahamas, nor, for the matter of that, to water warm enough for coral reefs. But she owns coral necklaces and bracelets, and she had seen photographs in *National Geographic* of the Great Barrier Reef. Magic fish and eels would snout their way through coral, but men would flay themselves on contact with the pointed nubbins of the rock. Their skin would shred and bleed and sharks would follow the blood trail and make a noonday snack of Samuel Powers and his new wife. She wonders, idly, if the sharks ate human hair. She wonders if they'd lop off his wife's head entirely, or leave the strands of orange hair to coil around the coral like weed.

She feels sleep slipping up. She has twenty minutes to rest. She switches off the electric blanket; "Lord forgive them their trespasses," she prays, "as I would ask forgiveness of my own." She thinks of Thomas Sherbrooke, as she does often before sleep. His knowledge of ships must have been meager; he had piloted a rowboat once, on Parrin Lake. He had learned to swim and had bought boats in bottles, she imagined, and watched the firelight gleam off their rigging and decks. He would have watched for hours, hands on his chin and elbows on the mantelpiece. He would have dreamed grandiose dreams.

Whales would spout to starboard. Dolphins would follow the ship. He lay on the forward deck, thinking of home, noting how the water underneath him was moving so much faster than water in the near distance, or at the horizon. There were bands of water. He knew the waves were demarcation points. ("Dear mother and father,"—he had sent one letter home—"Forgive me if you can. I'm off on what we sailors call the 'Bounding Main.' I have no regrets or uncertainty in making my fortune this way, and sure I am to do it because the ship runs four boats and is fitted out with 3500 barrels and for a voyage of 3 years. We are going round Cape Horn and to the South Pacific Ocean in a voyage after spearm whales with a crew of 27 men, and very pious Officers. I am very satisfied with my situation and Prospects except only in the grief I caused by manner of my leaving but *you must not worry* for me, not you particularly mother. There were contrary winds and averrse currents but we weathered them and recruited off Payta as also recruited off Tecamur and stand now at a full compliment of men. Tell Daniel to be a good boy and not to do as I have done unless he wishes also to be a burden to his parents tell him remember me."

She pictures him, gold-haired, blue-suited, laying down his quill pen to breathe and sigh and stare and brush away hot tears. The ship would heave in the windless swell; the smell of rum was rank. She pictures him rereading—as she herself has countless times reread—his single letter: "It is impossible to describe the misery of the slaves both here and at Rio in particular you would hardly conceive that with all its fine palaces and grand houses with the King of Portugal riding in his splendid Gilt Coach and officers attending him that there could be so much misery but while your eyes would be dazeled with all the splendor you will turn them away and see twenty or thirty poor slaves chained together bearing heavy burdens. Your soul sickens at the sight. But I am forgetting my story I went while there to see the place where the slaves were whiped there was one about to be Punished as he was tied to the post his back stripped and 150 lashes given him he uttered not a groan and when the horrible scene was finished the blood lay in pools at his feet and his body was so mangled and torn that he could not rise but lay senseless until he was carried away. . . . Give my love to all the children tell them to forgive my faults and if possible to forget them. Give my love to all my relations and friends if I have any. . . ."

He stands in the whaleboat, balancing. There are harpooners behind him. The harpoon is intricately carved, and the blade has a green sheen. It is polished. There is blubber and blood and, astonishingly, reefs that rise like candelabra from the troughs of waves. ("I have hopes you will forgive the rash step your son taken, signing on at Falmouth for which I am undutiful but repentant, and if ever I return again which God grant I shall endeavour to make good in esteem but no more for the present it is too much. . . . I get in common with the rest of us the 1.75 lay or one barrel out of 1.75. . . .")

Fins disport, cleaving. The harpoon shaft is on his shoulder, and the shoulder acts as a seesaw-fulcrum; it is tattooed. She peers at the tattoos but is unable to decipher them—they do not signify. They are black and red and bulbous. They are changing, self-wreathed shapes. His shoulder aches. He weeps. He fingers the tattoos. She sees them as flesh-hieroglyphs, the shadow and pattern of his manhood's rising prime—and knows there is a message there, but not for her to read. "Dear mother and father," he wrote. "I hope to be a steward shortly in the Captain's mess, and share his rations and musick what time he has musick to share. . . ."

VI

THEY EAT. HE EATS IN SILENCE, MOSTLY, WHILE HARRIET MAKES conversation-noise. "I want you to remind me," she says, "to have them plant shallots this spring. Shallots would be wonderful with meat like this, and I can't buy them anywhere—not Morrisey's, not anywhere. We could have them every day for months. They keep."

Finney has the three wills. He has followed Judah's instructions; they are letter-alike and brief. Hattie has her constant portion, and there are various bequests. The charities amount to one hundred thousand dollars—ten of them each getting ten. The principal beneficiaries, however, change; one testament allots the bulk to Ian, one to Maggie and one to an agreed-upon division, half and half of an assessment of the whole. There are copies; they bulge in the briefcase he brought. He will be one witness and will take them to his office, after signing, for a second witness and to have them notarized and filed.

He has learned not to offer advice. There are clients who request it, but it's wasted time with Judah and not worth the fuss. He calls himself a servant of the law. He knows that Ian had no chance, that this whole dispensation ceremony was no more than a charade. He had been tempted, almost, to try to reach Ian by phone. He had wanted to see Judah's face if both of them arrived—but then he thought that this too might have pleased his client, might have been intentional. And then he thought that Maggie might inform her son, or maybe the letter would anyhow reach him; then he thought the simplest thing is just do what Judah had asked. He takes his cut, whichever way, and each of them will be a legal binding document once signed. If pressed to it, he'd say that Judah's crazy like a fox. And if Judah wants to play a fox game, well, it's his own business. "Ours not to reason why," he says aloud, "ours but to do and do it properly." He'd set the briefcase by the sideboard and received a Scotch from Judah and ventured a joke: "It's your funeral," he'd said, and tilted his glass.

Finney drinks. He requires the hair of the dog. He needs an entire kennel, based on what transpires here, based on what these people think is sensible; he swirls the whiskey in his glass, watching the water separate out from Scotch. Maggie, he pronounces to himself, is one of a kind. The Big House isn't big enough to hold her; he'd known that; the state of Vermont isn't big enough, and probably she'd flown the coop as far as San Francisco, figuring the whole East Coast wasn't sufficient, thinking she'd try for Hawaii. Finney knows the type. He knew the ones who went to court with a black eye they'd got from a door or some Italian who obliged them, and cried and said it was their husband and could they please have everything he owned. He knew the ones who signed on late then wanted to leave early, taking fifty percent of the world. But though he knows this kind and heaps them all together—with the ambulance chasers and the malpractice people and the ones who ran to Canada, then wanted amnesty for that—she is the top of the heap. Finney figures her at fifty, and maybe a year or so past it, but you'd never know by looking and you'd have to do the arithmetic twice. She is Florence Nightingale tonight. She is all smiles and chatter and hot compresses and sympathy; Judah'd got what he wanted by getting her back. But Florence Nightingale contracted syphilis, Finney knows, and died in the Crimea of a dose. That was the hell of a thing—he finishes his drink and jangles the ice cubes and figures maybe he'd best pour the second go-round himself. You pick a model of charity and decency and selflessness, and make her a model for nurses, and she's got the clap.

He pours. He is there to safeguard the Sherbrooke interests. Heavily, he toasts her; she smiles up at him sideways, batting her eyes. But she is Sherbrooke also, and an interested party, and Judah's never even entertained the notion of divorce. He, Finney, had suggested it, and Hattie had no doubt suggested it often enough. But Finney got a flat-out no, and Hattie probably got worse, got a mind-your-own-business-not-mine.

"Are you glad to be here?" Finney asks her.
"Yes."
"Does it feel like home to you still?"
"Yes."
"Why did you leave then?" Judah asks her, interrupting, intent.
"You know."
"No, really . . ."
"Let's not start that, Jude," Hattie says. "Not now."
"Why not? What better time to start?"
"What worse time, Judah. . . ."
"No time like the present. It's what I always say."

"I never heard you say that," Maggie says.
"Why did you leave?" he repeats.
"What makes you ask that?"
"All right." He takes another tack. "What brings you here?"
"The love I bear you." She says this with recital precision, looking at Finney instead.
"Bore," Judah says.
"*Bear.*" She cites her letter to him. "And you said you bore me once."
"How was the trip?"
"When did you get my letter?"
"Monday."
"What did you do with it?"
"Tore it up," he lies. "Flushed it down the toilet. Gave it to Hattie instead."

She turns to Harriet, hunting complicity, asking how she's been and what's new with the world and how is it treating her now; Harriet asks for the salt.

It had happened to him with his sons. Feeding Ian, watching how his two-month-old learned to swallow or stick out his tongue, inserting the small spoon with its quotient of apricot or carrot or banana mush, Judah remembered feeding his mother—her on her final bed, drooling. She had lain there for five months, force-fed by him and her husband and nurses—eating from china, and with the best silver and crystal. But she too ate only mush or a boiled egg maybe on a strong morning, with a sip of champagne. She ate with the witless deliberation that signaled body function and not her spirit's purpose; her spirit's purpose, she announced, was to leave them all.

Judah fed her patiently, announcing how the egg was just as fresh as possible, as how he'd plucked it from the chicken coop five minutes before boiling. "Too soon," his mother would articulate. "Too soon. It should set up." She said the glass that she drank from stank, smelled of onions. He brought her day-old eggs, and she said they were too old.

For the rest of it, he manages well enough. Directly above his bedroom, in a third-floor storage hall, there are dresses. His grandmother had had the habit of preserving the year's most beautiful dress and selecting that single keepsake on Christmas Eve. She would give the rest away to charity or servants or nieces—or, if she were fond of the fabric but not style, would have the dress remade. The storage hall was cedar lined, and the commodes and chests were cedar, and therefore the clothes were moth-free; Harriet strewed camphor on the floor. His grandmother, commemorating, would pin a note to the left shoulder of the dress—thus Judah, holding a yellow lace-embroidered flaring full-length gown would read: *1882. June 25th The Adams Ball. I danced till 2 A.M.* In 1883 she wrote: *January 23. Reception for Anne Watts*—and chose a dress that was predominantly violet, an oriental-influenced arrangement of silks. There were ballgowns and picnic outfits and gowns she wore to christenings; after 1907, with her husband dead, she had worn only black.

Judah remembers her ear trumpet and the heft of her cane. She had shouted at him to speak up, and sometimes he mimed speech, making just the lip motions, and then he'd shout she was too deaf to hear. They took walks together, and she made him name the trees. For every type of tree he identified correctly, she promised him a penny—and they kept count. He'd tried to square that avid dancer with the impeding waddle of the woman he had known—and thinks of her wasp-waisted twirling gone defunct.

"Judah"—she would summon him—"what kind of tree is that?"

"A birch tree, grandmother."

"Yes. What kind of birch?"

"A silver birch."

"What other kind would it be?"

"A silver bitch," he'd mutter, and she strained to hear.

"What?"

"A white birch maybe, but it isn't. It's a silver birch."

She'd have her notebook out, and wet the pencil stub.

"Beech, did you say beech?"

"No."

"Hattie knows the answer. She could tell."

He put his hands in his pockets. He balled his fingers to fists.

"Fess up, Judah, you said beech—that's a penny less this morning. That cancels out the elm."

"*Birch,* I said. Silver birch."

"You got the popple," she would say. "You got the cottonwood."

He watched her make the plus sign and knew her teasing well-intentioned, knew she'd heard him after all and was content. She called their walk "the constitutional of the trees" and showed him the blue spruce tree her husband planted at his, Judah's birth.

Still, the room is peopled. There had been birthday celebrations and dinners for the Governor, when the Governor came south. There had been eighteen servants quartered in the servants' wing. He had had Margaret's clothes packed and locked. They are arrayed in steamer trunks, and he had the trunks stored in the boiler room, not storage hall. He did not want her leavings up above him when he slept. It pleased him, when he was sleepless, to think of his grandmother's portly promenading form, and the grave gaiety of Christmas Eve, when she made her selection. He managed sleep, thinking of that. There were hats and riding habits and gloves and shawls in profusion. There were mantillas on pegs. Everything was dust-cloaked, hushed, and there were no wanton ghosts to thump above him, naked. He does not believe in ghosts. He is haunted by flesh, not fleshlessness, and he twined his limbs' decrepitude around his young wife's limbs. She does not fade or stale; she took lovers twenty years her junior, as he had taken her. She tempts him continually, even in decrepitude, and is not dead but quick.

"I, Judah Porteous Sherbrooke, being of sound mind and body, do hereby declare," Judah says.

"Don't," Hattie says.

"I do declare," Maggie mocks him. The women lean together and are witnesses.

"And dispose as follows . . ."

"Jude," she says. "Remember when we married. You flustered the J.P. so—what was his name again, Thompson? Paul Thompson, that was it."

"Yes," Hattie says. "He lived in Eagle's Bridge. He ran for Sheriff, later, but he lost, remember that, and every time he did a marriage he warned about breaking the law."

"What I remember"—Maggie reached around the glasses and put her hand on his—"was when he came to the part about goods. I still don't know if it's 'earthly' or 'worldly' because you got him flustered . . ."

"You did," Judah says.

"It was you who pinched me!"

113

"Well, anyway," he says.

"What I remember, anyway, is how he mixed the two together and came up with 'worthly goods.' "

"Christ," Judah says. She will not leave off teasing. She takes his declaration on her terms.

"And then we were all on the porch. And he said he'd take the wedding picture and you focused it for him and came to stand beside me and he must have sneezed or something because when we developed it he'd missed us entirely."

"Legs," Finney says. "He got those."

"And three steps on the porch," Hattie adds.

"So what we have is 'worthly goods' and a bunch of steps that needed painting. That's what I remember," Maggie says.

"What's the point . . ."

"You don't have to tell us," she says, "every little thing you're planning. That's the point. It works out different, anyhow, it's never the way we expect."

"Amen to that," Finney says.

"He's got the papers," Judah says. "There in that briefcase. It's yours."

It is water, always, that he works his way through—water where she sports and luxuriates, the liquid that surrounds her so she is *of*, not *in* it.

"Ninety-eight percent of our body, Jude," she'd said to him, "is water."

"Fact?" he asked.

"True fact. And every single body cell is mostly water, Jude. And we come from it and swim in it our first nine months"—she pointed to her stomach—"like little Ian-Betsy is swimming in it now. So build me an enormous bath. And pool."

He managed swimming well enough and had been a strong swimmer. He flailed at the Battenkill, going upriver, and didn't give ground to the current. But it had been assertion always, and not relinquishing, not lazing on his back like some sea witch or whale. He gauged his progress by the river snags and branches and rocks on the bank; she gauged no progress and made none that he could see but wriggled and flipped her way past him with no seeming effort, with slithering ease.

"You're fighting it, Judah," she'd said.

A tune is in his head. He hums it and hunts the words. Mouse droppings on the carpet she had prized so highly, once, and squirrels using insulation for their nests . . . *"Way down in yon valley, in a low lonesome place, where the wild birds do whisper, and the beasts they increase. . . ."* He's got the tune to "Saro Jane" and can remember humming it (her wheat head on his lap, her eyes on his hand, fingers on the inside of his arm) but has lost the verse. He tries again. *Way down in yonder valley, in a low lonesome place, where the wild beasts do whistle, their flocks to increase.* That seemed more likely, somehow, and more in keeping with the song—that beasts would whisper, *whimper* maybe, while the wind was the two-backed beast.

"Talking of onions," Harriet says, "we're mostly out of them. There's water in the cellar now to three inches deep. It doesn't seem that way *above* ground, not the worst mud season ever, but it's bad enough below, I'll tell you, and lucky I looked."

"The wet went deep," he offers. "We were digging by the storage tanks, maybe four foot down."

Maggie bends to her plate. She fiddles with the cutlery. "What else can you tell me?" she asks.

He says, of course, no question; it has been in his mind all along. It had been the first thing he intended to discuss. But somehow he got sidetracked, someway it was hard to bring up the subject: when I'm dead, my darling, water the jade plants once a week but never more than that, and keep the Packard running. Do what you want with the house. Judah has no wishes, none that count. When you go, he tells her, you take yourself with you, and if they neglect to fix the storm windows it's not my worry, it isn't my affair. What happens happens anyhow, and no amount of meddling is like to matter much. They can burn bridges or build them or spill water over the dam. They can count hatched hens. A stitch in time saves nothing; the fabric rends. A bird in the bush is worth twelve dead ones in your hand. No question, Judah said, he'd been meaning right along to make some fitting dispensation and quittance for all claims. That's why he summoned her; that's why he'd wished each heir and legatee to show. Ian, of course, wouldn't come. Ian has been busy with whatever busies him. Nor did Finney have an address they were sure of; nor did they try much more than middling hard to notify that missing person of the chance he'd missed. You couldn't put a wanted poster up, you couldn't have the post office print an announcement: Ian Sherbrooke, come on home; collect your proper quittance, your parcel of the acreage and floor of the house and three hundred thousand dollars at the ticket window, please. That's what drove him off to start with maybe, and it wouldn't haul him back and if it did he wasn't the Ian they'd lost nor worth the finding now.

So everything gets sidetracked, he tells her; every talk they had would trail off into bickering and peter out. First he explored every trail, then every turning and then the dead ends of the trails at wells or pumphouses or where the tractor turned; then he followed deer paths, then by degrees forged his own. You get to telling someone how the jade plants needed water. You tell him how the axle on Harry Turley's Packard split like a toothpick once. It was like the differential was all teeth, like murder with malice aforethought when the front end dropped. You get to tracking little live things every which way, busy in the scurry of it, keeping up your prattle and dispensing kaopectate to the very young or elderly, and there is somehow nothing left, no time and not much inclination to sit to the rolltop desk and settle up accounts. Judah's been through that before. He'd worked through his balance sheets once. You do it to your satisfaction, toting up a deal more black than red, then looking up and squinting to see the angel of some sort of mercy or death hovering stork-legged in the hallway, waiting for your verdict as to which is suitable, water or the undiluted wine.

You'd been open-handed. You'd said why not, what the hell, there's plenty more where that's been borrowed from and you'd elected wine, said come along, step on it, Maggie, hop in, we're going for a hop-step-drive along the Old East Road. There are potholes. There is Larry Turley's Packard to remember. There is every blunder that you've ever made or might still make, ranked up and vivid, rankling so your ears would hum; there is this angel telling you Manhattan Island is a better place for bikes. It isn't memory. Your memory is good, is maybe better than most. They told you that in school or at the auction barn, and you never lost a number series once you learned it. But somehow Jude needs no reminding, knows the past is as the present's shadow, shortening and lengthening and mutable in the terms of perspective, changing with sightlines or on hillsides or pavement or light—yet truly immutable, fixed. And the present forms the future and is a kind of prophecy that will be history when future is also the past. I meant to tell you, baby, it's been in my mind all along. There is *yon valley* and her pursed lips on him and her hand and her thin cheeks puckered, and the strands of her hair on her cheeks; there is the mocking jingle of *adieu* and *whatever I do.*

"Please pass the salt," Finney says.
"Yes."
"It's excellent potatoes," he says.
"Yes."
"Are you still taking seconds? Is it still your habit?" Hattie asks. She surveys her sister-in-law. "I remember that you shoveled heaps of food and never put on weight."

Judah hears them hunting comfort in the topic of the food. He has his chin to his chest. His eyes are up under the ridge of his brow, protected that way from the overhead lights. He stares at her and sees where she has coarsened, sees the lines around her neck that had been seamless once. They talk about him now as if he cannot hear.

"I've been tending to him," Hattie says.
"Yes."
"Night and day."
"I'll bet he takes some tending to," she says. He takes this as a compliment.
"Seven days of the week," Hattie says.
"I'm glad I'm here," she offers. "I hope to be some help."
"I've not needed help," Hattie says. "I've done it night and day these seven days a week. He just needs attention is all."
"I know that."
"Maybe you've forgotten," Hattie says. She twists her mouth. "Lord knows it's been a weary time."
"Yes."
"You simply can't imagine," Hattie says. "I look at him sometimes in church. Or across the room from me, when he can't see I'm watching. And it's just the saddest face; you let him settle down and think there's no one watching and it's the saddest face you'd ever want to see."

He can remember toting water to the house; the wells went bad one summer, and he had to fetch and carry everything they drank. It meant that waste meant walking, and he'd learned to save on water, lately, so as to save on the trip. You didn't leave the faucet running or flush the toilet every time it filled; you took things as they came.

"I wouldn't want to see that," Maggie says.

"No. Of course not. Not if you can help it."

"We . . ."

"All you want is laughter and a good time Charley to, what do they call it, to rustle up the drinks. Well, he may have been your husband once, but"—and there is sniffing virulence in Hattie's face again—"let me tell you it's changed."

He shaves with a strop razor; that is consistency in change. He wears the same boot size and shirt size, though the boots and shirts would alter their shape's shape in wearing. What he touches is pliable and takes on his palm's sweat. The blue spruce tree he planted to signal Ian's birth was higher than Ian to start with, then smaller since it grew less quickly, then taller since it continued to grow. He wonders why he has no memory of pain. He would will himself into remembrance, or anticipation—but the pain is not corporeal, any more than pleasure is corporeal when done. Judah is glad about that. If he could balance pain and pleasure off, he figures pain would weight the scale considerably; he'd have to be drunk and sporting fifty times, say, to cancel out one broken leg.

He'd heard the heart stopped beating in three different ways. It stopped, Doc Wiggins said, when you sneezed or had an orgasm or died. You only die once, Judah said, and you come maybe five thousand times, maybe ten. In the oblivious intervals he tended to his business—not pleasure and not pain.

"Well, what about sneezing?" Wiggins said. You sneezed that many times, maybe more, but you could sneeze six times in succession if you breathed back hay chaff, say, and that would take a lot less time than sporting; that would wring him dry a whole lot more efficiently. So one was pain and one was pleasure and one was by and large indifferent, and he would choose, if forced to choose, that heart-stopping sneeze as the best way to go. "It's nothing to sneeze at," Wiggins said; then he told his ditty. "I sneezed a sneeze into the air. It fell to earth I know not where. But hard and cold were the looks of those, in whose vicinity I snoze."

Judah laughed. "Still and all," the doctor winked at Judah. "Still, judging by receptacles, I'd a deal sooner empty myself with that lower spraygun. If you take my meaning."

"Yes," Judah said. "I do. You piss-ant simple son of a whore. I take it well enough."

"What did you call me?" Wiggins said.

"If recollection serves," said Judah, "a piss-ant simple son of a whore. But I meant it kindly," and he grinned at Wiggins who backed off, bristling, abject.

"Jude."
"Yes?"
"Jude, I say."
"I hear you," Judah says.
"Judah, are you listening?"
"I heard you the first time," he says.
"What was I saying?"
"Well, what was I saying," he mimics, word-perfect.
"Before that?" she says.
"Jude-boy, are you listening?" His voice rises, parroting hers.
"Before that?"
"Only, 'Jude.'"
"You never listen," Maggie says. "You don't hear a thing that I tell you."
"I'm listening," he says.

Why does she counter him, she asks herself; what drives her to it, drove her north and to his side like a night nurse who prefers hot mustard poultices to balm, who uses rubbing alcohol to staunch each wound; why not submit if all he needs for peace is her enforced submission; she sees herself that way sometimes because he's looked at her so often in the guise of nurse and whore. The guises multiply and then persist and then it isn't clear which one is truthful, which disguise; *age cannot wither,* she remembers, *nor custom stale.* But age does wither and custom does stale and there's no infinite variety to what she's learned or where and who she's been (has said this to her analyst also—that she'd left Sarah Lawrence after two years, not seeing the point of it, not wanting to call Bronxville the Athens of the Bronx, wanting real grape arbors and not the hundred yards of trellised walkway they thought of as a conduit to universal learning, not needing little needy men to tell her there were large ones once, nor willing to believe that her breathless labored whirling was the present future of dance); her grasp and reach an octave only, and that's not enough.

So she argues with him just to keep her hand in. Forgive but don't forget; that's her motto, she tells Judah. You say tomato and I say tom-ah-toe; you say potato and I say pot-ah-toe, she says; *salad days,* the wilted scrap of what had seemed to her love's feast. We're oldtime adversaries, husband, and I'd rather disagree with you than agree with most.

So they each of them wonder, is this all? Is habit's hold a fastness and will they sit to supper forever and ever as if there'd been no past to pass—as if betrayal and revenge were topics like the quality of meat? Good manners, Hattie said, meant never discuss what you're eating. You can compliment the cook, but that's as far as it goes; you should never discuss such matters at the table. There had been stews, she'd heard, in which men were served up their sons. The proper thing to do would anyhow be compliment the cook and then, when you learn what you've eaten, provoke a duel. Discussing it at table would be anyhow too little come too late.

So politeness is the order of the day. Politeness means that Maggie serves Finney, and no one hurries Judah's carving when he drops the knife. No one says, "Here, let me help," or "Would you like to let me try?" or any of the phrases that might make things bearable (his shaking pronounced now, the blood leaking out of the undercooked steaks —not rare, not raw even, just bloody, just expensive pulp, the blade making no progress against that ten-pound fibrous lump, and none of them hungry anyhow, none of them able to do justice to Morrisey's best). No one of them refuses potatoes when the white slop sticks to the spoon; nobody mentions that the carrots should first have been peeled. It has to be deliberate, Maggie thinks; it has to be parodic of the meals they'd shared before. Yet Judah eats with concentration, chewing on his mouthfuls like something in a stable, shifting it from side to side in the forefront of his mouth. She watches his mouth skin bulge. She herself—she answers Hattie—has no appetite.

"Why's that?" the old woman asks. "You always used to eat."

"I ate on the bus," Maggie says.

"They've got nothing there."

"In Albany," she says. "At the terminal. There's a cafeteria and I wasn't sure what time we'd be eating."

"Correction," Judah says. "You weren't sure you'd eat."

"What does that mean?" Finney asks.

"It means she doubts I'd come. It means she worried where her next square meal was coming from, that's what."

There are candles. In the soft light and flicker of them, his skin smooths. Hattie toys with her food. She arranges it in segments on her plate, then shifts the right-hand portion left, the left right. She mashes her potato, the fork tines giving slightly when she forces. She makes a pyramid of meat.

"You're not eating," Judah says.

"Yes," Hattie says. "It's good."

"You're lying," Judah says.

"We call it table manners," Maggie says.

"Finish your food," he tells them. "It's the only politeness that counts."

So they try to please him, bending to their plates again, and suddenly this seems to Maggie her history entire: supervised consumption when appetite is gone. She straightens. She rejects her food. "Jude, I'll be sick if you force me to eat it," she warns.

He grins at her and says, "That's the little lady. That's the one I married. Sure it's slops and pig swill and you're right to quit."

"Why serve it then?" she asks.

"Because I need to see just how much shit these others will swallow," he says, and touches her arm, conspiratorial. "Because there's just no limit to what some fools can eat."

"Judah," Hattie says. "You'll make yourself sick."

"These slops"—he gestures. "These pig leavings. This shit I had prepared for you to watch you at the trough." He sweeps his plate backhanded and it crashes against the wall and falls and spills and rolls but does not break. They watch it teeter.

"I been waiting," Judah says, "for one of you to say just one thing. All this meal. Just once to tell me what you thought of what we put before you. Every step of it's been planned."

"So all right," Maggie says. "You serve us a second-rate dinner. Who in heaven's name cares?"

He had been making it, was faking weariness and sickness when it came to him that she needed someone young and hale as he, Judah, had been; he presses his legs together and feels his pants' fabric compress. He feels for the first time now and with terror's clarity that what he'd faked is real, that all the fraud was worthless since it also stood for truth, and Judah is in mortal straits, is mortal, is cut out to die. He does not move. He hears his heart's pulse amplify and echo from his chest to ears, then wrist. He is his own best audience, the kid who gapes forever at the card trick that he never learned, the one who always says "Again, again," and sits there openmouthed, letting flies feed off his tongue, big-eyed, a balloon-head with a needle who scratches his ear for the point. He says four queens, hell, that's terrific, hell, I could have sworn—and every second card is a queen, except he doesn't know it; riffle the deck in the other direction and it's only queens; so everything is foreordained and this sham sickness is the sickness unto death; his legs go weak. His lungs are weak. His arms that had been tempered steel in sheaths ("Like a sword," she'd say. "You draw your arms out from that undershirt like some proud swordsman") are rust-riddled, breakable now.

They draw back from the table. Judah says he'll sit a little while; it isn't often that you give the world away. He offers them camembert cheese. Maggie leads Finney into the room's far alcove, then turns to him.

"What is it you're after, Samson?"

"How do you mean?" he asks.

"You understand what I'm asking. Just tell me what's the point of this and I'll know how to play."

"It's not a game."

"It's not all that serious either," she says.

"For Judah . . ."

"Not that again." She turns away, half-smiling. Her lips are wide, he notices, and they turn up at the edges so that in repose she puckers, seems to smile.

"For you then," Finney acknowledges. "The point is that you're here."

"One bus trip. One afternoon. I didn't even have to change at Albany; they've improved the service."

"Yes."

"One one-way ticket. It's nothing to fuss about, Samson. What's the fuss?"

"The will," he says. "You heard him."
"Yes, it's mine. I've said my thank-yous; I'll say them again. So what?"
He stares at this quicksilver creature beside him and thanks God he never married, thinks it's simpler this way and less fuss indeed. There were times, he wants to tell her, when he'd been nearly on his knees and there'd been candidates for Mrs. Finney, just in case she thought the opposite, in case she didn't know. He eats a Ritz cracker, no cheese, and the crunching sound seems loud.
"You haven't answered me," she says.
"It's a legal document. I've got to get it witnessed and then notarized."
"And then?"
"It's watertight," he says. "It's like seeing snow on the ground and deducing that it snowed. Which would stand in court . . ."
"I don't . . ."
"Been thinking what to tell you," Finney continues. "You've got the place lock, stock and barrel once it's notarized."
"Aren't you forgetting something?"
"What?" He pops his tongue. He selects a second cracker from the bowl in front of them.
"Someone."
"Not that I know of. It's provided for. I'm sorry about Ian, but it's the way he wanted it."
"Not Ian. Judah," she says.
"No, Ian wanted it this way. He's the one who didn't show. If he'd come . . ."
"That's not what I mean," Maggie says.
Now it's his turn to stand there quizzical, awaiting explanations while he runs his tongue across his teeth to pick out cracker crumbs.
"It's Judah you're forgetting."
"I don't follow," Finney says.
"He's got to die first, Samson. That's what makes it legal and a —what did you call it—binding document."
He focuses. He had taken off his glasses when they sat to table.
"Until that time"—she nears him—"it's a piece of paper, right? Just a statement of intention, am I right?"
"Well."
"I could give it all away," she says. "Correct?"
He puts his glasses on. The room is recognizable.

"I could give it all to Ian, for example."

"In your turn," he starts to say—but she is hissing at him, so near now he smells the perfume and she has only one eye.

"Correct?" she says.

"Correct. There's no proviso . . ."

"But after. Not till after. While Judah lives it's his and I am his and he can rearrange it anytime. Just call you in one afternoon and say, for instance, Finney, my wife forgot to squeeze the orange juice, I want her out of the will. She talked back this noon so I'm writing her out, understand? He's done it before; he did it this evening to Ian, so who's to say he won't again?"

"People don't just . . ."

"Judah does," she finishes. "There's nothing changed here, Samson. So I ask you one more time, what's all the fuss?"

He swallows his answer since Judah approaches. He has no answer anyhow and studies how to tell her that. She puts her index finger to her lip and kisses it, then blows him the kiss. "Why, darling," Maggie says, and crosses to her husband. "How lovely you were well enough to eat with us. How nice you could come down."

Finney makes excuses. He has work to do; the bowling league started at eight. He likes the weekly routine of it—the competition and the feel of his personalized ball and the beer. Sometimes, with his second glass downed, he stares at his shoes on the sheen of the floor, watches the pattern his teammates make when running. The red-and-blue striped shoes tumble forward like trout, and he thinks the laminated wood beneath him is a triumph of carpentry, hears the rush and release and clatter of pins. This is all there is, he sometimes thinks; this is ballet, war, law, arithmetic, everything that counts. He has a one-hundred-and-sixty-three-point average for the last ten games; that's just this side of bad, he says, but preening, plucking at his coat sleeve, meaning just this side of good.

Judah says let's smoke one adequate cigar.

It has been simple for her, a kind of acquiescence not revolt: not so much for comfort's sake as for what in its worst light she saw as convenience, in its best propriety—and that the path of least resistance happened also to be primrose is a lucky break admittedly, but not her intention or fault. It has been natural, this sitting down to supper with her husband and lawyer and sister-in-law; fortune comes full circle like a wheel.

And there were surprises. She had watched him chew, bone-weary, head to one side and mouth making preparatory motions, as a blind man might or a suckling calf that stabs for the teat. And the attentive way he paused to swallow, the effort that it clearly was for Judah to down anything who when she met him gorged on flesh so first she called him cannibal—the weakness in him fortified some fierce protective tenderness she might as well call love.

"Should we talk about it?" Maggie asks.

He makes no answer.

"About how long I'm staying?"

"Yes."

"What's your opinion?" she asks.

"As long as you need to."

"And how long is that?"

"As long as you require me. Or maybe the reverse," he says, his eyes upon her now, his mouth at rest.

"Two weeks," she tells him. "Until tomorrow. I don't know."

"Make up your mind," he says.

"Which is why I want to talk about it."

"The doctors . . ." Hattie begins, but he is impatient, spitting smoke.

"Doctors know shit from shinola," he says. "As long as they collect the fee it's operation successful, patient dead. Don't give me a speech about doctors; if you're lucky you come out of there no worse than you went in."

"I wanted to tell you . . ." Maggie says.

"What? What? Don't tell me lies about doctors."

"That I'm here," she offers. "As long as you want me to stay."

So the seven lean years succeeded seven fat; so she sojourned in what Hattie would call wilderness. But the Big House had not changed and would endure till destroyed. Things within it feel unchanging equally, and Maggie feels herself the Megan of fourteen years back. Or Margaret at twenty-one, or Meg at twenty-eight years since, still pausing to shake out her hair. She is a high-school girl again with the two friends she'd kept from high school, and she goes quahauging in Wellfleet even if they call them littlenecks or cherrystones in stores. The fountain that she bent to drink from was still her head's height. Patterns are established, and she'd not know how they got that way, but knew enough to know the pattern had been set. And wisdom is seeing the pattern but not minding it, not fashioning assaults on what is easier to skirt. New York had faded from her as she neared the house, and the two years in San Francisco and year in New Orleans; the fruit fly lives and dies in daily generations, and she will be, she tells herself, each day's ephemerid.

Therefore she thought herself his golden-hearted whore. He would not use the word, of course, but every intonation meant he had reclaimed her when he claimed her for his wife. It was always staked claims for the Sherbrookes—they staked mines out, then office buildings, then women then farmland then line fences tended attentively. They took for granted what they took; she was chattel, she complained to him, and fief. "You are," he said, "my only prized possession. My prizewinning entry at the fair."

"That's sweet," she said. "You're sweet."

"I'm being truthful," he said.

"You flatter me."

"No."

"Yes. What a generous comparison. The best homegrown turnip. A cow."

"My prizewinning entry," he repeated.

"Impossible"—she spread her hands. But he deflected her impatience with his patience-shield. He was impervious, possessing her, as he was impervious to cows. He said they'll treat you how you treat them and there's a cow code; you get as good as you give. Now Sam, for instance, had no use for Ayreshires. And they know it and can use their horns; they're mean cows, Ayreshires, and he's got to watch them all the time, not like with Jerseys, they're sweet. I mean there's more than half a ton of cow, and you don't want it disliking you. . . .

"That isn't my point," Maggie said.

"What is, then?" He contrived surprise. "What am I saying that's wrong?"

"Oh, Jude," she said. "Oh, Judah."

"Tell me and I'll fix it"—he spread his hands, palms out. His lifeline was black.

"You should wash," she said. "I was trying to be serious. There's ways and ways."

"I'll mend my ways," Judah said.

So he joked and parried with her, inattentive. She never could touch him with words. She could make him see but not hear her, and therefore scrawled her body's signature across their shared space. He paid no heed to speech but heeded her motion and shape. She was angry at that; it was what they called sexist now—the body's degradation via compliment. She fell back on body claims and was angry with herself and angrier with him for forcing that language upon her —language she had learned since puberty, or since her first pink sheets. She had grown facile, using it, and fluent in her limbs' articulation when she walked. She knew that, where she walked, men followed her. They followed her with eyes or in imagined deed and some men followed her actually. She swiveled her hips, she sometimes thought, in comic counterpoint to the way that heads would swivel—or advanced across the room to elicit an advance. It was a time-tested game, and had been fun to play. But she'd been at it long enough, and there were other contestants now and—she hunted Judah's baseball terms—she'd retire undefeated, hanging up her spikes.

He had had, she told him, an engaging smile; his nose crinkled up when he grinned and made him the sexiest Roman, made him charming when he snorted, whereas most men brayed. His nose was his best feature, Maggie said; it was classic in repose and yet, in action, hooked. He should never pick at it, because picking widened the flange. It was, she said and pretended to shiver, a brutal, perfect nose.

She could delight him. She pleasured him in simple ways, but they were a complex delight. She wore no underwear, for instance, beneath her evening gown, or wore stockings only with her riding coat. She scented herself outlandishly and smacked her lips when watching him approach in the hot candlelit dark. She moaned and was appreciative when he entered her; she could write, he said, one of those textbooks of carnal accomplishment. She decked herself out like one of those magazine pinups, Judah said, she was every dream he'd lewdly dreamed. She wanted, she would whisper, to be his garden of earthly delights.

"You've got the house now," Hattie says.
"Yes."
"Congratulations."
"Thank you."
"May you have much joy in it. I wish you that."
"Don't be so serious, Hattie. Nothing's changed."
"That's not how I see it," she says.

"Why not?"

"You're thirty years younger than I am. You can laugh."

"I wasn't laughing," Maggie says.

"You've got what you were after. What you've wanted; don't laugh."

"If you say so," she says.

The phone rings. Hattie goes to it. "Hello," she answers. "Sherbrookes."

There is silence.

"Sherbrookes," Hattie says again. "Who is it?"

Their mother had said, "Sherbrooke residence" is for the maids to say, but you never just answer the phone with "hello." "Hi" is a way of measuring height, and "yes" is short for "Yes, who may I say is calling, please?" So Hattie had settled on "Sherbrookes" as a way to answer, and she says it a third time.

"Hello"—her voice goes querulous. "Is anybody there?"

In the instant it takes for her to cradle the receiver, Judah divines that the caller might have been Ian, calling his mother in code. "Nobody," Hattie says. "Just breathing."

"Maggie's back," he says.

"How's Ian?" Hattie faces Maggie. She drops her voice.

"How's who?"

"Ian. Have you heard from him?"

"Yes," Maggie says. "Last week in fact. He's fine."

"I'm glad to hear that."

"You don't have to whisper."

"I'm not." She points to where the men are puffing at cigars. "I wouldn't want Judah . . ."

"What?" Maggie says. "I'm sorry but I just can't hear you."

"Do you hear from him often?"

"Yes. Well," she pauses, judicious. "Not all that often."

"How often?"

"Well. If we're in New York at the same time, twice a week. Maybe less if he's busy."

"Too busy to call us," she whispers.

"No."

"Just one time. Just once in seven years."

"It's not that he's been busy," Maggie says. "You've got to know that."

"I don't," Hattie tells her. "I do not."
"Well, Judah does."
"Don't shout at me."
"I wasn't shouting."
"You were," Hattie tells her. "You are."
"This is silly," Maggie says. "We can do better than this. He doesn't ever call me, if that's what you're wanting to hear."
"I thought so," Hattie triumphs. "He's run out on every last one of us. I do so hope he's well."

Maggie believes, and tried to tell her husband this for years, that joy's a thing to share. You spread it around. You do that with butter, he says, not land. Good fences make good neighbors. She knows what he's saying, she says, but he doesn't hear her when she tells him the opposite, that bad fences make bad neighbors, and why this whole idea of neighborliness anyhow, why not everybody in one house always, sharing everything. A goddam hippie commune, he says, in the days when last they argued; nobody gets in my bed but the lady I put there, you hear? I hear you, Judah, Maggie says; I get the message. Loud and clear, he asks her, and she cups a hand to her head like an earphone, tilts it, saying, "Eh?"
But it isn't always comical, Finney knows that; it's been a bone of contention between them for as long as he remembers. If pushed to it he'd say, indeed, that's the rock they foundered on, that's the bedrock of the squabble where you push so far and no further and belief enters in, saying stop. They're peas in a pod as he sees it, two of a kind.
"You'll excuse us," Judah says, not making it a question. "I want to talk with my wife."
"Yes," says Finney.
"Good night."
"Night." Released, he gathers his things.
"You can go now," Judah says. "Hattie."
"I'm not the one who's tired," she says. "You mustn't mind me."
"I don't," he says. "I want to talk to this one who's come all the way from New York City. From Manhattan Island."
"Good night then," Harriet says.
"Good night."
"Don't tire him," she tells Maggie. "I'll wait for you downstairs."

"I ain't that tired," Judah says.

"He'll try to fool you," she insists. "He's tireder than he lets on. I can promise you that."

"Hattie, you could leave us now."

"I'm leaving. It isn't so easy"—she turns to Maggie once more. "I sit all day in some chair. And you can't imagine how it bothers the sciatica, how it irritates the nerve. It's probably a pinched nerve, Ida Simmons says. But the courtesy to let me take my own time going, is that too much, plain gratitude, a simple thank you . . ."

"Hattie," Judah says, and this time is commanding. Finney takes her arm; they make their way. And as Maggie turns to follow Judah, smiling at him, Finney, with a captive's sheepish smile who nonetheless would wash the feet of captors and dry them with her hair, the lawyer feels that Maggie wanted company not for the celebration but its mournful aftermath, not the night but day. She would cross that bridge when the bridge came; she would make the mountains come to meet her, shifting on their axis as the world continually shifts.

VII

LATELY, HATTIE HAS BEEN SEEING THINGS. SHE WALKED INTO A ROOM and the walls whirred. Cats flashed across the edges of her sight. Sometimes she saw birds there, flitting, with that quick lift and shift of direction that meant they sensed an obstacle, and sometimes she saw no beast she could name. She prefers to name them "cat" and "bird" than nameless changeling presences because her eyes are weak.

She can, however, name the ghost she saw. It was—she is sure of it—Seth. The Big House is not haunted, but her dead infant nephew is a presence at the windows and by every outside wall. She would not voice his name to Judah or ask if he sensed something too, but she is certain—in ways that beggar doubt—that the crib death was no accident. It would not have happened to another family or in another house. It had not been vengeance so much as a teaching for what they'd failed, before, to learn. The lesson was humility; they'd scanted that. They'd thought themselves above ill luck, but all the time it had been brewing; always it was there in some dark corner, fermenting, heating up. Always it was closeted and ready to combust.

The Sherbrookes had been fingered by a finger dipped in blood. It moved across the village, sparing the firstborn sons and families that lived with due humility, but paused above the Big House and wavered and then pointed down, like apple wood for water, or any dowser's stick. She sees forked lightning that way, sometimes, as if it were God's dowser stick, eradicating what it touched in order to point out the depths. Seth had been a candle that was snuffed before its time—that's what they said at the service—he was a bright little light. It had been God's hand come to fetch the unspoiled boy from this life of spoilage and iniquity, and to instruct those left behind in the hard lessons of bereavement. She, Hattie, had been bereaved. She'd mourned and wailed in silence for as many months as Seth had lived —not daring to commiserate with her sister-in-law nor comfort her brother out loud. They had not learned humility in front of this bleak proof. Judah's always studied gain and pride, not the difficult teachings of loss. And Maggie proved his equal also in that. She'd been flinty before, and sparky sometimes, but became rock-hard.

"I'm sorry, Maggie," Hattie would venture. "If you must make me say it."

"For what?"

"For what happened to Seth. For how it happened."

"We none of us know," Maggie said. "You're not responsible."

In the first flush, though, Hattie had tried to break through that stone surface, to touch and strike to where the water was.

"We're all of us responsible," she said.

"That's nonsense." Maggie turned from her. "We're none of us to blame."

Yet in her heart of hearts, Hattie knew there had been blame. Maggie said nothing, of course. She cast no aspersions and said nothing bitter and named nobody by name. It would have been simpler to dowse for water in the Sahara desert than to find the tear source in her, or to strike a rock and make it gush. But she was ravened, Hattie knew, by guilt. She, Hattie, could not sleep those nights and sat awake as now she sat, hearing lamentation fill the corridor. Wherever Maggie sat and rocked there was the sound of weeping; when she, Hattie, went to breakfast her sister-in-law would be in the kitchen already, wide-eyed, staring, fixing coffee as if there was nobody else in the room or in the wide world.

"Did you sleep?" Hattie asked.

"Yes, thank you; yes," she'd answer. "I only just this moment woke."

So they kept up appearances. They both pretended—as Judah too pretended—that nothing was so badly wrong they could not set it right. They said the doctor called it crib death and it cannot be predicted or prevented; "Crib death's as good a name as any," Judah said. And therefore Baby Seth was scrabbling at the windows still— for ceremony and the proper mourning period and Maggie's public tears—at her vision's outer edge.

Lately she has dreamed day-waking dreams. Thomas Sherbrooke tumbles, in her vision, through the ocean's depths and whirlpools the way washing does in a fluff-dry cycle. He spins past her, sleeve over leg. His sleeve is empty and unbuttoned but does not flap; it waves. This gravestone lies if it says that it marks the place of my burial, Thomas Sherbrooke says. She, Hattie, hears him out. He is mourning the sweet sun and how his eyes were eaten by the barracuda, and how he's been undutiful.

"You see me, Hattie," Thomas Sherbrooke says, "in Davy Jones's lock-up. You see me 'twixt the devil and the deep blue sea."

"Don't blame yourself," she pleads. "It's not your fault."

"Whose, then? Who was it went to make his fortune on the bounding main?"

"Put it out of your mind," Hattie says. "Don't blame yourself."

"The devil spar," he burbles at her. He is inconsolable. "That's what I'm tied to, me hearties. That's where I spend my time. Forever and ever and ever and . . ."

"Don't. I can't bear to hear it."

He silences. He raises his leftover arm at her with all the sweet grace of Ian, and he doffs his cap. Striped fish swim at his ears. "I'll have this dance," he says. "If you'll permit me, Auntie. It's written on the dance card."

"Yes," she says.

"It's what we call a hornpipe jig," he says.

She waits, collecting her breath. It is difficult to breathe. "I can't swim," Hattie tells him, but he guides her through shoals. The water, once she holds his waist, does nothing to her garments, and they spin together, laughing. He murmurs compliments. He says she is a natural-born dancer, and she says he lies. He says his whole life now is spent in the service of truth.

"That's right," she commends him. "That's as it should be."

Pilot fish maneuver past. He points to them and explains: "It means there's a big one. A killer whale, most likely. Some kind of shark."

She struggles. She is in over her head. He whispers courteous things to her, and his manner and decorum do not change—but what has been polite is terrifying now, and what has seemed a dance is writhings. His grip that has been loose is suddenly insistent. She falters. She loses step. She opens her mouth and the water roars in and she swallows, choking, while Thomas weaves himself around her like a willow branch, or weeds.

"Your manners, Mr. Sherbrooke," Hattie says.

He continues dancing, swimming, smiling his death smile.

"Please."

His hair, she sees with horror now, is water moccasins.

"A gentleman needs no reminding when to take a lady home."

But he is oblivious, as she knew he would be, had always known he would be when it came her turn to ask. His arm is an eel. His legs are octopus legs.

"I shouldn't have to ask a second time," she manages, but has no voice to say it since his tentacles are on her mouth and sucking out her teeth and tongue, and she remembers now, too late, what deviltry has been in him always, and how he'd bring her flowers in a beautiful arrangement and she'd say, Ian, thank you, that's sweet, and he'd say, Aunt, it's nothing, and she'd say, no, it's thoughtful, it's sweet of you, where did you ever find them? And he'd answer with that gap-toothed grin of his that charmed the pants off anyone, why, in the neighbor's garden, at Mrs. Pettingill's; why, she'll hardly notice and it wasn't stealing really since they're God's to grow and mine to gather, well, Auntie, isn't it a pretty time of day?

Seth had been, Hattie decides, the beginning of the end. There had been trouble before, of course, but every marriage has trouble, and this May-September marriage was slated for its share. Still, she'd thought it for the best and thought they'd handle trouble when it came; they'd talk it out and fix it like they talked out what supper to serve. In the first years of their marriage, it had seemed like continual talk. They gabbled over weather and the news and music and what Maggie was planning to do for the day and what Judah'd planned for the morning and, later, what Ian did and was about to do. They chattered and whispered and told the same stories until it seemed they'd wear the language out. They surely wore their tongues out, what with kissing and clucking and licking their lips. Those early years were difficult, of course, but if she'd been a betting woman and been asked to bet she'd have plunked her money down on luck and love lasting forever; she too forgot humility and dreamed no ill-omen dreams.

Then Seth died a crib death and was gathered up by God. Then the banter ended, and there was silence at meals. He could talk with his mouth full, she told herself, relenting; he could mumble nonsense all he wanted to at suppertime, just so he shared some of his bereavement and lightened it by sharing with those who were also bereaved. Ian took no notice or, if he noticed, didn't much care. That was understandable; he was still too selfish-young. But there was selfishness abounding in the silence of the Big House then, and it made a breach too wide to fill.

"He's the strong but silent type," Maggie announced to her, bitter. "Know why? Know what's the reason, Hattie? Your brother has nothing to say."

"Still waters run deep," she had said.

"Come off it, Hattie, still waters don't run. They sit there and stagnate, that's what they do. They get covered over with weeds."

And Maggie started traveling, who'd been a stay-at-home. She'd say where she was going and take a trip and visit friends to fill the silence. First she'd stay the day away, and then the day and night, and then stay days at a time, and then not bother to tell her, Hattie, where she was going or for how long. She'd find a note on the kitchen table, weighted by the butter dish, saying only, "See you soon." First Maggie took her son and he'd come back aglow from Concord, Massachusetts, or Mystic, Connecticut, or New York City, New York, with stories to tell of every ship they boarded and each museum and what the grizzly bear looked like, standing on its hind legs in the hall. Then, with him at summer camp, she went alone. Judah would be in the fields or at his accounts or off at auction somewhere, and she'd back the Packard up and race away and should never, Hattie thought, have been allowed to drive.

Maggie called the Toy House an extravaganza; she said it wasted men and money and time. They had had to have it repaired, but Maggie said the ruin was as picturesque as any finished thing. She asked, why bother with those pygmy slates; why mullion the windows just so? And he had told her that it wasn't so much a bother as duty; everything was imitation, and if he had had the patience for it, he would build a dollhouse inside the Toy House, and a midget dollhouse inside the dollhouse and so on. There were ivory elephants, Judah said, that split down the center to disclose further ivory elephants; he'd seen one set of eleven white elephants—the first ten hollow and segmented. They ranged from the size of his two hands to the size of his thumbnail—and were all of them hand-carved. Now why bother doing that, he asked; why worry over fit and imitation and repeating shapes?

"There's a difference," Harriet had said—still siding with Maggie then—"between what maybe takes one Indian man to carve in his spare time, or when he's got nothing better to do. And setting Albert Wills at a Toy House this whole summer, when you've got no toys. When there's no little girl to love it as a place to play."

He called it Maggie's Chapel anyhow; he called it the house cut down to size and a place to worship Peacock in. He called it a reminder that the Big House was the biggest, maybe, in their corner of the state but nothing by comparison to mansions he had read of in Newport, say, or Ipswich, or even up in Manchester.

"There's nothing so big that it can't seem little by comparison," he said.

"Tell that," Maggie said, "to a whale."

She had known that Maggie would come back. She knew it as she had known that time on School Street when the collie ran after the bus. Hattie saw it coming though she'd seen the collie go after cars and trucks and buses every morning for what seemed like years, and veer and fade off barking. She'd known it part of the morning's arrangement, part of the proportion of things that the bus would angle left because the Oldsmobile in front of the Carters was parked farther off from the curb, that the collie would maybe lose footing or maybe scent something for once on the wind or off the tire's rim that wasn't danger but delight, would hurtle ahead as the bus shifted gears (the driver so used to this noisy assault that he'd not even bothered to check, certain that the collie was in sham earnest only, more worried about Oldsmobiles than dogs in any case and not overly worried about either, worried most about his watch, which if it wasn't running fast was telling him he'd better). The pattern held; she'd seen it; the dog was entirely crushed.

There is also, Hattie knows, the question of his health. He shouldn't, she had tried to say, get over-excited; he shouldn't tire himself. The chills were mortal here in April, what with the weather changing and snowing the one day and raining the next and then being sixty degrees. "You'll catch your death of cold," she had warned.

"Don't baby me," Judah said. "Please."

"I wasn't," Harriet said. "I wouldn't dream of it. I only said you ought to be more careful."

"There you go again."

"All right. I didn't mean it badly."

"Again," Judah said. "Again."

So she'd wished him vanquished who had lately been invincible, and is glad now (she decides, scrubbing her teeth and then using dental floss and then mouthwash) that Maggie has come. Teeth are the mark of class distinction, Harriet maintains. They are the surest yardstick in these times of changing measure. No poor people have adequate teeth, and if poor or ignorant people have adequate teeth they are the exceptions that still prove the rule. She likes her sweets; she will not gainsay that. She keeps mints and toffee candy by her bed. But she attends to her teeth and scrubs and rinses them with a scrupulous regularity after each meal. She will die without a false tooth in her, and only a few teeth removed.

She hears the rain. She hears the last snow funnel from the eaves. It will accumulate at the edge of the house, and therefore they shield the yews. Snow lies there, humped, in April and even sometimes through May. Collapsing, it takes on strange shapes.

She remembers building snowmen with Maggie and Ian and one of his friends. They gathered and rough-shaped the snowman while she fetched the props. She fetched a scarf and porkpie hat and carrots and coal. Ian rolled his snowball down the hill, enlarging it, and by the time he reached them the snowball was up to his shoulders and would serve. The friend did the same and brought them what would serve as the snowman's head. They hoisted the head up and smoothed the balls together and Maggie said, "We need a belt. Hattie, is there a belt for this big-bellied man?"

"We need arms," Ian said. "We have to give him arms."

"And shoes," said Ian's friend.

"That isn't possible. He'd melt."

"His feet are fat."

So they set to it, smoothing and adjusting him and inserting the coals for his buttons and the carrot for his nose. She went back in the house to carve potato ears. She turned up the heat. She fetched a pair of Judah's boots and an old belt.

"His feet are fat," the friend called.

"And flat," rhymed Ian. "His feet are fat and flat."

They skipped with the pure pleasure of it, fashioning. Their gloves were soaked. Their noses, Maggie said, were just as red as any carrot, and dribbled a good deal more. "His feet are fat and flat," they chortled and placed Jude's boots, Charlie Chaplin style, pointing out at the snowman's base. Maggie tilted the hat down at a rakish angle, so that it shaded one coal eye.

"Now let's do Mrs. Snowman," Ian said.

"Mrs. Snowlady, you mean," Maggie said.

"Let's do you, mommy. Let's put you here next to Judah."

"Snowladies," the friend said. "What do they look like? What do they get to wear?"

"Well," Maggie said. "Coal and carrots and potatoes, like the rest. Then maybe an apron and bonnet and broom. You know, something housewifely, so no one gets confused."

"I'll get them," Hattie offered. "I know where."

"And don't forget the lipstick," Maggie said. There had been an edge in her voice.

"We'll build you, mommy," Ian said. "From the bottom up. We'll give you straw for hair."

So they set to work again and fashioned the snowman's companion. Hattie fetched an apron and a broom. The house was hot, it seemed, and maybe it had been the temperature change, or that the afternoon which had been cloudless was suddenly cloud-shadowed and her energy was spent, or maybe something evil in the mock proximity of this snow-thickened woman to man; maybe it had been the vengeance with which Maggie shaped and jammed on breasts and buttressed her ice hips—but what had been a game was earnest now, and not much fun, and she told Ian that she'd lost the stomach for it.

"Spoilsport," he said. "Hattie's a spoilsport. She doesn't want to play."

"She doesn't have to," Maggie corrected him. "Not if she's tired. We three can finish it."

"But where's the bonnet?" Ian asked. "You promised."

"I couldn't find one," she said.

"We'll just stick in the straw then," he said.

It had been evil, obscene. Her breasts were melon-large and pendulous already, dripping with the heat of hands, and Maggie forced the broomstick in between and gave her coal nipples and said, "Well, what do you think? Do you think that should satisfy Mr. Snowman? The lord and master here."

Lord knows where Ian has gone to, and she, Hattie, certainly doesn't and doubts that Judah knows. It was the gypsy in him, Hattie said. There were gypsies enough in the Sherbrooke generations, without adding Maggie's portion—his legs just built for running, his hand to wave good-bye. "You take yourself with you," she'd warned him, "wherever you travel. Ian. There's nothing you don't carry when you go."

"A backpack, aunt," he'd said. "A single suitcase, maybe."

"Lock, stock and barrel," she said. "It's foolishness to think you travel light."

He has always been her darling. They mention him in anger now, if they mention him at all, and she maintains to Judah that it is pure plain calumny. "If you've got nothing good to say, don't say it," she had said. "If there's no kindness in you for that poor forsaken boy."

"The kindest thing is to say nothing," Judah said. "That's right. He just about doesn't exist."

"He does," she said. "He does."

"Well, there's trouble where he's living, that's for sure," her brother said. "There's floods and earthquakes and general uprising."

"Judah," she protested. "He's your son."

"That's no excuse."

"He can't be all bad," she wheedled.

"Pretty near . . ."

He had been teasing, she knew. Ian was a chip off Judah's block. He looked the spitting image of his mother, and therefore those who didn't know him thought he came mostly from her, and even whispered sometimes, leaning to their cups or in their cups and insinuating, that maybe he was straight out of Maggie with no intervention, or maybe intervened with by some other blue-eyed blond whose last name wasn't Sherbrooke by marriage or birth. They had candidates. They listed them, though Hattie wasn't listening. Such talk was simple foolishness, and Ian was as like to Jude as son had ever been to father since the start of time. He was lookalike with his mother, she said, all surface angles and skinny and fair, but inside he was pure plain Sherbrooke to the core.

And so his enmity with Judah was the enmity of near and dear, not strangers. They knew each other's thoughts so well there was no need of talking, and those who heard the silence only thought it meant there's nothing between them to say. It was a man in a mirror, not needing to articulate what he tells the shaving mug, or how he feels that morning, but plain as the nose on his face. It was the prodigal's story all over again; there were those who left and those who stayed at home, and the stay-at-homes were wayfaring strangers when the stranger-son returned.

"Well, anyway he's growing up," she said.

Her brother drew air in his nose.

"Twenty-five years old he'd be."

"Thereabouts," Judah said. "I've forgot."

"You can't have forgotten," she said.

"Why not? It's not like there's been birthday cake."

"Whose fault is that?" she flared.

"Nobody's," Judah said. "He's twenty-five years old. I remember now, because that was the year the jerseys ran milk fever, and we lost every single lamb at lambing time."

They were peas in a pod, she maintained; they were spitting images which was why they spat. She remembered when Ian had the whooping cough, and Maggie nursed him until she too fell sick with flu, and then the whooping cough got worse, and the doctor said keep him quiet, keep him easy since we mustn't strain his heart, that's the danger with babies, and fever—then Judah sat by his bedside three nights running, not shutting his eyes and not letting anyone else use the washcloth or thermometer but only insisting on beef-marrow broth and grated apple and toast. She'd wondered where he learned that nursing gentleness, and how forgotten since the offer of the hand that three nights and all of the daylight had rested on Ian's racked head—but knows he's not forgotten, really, only learned to lock it in when he locked Maggie out, learned to guard against a second pillaging.

So she had known at lunchtime—what with his long delays and haircut and the way he'd fumbled with her maraschino cherries—that Judah had an announcement. He made announcement motions with each shift and set of his mouth. She'd heard him out often enough. He'd talk and talk and what would matter was the single thing unsaid.

She'd tried it out by naming Margaret Coburn—and knew, by his reaction, that she'd gauged the tide drift right. Margaret had called, indeed, but not to ask Judah to be the honorary chairman of the Library Committee Funding Drive; she'd white-lied though not really lied about that. Margaret had called to say his thousand-dollar pledge was welcome, as it had been welcome every year since she, Harriet, joined the volunteer staff. And surely Margaret Coburn would have been delighted had Judah (who rarely set foot in the building, who didn't read worth mentioning and then only agricultural circulars or biographies he took six weeks to finish, then forgot) been willing to serve. It would have meant a pledge hike and Margaret called about that. The Library expenses had increased. There was inflation everywhere, and books were hard hit by inflation and magazine subscription prices, and the cost of heat. She explained these things to Hattie—who had known them anyhow—and also knew that Judah would maybe increase his pledge but not serve as an honorary chairman of the Funding Drive.

So she'd sounded Margaret's name—calling her "Maggie" a-purpose, not risking much. He exploded as she'd thought he might explode. The cuckoo sounds ten times, then pauses, then sounds once on a higher note; it is ten-fifteen. She remembers her father's death face. It had a smile upon it that was past the art of any undertaker; it must have been the hand of God that turned the corners up. So natural, she'd said to Judah, so like him to the life. She'd prayed that he would leave this world with all his limbs and wits about him, able to walk without aid on the cloud grass that is the path to Heaven's gate. Their mother had had to be wheeled. She wished him in the full possession of his strength. And that wish has surely been granted, Hattie knows; she'd laid two red roses on her father's chest, and he'd seemed to settle in the coffin, dapper, smiling lightly, in the middle of a dream it was too good to leave.

VIII

SHE HAS BEEN HIS LAWFUL WIFE, NOW, FOR TWENTY-EIGHT YEARS. He had married at forty-eight years old, the second time, and Margaret had been less than half his age. He had amused her with percentages. In two years she would be half his age; three years before she had been, Judah told her, forty-four percent his age, and eight years before —with her fifteen and him forty—she had been thirty-six-percent. So she was catching up but would never quite catch him—last year, for instance, she had been sixty-seven percent.

But there was no percentage, he had told her, joking, in waiting around like the hare for the turtle; he was plodding on and making up a fraction of his allotted distance week by year. She'd been worldly-wise before her time and could run like the wind till she got winded, but he was slow and steady and would win the race going away. She had been his lawful wife for thirty-five percent of his life, and better than fifty of hers. But there were lawful wives and actual wives, and she had been his actual wife for less than thirty percent.

He had thought her likely to continue. He had been a gambling man and thought her worth the bet. He had known the odds against them and been lectured on the odds—though not aloud; they'd not ventured that; he'd been instructed instead, in the bars, by his friends' backslapping hilarity and praise, been lectured by his sister's noisy silence, and Lawyer Finney's attention to detail when it came to rewriting the will. It was a good deal more expensive than betting on an inside straight; he told Finney that. He knew it was a deal more risky than bluffing a four flush; he needed no remonstrance lecture, or reminding of the odds. So Finney grinned and said, "Judah-boy, you were always unlucky at cards," and then rewrote the will.

With Ian and Seth born, he thought his gamble won. Meg would spend glad hours with them, suckling, crooning, contained in the enclosure of her sons' small reach. He reclaimed Daniel Sherbrooke's cradle from the borning room; it was birdseye maple, and had spools for slats. Ian had been born the third year of their marriage, and Seth the fifth. Meg sang: "Mama's little baby loves shortnin', shortnin'; Mama's little baby loves shortnin' bread." She made the song an incantation, using only that verse. He watched her, never breaking the rock-motion or the rhythmic chant. She bent above them, her hair cascading like some hay bale with the twine not tied, her breasts unbound. Ian had been fierce at feeding time. He kicked and squawled and raked his nails across his face; they had to cut his nails repeatedly and glove his hands at night.

"He's got your spirit," Judah said.

"Your stubbornness." She smiled.

"I hope he gets your looks, leastways."

"And brains," she said. "Don't forget brains."

"He'll get them also, woman, if he's got a brain in his head."

It hadn't all been prideful then, or easy rearing, or companionable banter while she gave the baby suck. But he remembers it mostly that way when remembering. She would sing "Mama's little baby," and his sons' eyes glazed with that same distance film she had when beneath him, in bed. He is glad by now they'd had no daughter. She would have been, continually, a torment and remembrance; she would have been echo and shadow and an adversary always who called his four-flush bet.

"What about Ian?" he'd asked her, the first time.

"What about him?"

"You can't just run away like this."

"I'm not," she said. "I'm taking him. Just give me time to find a place; I wouldn't leave him in this house a minute longer than I had to. Not one week."

Yet when she left she took a single suitcase only, and wore her slate-blue traveling suit. She could, when it came down to it, travel light. He forced himself to keep from her closets, or from ransacking her bureau drawers to find out what she took. She would have known, or wearied him with asking, if he touched her clothes. And Judah could guess anyway, could rub between his empty fingers the silks and lace she would have been wearing so as to have them torn off. . . .

"Bring fine clothing," Peacock wrote, "when you come to settle here since Coarse Cloth is available, and Linens. When you travel through the Isthmus, I should advise wool Underwear, since it proves far more healthfull even in the heat. And make certain to embark before the Rainy season, if Providence and Planning permit, since April is the time when Vapors do not cling to the commercial Pilgrim as more than a Miasm of the coming Judgmental Storm. But June is Tempest Weather for that which you consign to Cargo Ships round the horn, & you must hazard Cargos and be sanguine of their quick Arrival, else the brine encrust our Bounty, as with so many ventures before. The Land Grant Commission, Judge Hall presiding, has made good my claim on the two thousand acres at San Rafael. It is a healthful Place."

She had left town driving, taking the Packard. He subdues the memory but cannot dismiss it—her soft-brimmed hat angled toward him, the Packard spraying gravel as she pitched it down the drive—he, Judah, at the French doors, holding to the handle so as not to put his hand through glass, thinking he could open the doors and in two strides be at the railing and in twelve strides at the car. Maggie would lift her foot in shock and the Packard would sputter, throttled, and he'd reach in through the window and break that if need be, reaching, and take the keys and throw them over the house roof—but knowing that it wouldn't work, knowing it was best though worst to let her be, to let her go and locking the door handles therefore, holding himself at attention, biting on his pipestem till it shattered, then spitting the black fragments out, hating pipes, praying: *God deliver me. Deliver me from this witch-woman and her beauty spell. Let her drive the car to Nevada or to Mexico and buy whatever it is they sell there that passes for a severance, a sundering in Your sight. Deliver me again my peace of mind and solitude and I shall dignify your name, believing it.*

The chandelier behind him had been lit. He stood, not seeing anything, not moving since the dust of her departure settled and aroused again, the wind rigadooning so that even her tire tracks had been erased. All else will be, he had promised, erased. Then Judah focused on himself, the glass become a mirror with the chandelier's reflected light. He studied his face lineaments. He brought his nose to the pane's nose, and pressed.

They called it, Judah knew, the green-eyed monster. It had a wintry aspect, but the man who courted jealousy was skating on thin ice. There was a joke about Canucks. One Canuck went ice fishing, but he was so stupid he never cut his ice hole and stood there freezing for hours, catching nothing. A friend passed by on a snowmobile and called "Hey, Pierre, any luck?" Pierre said, "No. Not a bite." So the second Canuck pointed to his snowmobile and said, "Hop on. We'll go trolling."

He told that joke repeatedly. He liked to think of the two men zigzagging over the ice floes, slapping their arms as they fought with the reel, cursing at the weather and the fish that would not bite through ice. He told the joke to Finney, and Finney got the hiccoughs from laughing.

There were jokes about jealousy, but Judah never laughed. There were jokes about husbands with horns on their head, and faithless wives, and the inefficacy of chastity belts. He knew it silly not to laugh, knew the joke about chastity belts and the queen with quadruplicate keys was as funny as the joke about ice fishing. But he had no stomach for that kind of humor—has never had, not even with the tables turned and himself, Judah, the lover of some faithless woman, gilding her husband's cuckold horns while he plucked and gilded the lily. He couldn't stomach it. He stomached it no better than his sister brooked jokes about family pride. There were certain things you held on trust, and certain things you trusted in, and he had trusted in the notion of fidelity, once wed. There were jokes about men in closets, and stories about the milkman or television repair man, but anyone who knew him, Judah, knew not to tell those jokes.

He remembers Maggie in the rope hammock he had strung between two apple trees. He sat beside her on the grass, and she used her horsehair riding crop to ward off flies.

"You've got nothing to complain of," she had told him.

"Nothing?"

"Nothing. Not any single thing."

"The thought's the deed"—he pressed her. "You've sinned in thought and that's as bad as deed."

"Come off it, Judah," she said.

"I'm not accusing you," he said. "I'm just observing that the thought's the deed."

"You're positively biblical." She pushed the ground with her left leg and started the rope hammock swinging.

"No."

"Yes. It has to be Sunday today."

He watched her body's pumping motion—the whole of her rhythmic, suspended.

"Yes."

"Yes it's Sunday and yes you're vengeful and jealous and biblical and no you have nothing to complain of," Maggie said.

"Jude-ass," they'd called him once. He'd broken the right arm of the boy who started that. It had been Billy Harrison, and they were both thirteen, with Judah half a head taller but fifteen pounds less fat. He'd taken Billy's arm and twisted it behind his back and elevated it till Billy shouted "Uncle!"

"Uncle what?" Judah asked.

"Uncle Jude-ass," Billy said, and Judah took his arm and raised it to the shoulder blades until he heard the muffled bone-crack.

"Uncle Please," Judah said, and let drop.

She was wearing riding boots. He helped her pull them off. She splayed her toes.

"You've got to trust me," Maggie said. "Just like your bank"— she grinned at him. "Bankers Trust."

So he had worked at and endeavored trust. It had seemed plausible then. She rubbed his cheek with the black horsehair crop.

"All right?" she asked.

"All right."

"All right as rain?" she cajoled him. "Or just all right all right?"

"As rain," Judah said. She could have sold the Brooklyn Bridge twenty times over with such cajolery. She could get water from a stone and gifts for the asking, and there'd be no cobra that she couldn't charm. She'd blandished the pants off of him often enough, and no doubt she'd done it with others and no doubt could do it again. He acknowledged that. She'd have taken him at poker for every cent he was worth. She'd smile and stare at him and he'd forget his witness proof, would twist to her finger like string.

"A penny for your thoughts," she said.

"I'll give them to you free."

"A penny anyway. They're worth that much."

She twisted, set the hammock jumping and reached for the pocket of her riding breeches. They were tan, and tight.

"I can't quite make it," Maggie said. "Not from this position. You reach in and take what you find."

"I'm thinking," Judah acknowledged, "this isn't the worst way to be."

She offered her cheeks up to him like bait. He cupped his hand on her and pushed. She swung away from him, then back to his hand's shield.

"What's better?" his wife asked.

"What's better is believing what you tell me to believe."

"Believe it," she breathed at him. "Jude. Judah P."

So jealousy was slaked. He was an old, fond, foolish man, with nothing to mourn for and nothing amiss.

"You've got no right," she'd say, "to worry me like this."

"It's me who's worrying," he said.

"You've got no right to that either. You'll give yourself ulcers, baby."

"It's not a joke," he said.

"No more are ulcers," she teased him. "My baby Judah P."

So he took the bait she was, and every love hook and the crookedness. She called him her bigmouth bass, just waiting in the shallows for her to flit by near enough. He would lie there, Maggie teased, disguised as some mild mud stick till he lunged. He had thought himself the catcher but was caught. He intended to swallow her whole. But she was barbed, he knows now, and full of false enchantment and had been playing him out. She fed the line expertly, letting the line slack and reeling it in and always attaching him while he thrashed. Still, her love hooks have impaled him; still she is his long-legged gaudy catch.

Judah had been married once before. But looking back he finds it hard to remember that marriage, the two years spent with Lisbeth McPherson before she died—when they were both beginning. He'd put it out of his mind. He consults her portrait sometimes, seeing, yes, she'd had brown eyes and a firm-fleshed face which would, he thinks, have ripened and rotted in time. She wears amethysts. It is a strand her mother gave her, set in gold and imitating every fruit—so that one amethyst is pear-shaped, one shaped like an apple or banana and one with gold tooled around it in order to resemble grapes.

Lisbeth would have made him, he supposes, a proper wife. Their courtship had been proper, and the engagement no surprise, and the marriage ceremony had been a sort of contract for the families to sign. It had been their wedding, not his. It had been, somehow, their idea. He had married the McPherson place, and the McPherson's second daughter and a resistant spongy piece of flesh to press. There's loneliness, he knows now, and being alone together; there's a way that solitudes can border and protect. And he'd been alone but not lonely for twenty-two years, then part of a company they called Sherbrooke that incorporated his wife. But when she died it was no flesh loss or any sort of amputation; they'd not kept company for long enough, he knows now, so that he knew how to mourn. She'd been soft-spoken, dutiful, and no doubt kept her eyes shut when he came to her in darkness and had had them lowered when she crossed the street. Therefore she noticed nothing when the truck jumped lanes and swerved to miss her, hitting the tree that hit the power line that fell—snaking, making a murderous skip rope she caught her ankle on and tripped.

Yet loneliness when Maggie left was absolute. It was as if his fingers were divided down the center, nail from knuckle—as if his arm were wrenched from its socket and he walked one-legged. There was nothing of his body that had not been their body, no part of him not ransacked. He falls back on arithmetic. *Integrity,* he tells himself, *means oneness, wholeness, the number as is. One is not a fraction; it's indivisible*—the unit that he started with and is again and must be forever and ever. . . .

Lisbeth sewed. She constructed lavish dresses that she dared not wear. She knew her place, as Hattie said, and kept it at the bottom end of the table, and when she left there was no absence, nothing to replace. So for twenty-five years Judah said he had been married but would not marry again. He missed nothing notable. He'd learned about the nuptial state and wedded bliss and what they called uxoriousness. Nothing of it had mattered much and he felt no need or wish to double his integrity. She had had dark brown hair that, when he came to her in darkness, framed her face.

Still, there are memories. There is the time he found her in the summer kitchen, with an armful of flowers to dry. He said they would not dry well, and she said that as far as she knew, these flowers were perfect for drying. He said she didn't know far enough, and Lisbeth bent her head, submissive, and he took her in his arms to take the edge off insult. She seemed entirely compounded of lilac fragrance then.

There is a memory of mourning clothes, her stiff-faced family about him and the oak box that she lay in, scarified. He gripped the coffin rail in order to feel something, *anything,* he tells himself, *whatever it is that bereaved husbands feel,* and makes his knuckles white with gripping and pops the seam on his shirt. There was music; there were the comforts of faith. There were professions of sorrow, and Judah waited in the parlor, in the stillborn center of his infant marriage, professing sorrow with his upright silence and hearing them tell him: "Too much. It's just too much to take." And even then they'd called it freakish, called the accident a freak, said somehow something intervened to blight his purpose, bring him to his knees who stood a head taller than anyone there, who cohabited on the top floor of the highest house on that high hill. They whispered, Judah knew, that the Sherbrookes had had their comeuppance, and it was a long time coming. . . . Add it up, they whispered later; he gets one twenty-three year old because he's lost one earlier; it all of it adds up.

And, in a sense, this was so. Yet his comeuppance came with Maggie; he'd learned of loss and bereavement with a lively wife. He sometimes thinks there is a Woman's League, a kind of bluestocking alliance to get even every single way now that they've got the vote. And Maggie was the last, best version of Lisbeth—though Judah had thought them opposed. He'd elected blond for brown and tall for short and hard for soft, forthright for retiring and fire over smoke. He thought he'd voted for life's party and could hold it in a passionate embrace. And he had been watchful, watching Maggie at the door or on the carousel or, ten years later, at the cheese counter in Morrisey's. But what he watched, he knows now, was his passionate embrace of error, was their last best chance to bring him down. So Maggie is Lisbeth incarnate and their shared revenge. When his first wife jerked like a puppet on that electrified string, convulsive to her very hair ends and he felt no sympathy, or when he was convulsed atop her, emitting what he thought was life into that doomed receptacle—when he stood unbending by her open grave to wonder what was closing now (*What stops,* he'd asked himself, *what ends with this beginning?*), Judah had broached rules. The rule is do unto others; the rule is where there's smoke there'll be a fiery second wife to flame at you from every recess of your house and Toy House and the barns. The rule is press dry lilacs and they'll turn into perfume, and men will lap that scent up from behind your wife's earrings like dogs; scorn not lest ye be scorned.

Later she flaunted faithlessness in front of him, bringing what he knew were suitors to the house. Still, he had restrained himself. The meat knives trembled in his hand, sharp enough, and he dreamed of carving off her guests' meaty protuberances. Ian had admired and then emulated his precision with the carving tools. "You keep your brush hook sharp," Judah had said. "And sickles. And your axe blade and your hatchet, right? So do the same with knives."

He, Judah, would simply lean across the table and take the piano teacher or Cousin Alexander or Andrew Kincannon by the throat and, holding them with his left hand, slice off their earlobes and nostrils with his right. He'd use downward strokes on the right-hand side and, inverting his wrist, upward strokes on the left. Then he'd release his choke hold and they'd cover their faces, moaning, and try to staunch the blood; then he'd reach down and geld them, removing the creased, cloaked parcel that had sought its pleasure between his wife's spread legs. They had rooted at her, and he would stick them like pigs. He'd put their mangled, fabric-swaddled manhoods on the salad plate.

"It used to be a delicacy"—Judah had worked out his speech. "Leastways some of us present here thought so." He'd impale the shriveled remnant on his knife. "I insist, sir. Take a bite. We're ever so proud of the blood sauce, though you might prefer the stuffing. My wife preferred it, once."

They made conversation. Margaret chattered about George Szell or whether Horowitz would play again.

"I don't think so," her piano teacher said. Judah cannot now remember his name. "That's my opinion."

"Why?"

"It's only my opinion, mind you, but it's a considered opinion. I think there's just a limit to the pressure. We go so far and snap, if you see what I'm driving at, like a string, say—yes, like a string. We replace it, do you see, we don't just knot it up and start again."

"We tune a piano," Margaret said. "It's a question of degree."

"Yes. A good point there. I see what you're driving at. But it's a false analogy, if you'll permit me, Mrs. Sherbrooke. The point is really one of snapping like a string."

"Well, what about Rubinstein?" she asked.

"Now, him. Now, Artur. He'll bend and stretch forever but he'll never snap. That's my considered opinion; he'll be playing piano till he's ninety-five years old. And enchanting the audience too."

"There's so much hair oil there," she laughed. "There's ever so much lubrication for the moving parts."

Judah snapped his wineglass. He had tightened his hand on the stem. The crystal shattered and his red wine spilled.

"I'm sorry," he apologized. "I didn't mean to do that."

"Darling"—Margaret had half-risen—"Darling, are you all right?"

"Yes."

He watched the wine stain spread.

"You're certain you didn't get cut?"

"Yes. The goddam stuff's so thin you break it just by breathing," he said.

"You're absolutely certain?"

"Yes. Don't mind me. Just pay me no mind."

So she would ring and summon a second glass and bottle and the maid would bring them to him and pour salt on the stain. He would note with satisfaction how the gossip lagged. The piano teacher's windy exuberance would slacken, and Margaret would focus on her plate again, and Andrew Kincannon would go thoughtful, toying with his cutlery and glass.

"You were saying?" Judah prompted.

"We were talking," his wife said, "about concert careers. We had been discussing that. But we don't have to, really, there are other subjects. We could discuss, for instance, the quality of shit you had them spread today on the fields."

She was feisty; he granted her that. She had had more balls than all of her suitors combined. That was why he spared them, not bothering with the knife; they were just accessories, like hats she tried on and discarded or lace mantillas that she stored against some dress occasion. She sat at the table's far head, lit by candle glitter, and was his equal adversary—crystal he could neither warm nor crush.

"My cup runneth over," he said—and proposed it as a toast to both his wife and guests.

He reaches the lumber trail's end, or not its end so much as evanescence, the track of it faded, those wheel bruises finally healed where first they leveled trees then leveled the undergrowth, hauling trees down. All Judah sees is second growth, or even third growth maybe, the hardwood stumps his body's breadth, extended, but the biggest standing tree his body's girth only, trunk congruent to trunk. He thinks of the gigantic labor once it was to raze these hills and how his great-great-grandfather's logging teams had spent the summer cutting and the winter using ice sleds, clearing, season by year till the mountain shed growth like a man going bald and was its rock face only, with streams for the blood lines and high white patches and the skull showing through fuzz. Daniel Webster spoke once, Maggie discovered, at Glastonbury, at the confluence of valleys that was the Woodford Mountain Pass, and forty thousand men came to hear him, she said, and even if she multiplied by twentyfold his true attentive audience, even if there'd be no man without a megaphone who could make himself heard, no matter how high the soapbox or how high-pitched his bellow, over the stertorous breath of the wind; even if she multiplied by forty how spellbound he held them and how long without coughing or pausing to swallow he spoke, the speech presumed vitality where all was death-thralled now, and absence, no living thing beyond Judah's voice range but sparrow or sparrowhawk, squirrel and deer (there were mountain men he'd heard of who ranged these hills still, toothless, unlettered, begetting new idiot-get). So he bears left from the lumber trail and finds the beaver bog he recollected, dams intact, the three beaver houses seeming empty but trim, and he knows them therefore not empty but that his crashing passage through the undergrowth signaled the beavers to take depth shelter and wait this his alien presence out in their wet safety, chittering, remembers having ridden there with Maggie (she was the better rider, really, though he could stick to any horse he's known or force it to yield to his own unyieldingness, who had been thrown often enough but not beaten, who clambered back grinning and clamped his legs to that shallow-breathing belly like glue—though that was not the point for Maggie, never at issue somehow; the horse would be completed by her, suddenly intact, so that when once again riderless it would look halved, bereft, deprived of that airy and sweet-smelling burden it had been released by, not burdened) taking picnics, with maybe a chicken and wine in the hamper, and hard-boiled eggs and cheese and fruit, and they'd clear themselves an area and tether the horses and spread out the blankets, then use the blankets both as a table and bed—"A jug of wine," she'd said to him, "a loaf of bread and thou." "What's that?" he had asked her, incurious. "And thou beside me in the wilderness," she'd said. "That's poetry, you dodo, thats the *Rubaiyat of Omar Khayyâm.*" "Makes a pitiful picnic," he'd said, and she flailed at him, laughing, pummeling, till he folded both her fists in his one hand and held. So Judah torments himself, returning, looking for the flattened grass where last they'd lain, a score of years before, where a century previous maybe Daniel Webster also took his pleasure, the beaver bog a streambed then, with limpid and inviting pools to slake the body's thirst, and falls to his knees in the thicket and is assaulted by mosquitoes and the branches lash his arms as he scrabbles beneath them for some sort of signal, *her trace.* What is it he hunts there, he asks himself, ravening, and answers with what he can't find. First, and predictably, the ground has shifted, grown over so that he won't even know (except this is the southern bank, their chosen exposure) if the patch of earth he picks is near the one they sunned and spawned on, if that tree was the sapling at the center of her Morgan's forage circle, if the brackish water before him has not receded or advanced, making the lakebed their bed. Second, he remembers losing nothing and strewing nothing that lasts (stowing the wine bottle back in the hamper, though empty, forgetting neither shoes nor watch nor anything corporeal, but *everything,* he whispers now, *every single thing that matters*) for chicken bones won't make a chicken, nor cheeserinds the cow nor eggshells the egg, the fruit pit turned to humus maybe but surely not an orchard. Third, his memory's gone fitful and he can't distinguish now between dream-wish and remembrance, so she torments him only incarnate as mosquitoes, the flesh he presses flaccid, long since slack. Yet Judah makes obeisance and rims his poor perimeter with stone and kneels facing in the four directions, arms at a northwest axis and feet splayed, pointing south-southeast, and shuts his eyes and bends his head and rends her garments gently, kissing the breast-dust.

IX

SHE CAME FOR HER OLD LOVE OF HIM, SHE SAYS. SHE CAME FOR HER continued love, and because he'd let her.

"Come running when I call?" he says. "That isn't like you."

"No. But it's been some time."

"Yes."

She smiles at him, attempting to kindle an answering smile. "Since last you called, I mean."

"I didn't have no telephone number," he says. "Finney did."

"You could have whistled." She bats her eyes, slipping back into their mockery like camphored clothes.

"Yes."

"You still got all your teeth."

"Yes." He purses his lips.

"You're a handsome old goat, J. P. Sherbrooke, even if you were my husband once."

"I thank you, Mrs. Sherbrooke."

He inclines his head, and she watches him carefully. He does so out of weariness, Maggie decides, and plays their courtship game because she prods him—indifferent to the play.

"Don't take it as a compliment," she finishes. "Take it as the truth."

She sits beside him, takes his hand in hers and traces the lines on his knuckles. There are cross-hatchings and little white hairs. There is dirt in the pores. Always, no matter how hard she had scrubbed at him—or he for her—with soap and pumice stone and nail brushes, there had been dirt in the pores. She thought of Judah with his hands plunged to the wrists in loam, fingers spreading like roots and his thumb the taproot, extending. It was, he said, cleanly dirt.

"That's a contradiction," Maggie had argued. "It doesn't make sense."

"There's dirty dirt," he said. "There's filth and not all of it's sweet-smelling."

"You're making distinctions," she said.

"Yes."

"Well, it's distinctive dirt," she said. "I grant you that. But still an insult to the chef."

They had argued then for conversation's sake and not because it mattered, not because she meant it or would hold to her argument's side. Had he apologized and said Maggie, I'm sorry, I just can't get rid of it, she would have told him, why should you, it's honest and justified dirt. The house is built with bricks and wood, and both of them belonged to the earth once; why try to hide where you come from or what you did today?

She feels Ian is correct. She wishes she could be with him more often. He sends her postcards and, every few months, places a long distance call. He has severed himself from their lives with a finality so absolute he can even afford to be kind. His postcards are cheery, always, as is his voice on the phone. She wonders how he knew so much so early—knew to get out when the going was possible, knew the Sherbrooke knots around him would tighten not loosen with time. She dreams of him sometimes, resplendent, in rodeos or bank board meetings or in the Himalayas, coiling rope. She knows no context for him and therefore has various dreams. Always his eyes are the same glacial gray; always he calculates odds. Seth remains her suckling infant, doomed by crib death to consistency, but Ian is the principle of change. He sends her cards from Mallorca and Dakar and places collect calls from Albuquerque or Bombay. She too has many addresses, and sometimes she wonders if Ian might not try to reach her, needy when she is unreachable—sometimes worries that he'll fetch up penniless or sick or hunting sanctuary that she isn't there to provide.

By contrast her own severance felt sham. She maintained it urgently, knowing anyhow for certain she'd see her husband again. His hand is heavy. She hefts it. They are in his chosen room, though she had expected he would lie in their shared bed and not in this single gray relic with cotton sheets. His weight impedes her; she finds the phrase "dead weight." Alive, she danced and jumped and pushed herself away from the earth, opposing gravity—yet Judah's hand is without resistance.

"Husband," she says.

He makes the throat sound that he made to signify assent.

"You warm enough?"

He clucks again.

"Or are you too warm?"

"Just right," he says. "I thank you."

"Tell me," she says, "whenever it changes. All right? When you get too cold or hot."

His fingers move. They have their own volition. They cramp and curl.

"I'll tell you that," he says.

She remembers his intricate probing. She shifts her weight.

"I'd rather be night nurse than Hattie," she jokes. "But I'll catch it good and proper if you get chill."

"She's a taskmaster," he says.

"I know that. She doesn't mean us harm."

"She'll kill you with kindness," Judah says. "Or curiosity. That's the danger in it."

She asks herself, this night, what is she trading for what. Put safety in the scales against the sweet wine of risk; put roots against pure rootlessness, habit against habit, the determined creature against the self-determined. She thinks somehow it's in the balance now. She looks back for turning points that she'd not clearly known when turning—for what their poet called two paths within one wood. There had been options, of course. But Maggie knows (in this first year of the second part of her life's century; who was it, she tries to recall, which friend that said the first years of any decade are the difficult ones, so she's spent time preparing, through the last five years or so, for being fifty, can handle it, is managing nicely I thank you) nostalgia tricks out truth. So now she can't be certain if the stage or Hawaii were real, if the man who'd said to her you have a great career ahead, you ought to be an actress, here's my card—if he were just the preening fool she'd taken him for at the time, saying thanks but no thanks, or some dim god who might have managed it. . . .

Therefore she tests herself in mirrors and men's eyes. She needs to gauge her effect. The mechanics of flirtation are easy for her still, as the gearshift is simple for garage attendants and the heating system for the fuel oil man. She knows which strings to pluck.

"You've been hearing from him," Judah says.

"Who?"

"Ian Sherbrooke. That's who. Our son."

"Yes."

"Well?"

"I never denied it," she says.

"How often?"
"He sends his best. He wants you to know that he's thinking of all of us here."
"It's big of him."
"He's busy now. He's got a life to live."
"So where is he living it at?" Judah asks. He picks out a thread from the coverlet. The thread is brown; he winds it round his index finger, tight.
"In New York mostly."
"Where?"
"He'd tell you, Jude, I'm certain."
"I'm his father," Judah says. "In case you've forgotten I'm fifty percent of his parents. I've got a right to know."
"No one's denying that."
"Yes. You are. You both of you have got it figured so he'll be a stranger when I die."
She lifts her eyes. He reverses the spool on his finger and jerks it so it snaps.
"Tell me what he says," says Judah.
"I've already told you that. He sends you his best wishes."
"For a speedy recovery, right?"
"For everything."
"Well where's my card? Where does it say 'Get Well Soon'? Why doesn't he call us just once?"
"That's his business," she says.
"It's what you put him up to. It's you who's estranged us. Why can't he just come visit once?"
"He's not a child now, Judah. It's his choice, his decision."
He sees her eyes are puffy and the lids are pink. He'll stop this hectoring, he tells her, just as soon as Ian comes, or if she'll let him talk to his own son just once.
"I can't do that," she says. "It's not my decision to make."
"I've got his telephone number."
"Then use it. Then see if he answers your call."

The water is warm. Maggie is swimming at night, in phosphor. Her feet and arms are wands. He snorts and wallows, sonorous. She noses through the incandescent water, igniting galaxies of diatoms, light-limned. She has a mussel steamer and they hunt mussels on the rocks near shore. He fills his sea pail and empties the pail at her feet. There are weeds and kelp and crabs attached, and she separates them carefully while Judah dips and tears. She distrusts free-floating mussels, she says, and one mussel filled with mud not meat can spoil the entire concoction. Nor should there be grit in the brine. He says, "You know so much," and means it, not scornful, humbled by her shoreline certainties. She takes it not as compliment but challenge anyhow and says: "I've lived here, you know. Not here I mean, but by the sea. Always by the sea in summers—with that one single exception, that time in Vermont."

Their honeymoon house is on stilts. He likes to lie face down on the porch, watching the sand through slats. The gray sand eddies with wind, and the spear grass traces perfect circles beneath him; he cuts his feet on the sharp speargrass points.

"Are you glad about it?" he asks.

"About what?"

"For that single exception. That time they hauled you to the mountains."

"Kicking and screaming." She smiles.

"And giving you a bicycle."

"I'm glad," she says. "I wasn't then, you know. I wanted a canoe."

"We'll get you one," he promises.

"Oh, Jude, you promise?"

"Yes."

"Cross your heart and hope to die?"

"Not hope to die," he says. "But cross my heart."

For which she rewards him by kissing his hands, then putting his hands on her breasts. "Cross mine instead," she says. "My heart."

Judah, she knows, has set traps. He has baited the testament pot. His enticement is his legacy, the land and houses and wealth. He had been scornful of such trappings but learned to flourish them now. Whoever wants, he seems to be saying, to get into this house of mine must eat the fishhead at its center; whoever backs in can't back out. He rehearses praise of Maggie, and her answers are ordained.

"What do you want of me?"

"Nothing that I know of," Maggie says.

"You can't mean that."

"I mean it."

"They all of them want something. They're sniffing around this place."

"For what?" she says.

"For real estate development. For the state highway extension."

"Don't let them do that," she says.

"For high-rise dwellings, I believe they call it. Condominiums. Museums. Doesn't matter what they call it, they all of them want something."

"Not me," she says. "I don't even want to be questioned."

"Why not? If you've got nothing to hide."

"It isn't a crime yet," she says, "to visit your husband."

"You're here for a reason," he says.

"We've been through that."

"Not properly."

"Enough."

"Why did you leave?" he asks her, insistent. "And why did you come back?"

She tells him that she loves the house, making her mouth work. She had had, that afternoon, to change the bulb in her bathroom light; it had burned out. She went to the pantry and selected the right size—and standing there, among the insignia of some strange family order, in her chill shuttered seclusion (the tomato soup next to the peanut butter where she, Maggie, never would have placed it; the lightbulbs stacked by salad oil and aluminum foil) she had been illumined, at peace. There are systems she is part of though they seem like foreign systems; there are other lives she lives. There were orders and disarray through which she ranged, inviolate.

"You look well."

"Thank you, Judah."

"You do. Really."

"Thank you. I'll believe that. Flatterer," she says.

"Every compliment I paid you was the truth," he says. "You do look well."

"It's nice of you to say so. Nice of you to have me here."

"It's your house," Judah says. "You didn't have to wait."

"My goodness," Maggie nears him. "You've gone and gotten courtly."

"Just paying dues," he says. "Giving out praise where it's due."

"You didn't used to do that."

"I would have," he tells her, triumphant. "You just didn't used to deserve it."

Then there was the hole he dug and covered over carefully, with brush laid crosswise and long grass and leaves. It looked to be substantial ground, but was a pit with thorns. There was the net he slung and covered with branches and leaves and when his prey ran through he, Judah, chopped the net's drawlines and hoisted his catch. There were decoys to set and red herrings to drag on the trail; there were sitting ducks. There were chipmunks who would tackle muskmelon rind, if winter up ahead looked difficult enough.

"The time is past," she ventures, "when we should beg for favors from each other. When common human kindness is a bone you throw to dogs. When everything you have the right to ask for is denied."

"It isn't my intention," Judah says, "to beg."

"No."

"There's things I own and things it's mine to give away. And there's been a pack of them after it, believe you me."

"I believe it," Maggie says.

"You see them off in corners whispering," he says. "Or dickering about the best approach. Which way to sidle up to Uncle Jude. Which hand to hold out when they're holding hands."

"It can't be pretty to watch."

"No," he tells her, triumphing. "Not half so pretty as you."

So squirrels hoard and sleep; so the bears accumulate fat and go lethargic and sleep; so everything about him, that had slept a dull slow season, stirs and is grasping and trapped. Judah hears them plotting; they are making wallow-laughter noises in the mud below. They rooted for his leavings and shat tomato plants. They were mistaken, he told the town planners, to think they could reap what he sowed; a man's entitled to the distance he can travel in a day, on one horse and in one direction; then take that line as radius and cast it in a circle, not forgetting mountains, not forgetting riverbanks and the valley that they fashioned, not forgetting trees.

Now Judah raises himself. He sits upright. He rises with a smooth swivel motion, shifting his hips. It is the gesture of a farmer—rolling out under the tractor or carrying a feed sack or vaulting the pigpen's gate.

"Hey," Maggie says. "I thought you would be sleeping."

"Maybe."

"What woke you?" she asks.

"I don't ever sleep these nights. I give myself twenty minutes. It's a way to let Hattie get rested, see, to tell her I sleep straightway through. And"—he moves his mouth—"to give me some left-alone time."

"All right." She stands. "I can take a hint."

"I didn't mean that. Not you."

"You want a dance band?" Maggie asks. "You moved like you've been practicing."

"Sure," he says. "What do they call it? The Twist?"

"It's the Black Bottom," she jokes. "That's what's in fashion now."

"I knew you'd know it"—Judah is bitter. "You'd know every one of those gyrations. Be in on the latest."

"The Black Bottom isn't the latest," she says. "It's been replaced."

"The Yellow Belly, then. You'll know them all."

"Why did you let one come back?" she asked. "If that's how you feel about company?"

"Two's company," Judah says. "You're my wife."

"Yes."

"You're not some moneygrubbing climber come to lick my hand and bite it when they think I'm sleeping; you're not that."

This is said in accusation and with a spitting venom that makes Maggie stare.

"You wouldn't show up smiling just to wish me dead, now would you; you'd not quit the house then come back smiling when there's money in the wind. When I've got a will for notaries to stamp. There's others who might do that, but not you."

(Seth suckled at her; his perfect hands had ten perfect fingers with perfect crescent nails. They fitted themselves to the curve of her breast and were a perfect fit. His eyes were blue as blue could be, and he shut them in appreciation while he drank. They stayed that way. Then the suction lessened; then his lips stopped working; then the action of his throat, in its turn, ceased. She wished it would not cease. He slept. She wished he could not sleep but was grateful for the rest he took, and waited for his breathing to begin.)

"You let me come," she says.

"I know."
"You haven't got to wreck it," Maggie says. "We could maybe like each other, Mr. Sherbrooke."
"I know that too. Don't take me for a fool," Judah says. "That's all I'm asking, all I ever asked. It isn't too much to ask, now is it, just don't take me for a fool."
"I won't," she says. "I never have."
"Miss Black Bottom. Miss Yellow Belly," he derides her. "Queen of the hop."

Then he shuts his eyes. He is, he says, conserving his strength. There is a regularity in his breathing that makes it seem sleep. He wheezes each seventh breath. She imagines husbands a century or so before who'd leave for seven years and go to cross a continent or ocean. Gone to make a fortune or shore up failing fortunes, they would come back wearing earrings maybe, and carrying parrots or Malacca canes, smoking strangely fashioned pipes. Or centuries before that, even, bounding back with the splaylegged gait that told of wondrous voyages, and three-legged natives wearing palm fronds for shoes, and nothing else but musk oil to disguise their animality. There would have been tales to tell and news to give and get in abundance, then, and the oil lamps would have flickered and the windows misted over just the same way for that pair of strangers, those fraudulent avatars also. . . .

(Judah tends his affairs. He keeps his ear cocked though she thinks him heedless, and keeps his right eye open behind the lashes' web. He is peeking out at Maggie like a schoolboy, inching the curtain aside. She would be his audience and will applaud him, would be flabbergasted and rolling in the aisle. There are others. It is dark. The footlights flare at them, not him. They are enthusiastic. He will leap to her side with agility—and not be caught in the bedclothes or crippled, or spavined by arthritis like some out-to-pasture Clydesdale collapsed with its own weight. You have to be quick-footed to steal a march on Jude.)

And sons would visit mothers who had lost their sense and sight. Sons would come to fling themselves after the last earth handful on a new-dug grave. They would return, Maggie thinks, with a week's hard ride and the frost-stiff ground their bed, with no chance to favor their horses or thank the ferryman sufficiently (who was not used to night trips, who didn't like the weather and was half-deaf anyhow, who heard no apologies therefore and waved the tip away in a gesture of derision, muttering about the horse puckey on his loading ramp). Sons returned without left legs or six inches taller or bearded or bald, returned through malarial swamps taking the shortcut past the tamaracks where two thousand died, they said, in that first August pilgrimage—skirting the bogs and rapids, but losing their packhorses anyhow to gopher holes, a kind of indignity always attendant, mosquitoes rampant and the storm-felled oaks impassable, the message ("Come Home if you Can; Mother Faring poorly and would like to see you Once") ciphered out and deciphered, worried over endlessly, the paper of it worn and rubbed dull with folding, edges furled. . . .

(He feels a man's life signifies; he feels it matters how he walks upon this earth. He has been schooled from childhood to believe that actions ramify, and a Sherbrooke's more than most. He says the Lord giveth and taketh away, but so does the Federal government, and so can any man not merely an automaton but self-willed, self-reliant, self-defined. Therefore he will give his house and barns and land for love; therefore he withdraws from anxious husbandry. His world is the visible world. He owns all he can see of it, and that's enough. Standing beside him—two feet to the side, and half a head shorter, she sees a different world. It's only natural, he tells himself, it's one of the laws of perspective. But he owns all *she* sees to boot—even lying, feigning sleep, in the bedroom of the house he fingered in its replica that morning. He can confer it, and does so. She takes it as her due.)

"I'm dying," Judah says.
She makes no answer.
"You know that," he says.
"No."
"Finney must have told you. You got to know that much; I'm dying tonight."
She takes his hand.
"I'll die if I sleep here alone," he says.
"We'll watch for you."
"Will you?"
"Yes."
"How do I know that?"
"I promise." She spreads his fingers with hers. She strokes his palm.

"How do I know you won't leave me?"

"You don't."

"You always have."

"I always came back," Maggie says. They are adept at this gambit also, and she marvels at how quickly she traverses time. Men returned from wars and bounty expeditions and mental hospitals; their parents said, hey, boy, fix me this gatepost, hey, boy, go brush your teeth.

"Don't leave me. Don't run out."

"No."

"How can I trust you?"—he stares at her, unblinking. She waits for him to blink.

"You can," says Maggie.

"Sleep here. Sleep with me."

"All right," she says. "I'll get an extra blanket. I'll be back with pillows."

"No," Judah says. "In this bed."

He releases her hand and pats the space beside him.

"I need someone here to hold me. When I die."

She steadies herself. He would, she knows, spare her nothing; he has worked his punishment out in every fierce particular.

"Please," her husband says. "I need that."

"If you ask me"—she deflects him—"you're a mighty lively corpse."

"I'm not asking your opinion," Judah says. "I'm asking for your help. For charity's sake."

She smiles. Her hands are shaking. Her voice shakes. "The condemned man ate a hearty meal."

"All right," he says. "Send me up someone who'll do as I ask. Find me some companion."

"No," Maggie tells him. "I'll stay."

He looks at her. She could swear he smiles. It is a grin that he turns—she could swear intentionally—into a cough.

"Go," he says. "I'll manage. Just find me someone else."

"Who else would have you, Judah? I'm your wife."

She tries to comfort him, who has little comfort to spare. She tries to say the world is full of things that frighten her, because you're never certain where they go at night. Best keep the closet doors open, she whispers to him; best keep drawers pulled out. Best call everything an ostrich that puts its head down under and snuffles after worms. Best close your eyes; best pluck your brows; best wish upon and blow the lash that falls.

"You win," he says. He lifts his hands in submission.

"And you."

"I'm tired," Judah says. "Let's get to bed."

She sits beside him. She felt the same way, sometimes, after drinking too much or not good enough wine. Her very bones are stiffened and her body a rust-sack. Nothing works. No single thing makes its customary motion.

"Get in," he says. "Under the covers."

"It's hot here," Maggie says.

"Not for me," he tells her. "It's as cold as that night was we slept out in the winter. Remember?"

"Yes."

"Get next to me," he says.

She starts to obey.

"Not that way," Judah says. "If you're so hot and I'm your husband anyhow, take off your clothes."

She is sweating.

"I'm not hot," Maggie says.

"Of course you are. You're sweating. You're a furnace."

"I'll get used to it."

"No," Judah says. "Take off your clothes."

She tells herself it doesn't matter—that it is her husband in his health, not sickness; in his prime, not mad old age. She unbuttons her blouse.

"I'm dying," Judah says. "Tonight. You'll see."

"Please," Maggie says.

"Please what?"

"Don't say that. Please."

She drops her blouse to the chair by the bed, and lies back.

"I'm not trying to scare you," he says.

"But you're succeeding, Judah."

"The skirt," he says. "What about that?"

And so he wheedles and coaxes her out of her clothes. She lies rigid beside him and watches the gooseflesh on her arms prickle and subside. It is, she tells herself, a caricature scene; it is *Death and the Maiden* or *Virginity Defended and Preserved*. But there is only his breathing and the oil lamp's rasp for music, and she had yielded up her maidenhood with pleasure, thirty-four years earlier, in the changing room of the cabana in Alan Seligman's Easthampton beach house. "Hold me," Judah says.

She holds him. She busies herself with memories: the way that Alan Seligman's swim-trunks elastic intaglioed his flesh, and the burnished gold his body was above the line contrasting with the flaccid fish pallor below. He had pretended competence but was a virgin also, and they fumbled and poked at each other. Maggie shuts her eyes. He, Alan, had been eighteen and won the free-style relay and flexed his pectoral muscles and biceps for her; they went steady afterward and improved their shared technique.

(They seek bluefish. His host had had no luck with lures. There are menhaden in the harbor, and the bluefish are after menhaden. They snag menhaden therefore, and then implant double hooks. The menhaden are after plankton, and Judah casts for them repeatedly, thinking of their aimless, guzzling progress. He jerks his line the way their host explained. He imagines the barbs responding late, refracted, slicing through weed then flesh then bone. It is no problem. There are many menhaden, and the water is discolored where they swim. They roil and slap at the surface; there are blues beneath.

"It's Barry Blue we want," his host says. "Not Mickey Menhaden. They're an oily goddam fish. They're only good for catfood, only how we get to what we're fishing for."

They die, however, on the line, or slip the hooks. Or he snags them in the gill, and then they die in the boat. "They've got to get back to the school," his host explains. "And swim along. Only slower. That's what Barry Bluefish wants."

"The sucker suckered in," she offers. It is their honeymoon.

"Pound for pound," his host announces. "The best goddam fish in the sea."

Menhaden thump about him. "Photosynthesis is marvelous," she says. They play the menhaden forth, back. Suddenly the line hums and gives and the fish is quivering, racing, light, and he reels it in to find it headless, chopped cleanly off at the hook.)

X

HATTIE FINDS HERSELF WITH SLOGANS NOW WHEN SHE WANTS words. She hates supermarkets, and the jingle songs she finds herself singing in aisles. They pipe music from the four corners, and Hattie is pursued by echoes, hunting rope or camphor or tomato juice. In these newly built and lavish emporiums, she feels her age. She stumbles down the corridors of canned goods and household supplies, pushing her pushcart as once she had her mother's wheelchair, but with a deal less agility. She—who'd admit to many faults but not to indecisiveness—is assaulted by competing claims and labels and products and stands there indecisive, trying to sort matters out. Like as not she'd reach for camphor and there'd be mothflakes and mothballs and mothcakes to choose from, and when she'd choose at last and reach she'd knock the stack down, or scatter the cans. She did the bulk of their shopping at Morrisey's still, or had it done by Judah—but once a month, maybe, or once every three weeks she'd negotiate the shopping plaza, tormented by such opulent look-alike choice. Soda water, for instance, would be marked at thirty-five cents the bottle. There were five- or ten-cent additional deposits to pay. So she'd accumulate bottles at forty or forty-five cents the bottle, arranging them in her shop cart and checking the stamped price each time. One time she found one bottle at eighty-five cents and therefore was continually wary and pointed out the error to the girl at the check-out machine.

"Look here," she said. "Someone marked eighty-five cents."

"Where?" she asked.

"Right here," said Hattie, pointing. "Right at the spot where my fingernail is. On the cap."

"I'm sorry, ma'am," she said. "I'll charge you for thirty-five cents."

"I expect so," Hattie said.

But her point would be lost, and her precision wasted—except for the fifty cents saved, and that was hardly saving. She'd sweep her goods along, and someone else would pack them, and Hattie would be out of there before she knew it, sweating, sorting the change. She'd be out on the tarmac, hunting the taxi she'd ordered, still hearing the loudspeaker bray organ music behind her and take her first deep breath and breathe in gas fumes and heat and the smell of hamburger fat from the restaurant section.

Judah cursed modernity and every tinsel accomplishment; they were saving nothing of importance, he would say to her, although they salvaged time. "A stitch in time saves nine" had been her slogan-motto and her emblem of frugality. He asked her if she truly thought they needed this gleaning frugality, and what did it save anyhow—nine stitches or nine times?

"Nine stitches," Harriet said, "and don't forget who does the stitching"—and he granted her that argument but said she should throw the old clothes and sheets and tablecloths away.

"If I did that," she said. "We'd see how long you'd let me do it."

"Long enough," he said.

So she hoarded their history's leavings; she is like a magpie, he complains, lining her room with silk scraps. "A penny saved earns pounds," she said. "Waste not, want not," she urged. Then Judah told her that they earned each year more than they knew how to spend. She said that wasn't possible, and he explained to her that money made money without half trying, that funds accumulated on the trust funds, and even after taxes there was all they'd ever need. "Necessity's a difficult teacher," she said, and mended the living room curtains when he didn't see they needed mending, and wouldn't have cared if they did.

Maggie had spent money like she spent herself on everything—flat-out. It was as hard to hold to, Judah said, as a greased squealing pig. Not that he minded it, either; there was as much fun spending as there was in getting, then, and he lavished gifts on her with what Harriet called luxury. He gave her earrings and bracelets and cars and would have given a fur coat if she tolerated furs. "I can't abide it," Maggie said. "Shooting and trapping and poisoning those animals."

"Which ones?" he'd asked.

"Whichever makes a coat. A seal for a sealskin coat, a lamb for lambswool, and all of those minks. Leopards. Tigers."

"They ain't defenseless," Judah said. "And some of them is pests."

"Don't play the trapper," Maggie said. "Did you ever notice that you put your bumpkin accent on whenever you're not certain?"

"Sartin," Judah pronounced. "Shorely."

"Well I don't want a coat," she said, "that comes from killing. Thanks anyway. No thanks."

Words were a kind of coinage they melted down from slogans, then minted their bright love words for exclusive use. Hattie listened, envious. There was the warble and hum with which she spoke to their two sons when suckling, voice high-pitched. Now Hattie runs through supermarkets like the aisles or obstacles, or gauntlets like the time that Ellen Wills was at the altar, waiting. Ivory Snow is a dish soap and Gleam and Crest are toothpastes, and Joy is a detergent.

Hattie moves with caution, soundlessly. She readies her bed. It is a tester bed, not canopy, because there is nothing inside it to cover—no shameful goings on. The fringe around the bedposts is pink eyelet lace. She allows herself that. It is an extravagance, of course, and frilly the way little girls dream about frills. Sometimes, staring past the bed's frame at the rectangle of ceiling, Hattie thinks maybe that's how you get to heaven, maybe that's what ascension implies. Maybe you go through a space that's called a tester shape because it doesn't close you in and is a trial. There's tribulation inside, and pleasure for the best part of a quarter of your life. Lately she's not been sleeping long or well, but still she calculates six hours on the average for, say, sixty years. She's done better than that to begin with, and worse than that to end, but it evens out. And on the way there's temptation that comes in many guises—call it luxury, then restlessness, then sloth. The eyelet lace would be a comfort-temptation and test, but her soul would hurtle past it into the cold space beyond and butt against the ceiling and knock for admittance. It would be smoke without a chimney, looking for the topmost part of rooms to hover, coil and dissipate—or birds caught in a barn or like the bluejay in the entrance hall that time, battering at windows, seeing only the blue sky beyond but not the translucent obstacle that was a just and upright judge sitting in absolute judgment. It was like the way heat rises to cool upper air, or the way she went lightheaded after bending and straightened up and thought she'd grown six inches. Everything would rise about her, and what seemed like plaster with a crack in it would be, entirely, smoke. Where there's smoke there's fire, but this would be a smoke screen to shield her from impurities and smoke the hellish remnants out and leave her in the perfect welcoming empyrean, breathing without luxury or sloth.

Hattie smiles. She permits herself day-waking dreams if the visions are not harmful, and no one could claim heaven daydreams ever did anyone harm. Her heaven is snow-white but warm. It is a storm of miracles, with everything unblemished and intact. Vermont is her heaven on earth. It is a kind of paradise, free from the disasters that beset the countries she reads of and almost every other state. It has no tidal waves or hurricanes because it has no ocean; it has no poisonous snakes. There are no earthquakes and no one dies of jungle fever, and no one dies because of rabid bats. There are rabid bats, all right, behind the Big House shutters, and she hears them squeak and rave but knows they will not bite her if she offers nothing to bite. Nor is there one recorded case of death by bat bites that transmitted rabies. There are no floods worth mentioning, or not enough to kill you, and there are few drought years in Vermont. It is Eden on earth except for a blizzard that maybe could cause you to freeze. But even then you had to be improvident and not amass the firewood, and there are no avalanches like she'd seen on TV in Canada or the Swiss Alps. Men fire off their guns and mountains fall. There are wood ticks in abundance that Judah picks off the dogs, but they do not carry Rocky Mountain spotted fever. He'd sit there squeezing and applying rubbing alcohol or matches to the ticks, and she'd be appalled at their bloodsucking tenacity—but it is not fatal in Vermont.

And so this earthly paradise stretches around her, comforting. There are high winds, admittedly, but not so high you perished out of breathlessness, and if you stay away from falling trees. No place in the Bible did it say what happened to the Eden tree when they ate the apples, but Hattie thinks the tree went rotten probably and was hollowed out by woodpeckers and fell in the first high wind. Eve knew enough to get out of the way, but Adam cast a backward, rueful look. Get thee behind me, he seemed to be saying, at least until I'm full of my wife's teachings and sinful knowledge and have honed my axe.

Still, paradise is warm. It is a stepped-up version of September. There are skies so deep that the deep she knows means shallow, and no bitter cold or natural catastrophes or enemy to man. If only for that single fault, the landscape would be Eden, so she warms it up in daydreams just the way that New Orleans is warm—and then the snow is duck down in angelic sheets.

She'd people it differently too. She'd pay no attention to color or creed, since paradise is democratic and without regard to that. But He regarded manners at the entry portal, and if your hands are presentable, scrubbed and cleanly after labor. He regarded works, of course, and kept them in a ledger, keeping neat accounts. But mostly He regarded if you'd done willful harm, and if you've done no willful harm in thought or deed you were just about guaranteed access to eternal life. It would be bliss; it would be cherry trees in blossom and no neighbors running neighbors down and nothing spoiled or soiled. It would be a profusion of delights. The people would be openhanded and glad-hearted and their wings have eyelet lace through which you can see arms.

She waits at the window seat. She had never been a lazy woman; no one gainsaid that. No one denied that she woke at first cockcrow and worked at the day's tasks unflaggingly—glad for the chance to be useful and not meddlesome or lazy but only helping out. Busy hands keep out of cookie jars, she said, and empty hands are never full and weak ones aren't worth shaking if they daren't shake you back.

But this night she is lazy and will stay that way. This night there are others in the house, and Judah'd made it plain enough her presence was crowd-company, and that he'd do without her now who hadn't done without her day or night for seven years. She'll take her ease, she tells herself, and yawns. There is no ease to take. There is nothing to do in the room. She'd stay in there till Maggie left, or noon, though she doubts that Maggie will make it till noon. She'll stay until they come to get her and find the door locked. She pockets the key.

Now she is in exile in her room, with nothing to read that she wants to read and no television set or silver to polish, and her afghan in the billiard room. She ought to have remembered that. She could have swept in, leaving, and swept it up and taken it but couldn't creep back down there now and get her work. It is purple and yellow, which are Mrs. Ferguson's favorite colors, and Hattie plans to finish it by Mayday, for Mrs. Ferguson's niece. It had been an outrage, but she wishes no willful harm. It had been unkind of Judah, but she was used to his unkindness and inured long since; his wife should intervene, however, and take Hattie's part. Yet she wishes Margaret no willful harm either, for having failed to intervene or say with loving kindness, "She's your sister. She could stay."

She sniffs. She wouldn't have wanted to stay. There had been goings-on enough in that room, and will be likely again; she, Hattie, has no need to know and doesn't wish to anyhow. Curiosity, she used to tell Ian, doesn't always kill the cat, but if he sticks his nose in garbage cans he'll come up smelling bad. It makes no difference, Hattie said, if there's a pile of roses; sniff around it long enough and you'll find thorns and the compost and stench.

So she is glad of her privacy and has willed it so. She'd left the room of her own free will and not been ordered out. She composes herself for sleep. She wishes she had the silverware or afghan anyhow; it would have passed the time. They huddle in the rooms beyond her, bickering or reconciled or lustful because Maggie always signaled lust, and everything would be arranged and rearranged in her despite. "There's no natural catastrophes," she'd said to Judah. "Not in Vermont."

"But what about *un*natural," he'd asked her, only half joking. "What about my wife?"

"That's not fair," Hattie said. "You don't mean that."

"I do," he assured her.

"Not really."

"A manmade disaster," Judah finished. "Just like her son."

Ian, their glory, their hope; he who would reconstitute their failing fortunes, she wanted to say—who'd make all well in this world and was an image of perfection in the next. She kept her peace instead. She left the room not reproachful. A long while after Eden, she had been bursting to say, there were lights in the house that the first family built. There was someone inside sweeping up. There was silver to polish and caning to do and the sampler for the downstairs hall is frayed along the edge. There are letters to answer and invitations to explain about refusing or accept. There are bills to pay. There is always someone leaving and someone left with the leavings, and ingratitude rides on the train of departure like thistles on her skirt. You pick your steps and have picked them before and know the way the path heels over and where it would be, likely, mud, and anyhow the thistles find you out and follow you and find themselves a brand-new site at breeding time.

She hears house sounds. She listens for the furnace and can distinguish that. Water clanks in the pipes. It sounds, Hattie thinks, like iron croquet balls on carom shots. She loves croquet. She'd beat Judah handily when he consented to play. She knows the pitch and obstacles and takes on every corner and never ever had lost. "You're a tough customer, ain't you," she'd tease Ian—and then go through five wickets without losing a turn and knock his ball into the uncut grass for good measure on her last. "Some tough customer," she'd say, and wipe her hands on her handkerchief, since they'd grown damp on the stick.

Hilda Payson had beaten her, once. She acknowledges that. But she, Harriet, had been overconfident and lazy and let Hilda get the jump on her and then was knocked into the wet uncut grass herself, and was just getting over a cold. So her shoes got soaking and she sneezed and missed the recovery shot, and then Hilda who was gleeful and cantankerous and not to be trusted with the liquor cabinet key had knocked her back again. She nearly lost her temper. She said dreadful things, nearly aloud. Hilda Payson had pretended not to care. But Hilda cared—she, Harriet, could see that—cared tremendously, was cawing to herself in delighted triumph and her knees were set so far apart you'd think she sat a horse.

She said, "Croquet's a game. You win some when you're lucky." Harriet was ill and shivering and her next shot hit a rock and bounced right back. That was the trouble with Vermont; no matter how you fine-tooth-combed it there were always, anyhow, rocks. It was inhospitable country for croquet. "It doesn't matter," Hilda chortled. "You'll have better luck next time, I'm sure."

"It isn't luck," she'd said. "It's skill. I'm off my game."

"You couldn't know about that rock," Hilda said.

"I could. I did."

So Hilda inched her out. She, Harriet, is near to sleep now and upholding truthfulness and therefore bound to qualify that. It hadn't been close. It was closer to a country mile than inches, and Hilda brayed with pleasure as she hit the stick. Her upper plate was loose. Harriet pointed that out. "Don't be a spoilsport, dearie," Hilda said. Harriet had not been any sort of spoilsport, then or ever; it was just she'd had no practice losing at croquet. So she'd had the borders trimmed, and Judah levered up the rocks for her and she took every corner on again and beat them handily—but she had lost her taste for it and was glad, that year, for snow.

Ian was meticulous. He had spent hours preening—or what had seemed to Hattie like hours—turning in front of the mirror, studying himself with what at first seemed vanity and then something harder to name and accuse. It was the kind of study he'd accorded puzzles or spelling, or the internal combustion engine when he took his first motor apart. There were parts and wholes, and somehow the sum of the parts, Hattie knew, had to add up to the whole. Somehow those eyes and ears and eyebrows made up the whole of a face, and Ian studied it to puzzle out the mystery of things. So she hesitates now (though she had not at the time, had teased and taunted Ian mercilessly if without avail) to call it vain. There was nothing personal in that slow study, as if Ian might have studied any available skull—providing that the skull would smile and wink and scowl on order and not lose patience, not leave. It was as if he knew there'd be a dearth of mirrors, that someday soon he'd be in some desert with nothing to reflect him back, no proof of his existence except memory. And that he'd better stare his fill while there was something to look at, better trace the lineaments till instinct would assure him there were distinctive lineaments to trace.

For he had learned distinction. Hattie made it clear without saying; her lessons were none of them spoken but written on the blackboard of the air, and just as quickly erased. So he'd be staring at the traces of instruction, trying to learn what he, Ian, needed to know—while there was only her blurred mouthing, only the spoor of the sentence she'd thought and no blackboard and no chalk and nobody there to nudge him with the answer. Still, he picked it up. He lip-read, thought-read, read without reading; if only he'd been half the student in school that he'd been of her manners schooling, Hattie said, why then he'd be adept at fractions and geography and penmanship also. He learned degree and size. The neighbor's homes are none of them big as the Big House, and his is the biggest around. The Sherbrookes that spilled over went to Canada and started up a place called Sherbrooke there. Our family was sitting here when neighbors came in wagons, and they took their shoes off when they came into the parlor, and it was a shoe that still fits.

So that way at least they were similar; that way vanity was utilized by each. When Hattie closed her eyes, she persuaded herself it was night; when the sun sinks over Woodford Ridge it is the sun, not Hattie's world sinking, and no one speaks her name if she isn't there to hear. Ian, of course, had had occasion to be vain. He was his mother's picture in a man. Everything that passed for beauty or handsome was his, and handsome is as handsome does, Hattie said. You couldn't help but notice how the phone rang nightly, and how they always picked him in the partner's choice.

There is the sough of Judah's toilet, and the trickling refill in its tank. There are voices raised in what she thinks is argument, then thinks is maybe song. If her Creator lived, He knew without half trying all the goings on in the Big House, and he too clucked his tongue. Pins dropped in a haystack are quiet, she knows. Yet she can hear a pin dropped in a tin pie plate at twenty paces; it is all a matter of degree. Across the hall, in his room, she hears the sound she loathes— the cry of "Judah, Husband," and what sounds like springs, like slammed doors, the sound she's heard unceasingly and even in this seven-year silence, the familiar slap of flesh on flesh like heels on flooring, *Judah, Husband*, while the woman moans through every thick partition, and Hattie curses her hearing, her ears that have to endure this, *Judah, Jude*. The slap and bustle of the two-backed beast is paramount, continual, is all she's ever listened to from that cage three doors across where Maggie prowls—and she places her hands on her ears and hears in her cupped palm chamber the sound again, blood thumping *Husband, Judah*, and presses her elbows together like knees and forces her ears shut.

XI

"I'M DYING," JUDAH SAYS.

"Don't say that," Maggie says.

"I'm dying."

"Fifty years from now." She snaps her fingers. "Just like that. It used to be your joke."

She presses herself to him and is again the cocksure twenty-three-year-old who's met her husband match. Then Judah had been superb. He was the strongest man she'd ever known or would have wanted to know—with that near-surface fury. He set her teeth on edge. He set them chattering, then ground them down, it seemed, until her teeth were nerve ends too. When he hugged her he hugged with such suffocating pressure that even her teeth felt compressed. He'd cracked two ribs those years—and when she remonstrated or drew back he was, absurdly, hurt.

"It's me who's hurting," Maggie'd say. "It's me who can't breathe deeply anymore."

"I'm sorry," Judah said.

"You don't, like they say, know your own strength."

"All right," he'd promise. "I'll quit."

But he wouldn't quit, would never leave off pawing at and pressing and compressing her until, for sanity's sake, she made him keep hands off. He called her "Hellcat" since there was a play out then about a football hero, and his wife who was Maggie the Cat. Elizabeth Taylor played the movie part, and they went to see the movie and he told her, meaning it, she was better than that Maggie or the movie actress anyhow, and by a country mile. She rewarded him for that. It came to be a system of reward. When he was submissive she'd submit in turn to his huge manhandling and lie there underneath him while he worked his ardor off. It wasn't all one-way, of course. She took pleasure enough for herself. But there was always panic at the edge of it—that he would annihilate some inner reticence, would take more than she had to give and leave her sucked dry, dessicate, bone pounded into bonemeal and her pelvis crushed. She'd seen a dog that way once—run over on its hind legs but not yet dead, but howling, running with no way to run. Hattie came and fetched her, seeking help. It lifted itself impossibly from the roadbed, swiping at its body ruin that had no dimension left—and she, Maggie, ran to the house and found and fetched Judah in her turn and told him to bring his rifle. He did, but the collie was dead by the time they got back to it, with the blood not running now. He shot it anyway, point-blank, twice in the head.

"Hold me," he repeats.

"How?"

"Here," the old man mutters. "Here," and places her hand on him.

"Judah . . ."

But he makes no answer, turning to the wall. So once again she is his helpless totem, sprawled beside him while he violates things. The dog had shifted twice. There never had been danger in her early lovers or her love affairs. There was danger at the edge of them only—since Judah licked at her paper-thin lovers like flame.

"Harder," he says now. "I'm dying."

"I can't," she says. "I'm frightened."

Maggie weeps. It does not work. She tries to picture him huge, in his towering possessiveness and marbled perfection, stripped to the waist while he sponged himself clean after work. The sun line on his arms was absolute. It is not working. Nor can her gentle memories—of Alan Seligman's enthusiasm, or of Michael's enthusiasm, and the love litany they've chorused at her since—seduce her from the present horror, his spittle at her lips.

"I don't know you," Judah says.

"Yes."

"No. You're a stranger here. This isn't my wife."

"Oh, Judah, yes but it is."

"No. Outen here," he warns her. "This isn't the way my wife works."

"What way then?" Maggie says. "I'm humble before you. Just give me one chance."

"Don't cry. Be glad," Judah says.

She knows when things went bad. She knows when the whiff of mortality became a mortal stench. All things had seemed possible till Seth. When he died her world went bitter, difficult, and everything that seemed to fit was formless after that. That was the path's true turning; that was when the woods grew dark and trails crisscrossed and doubled back and things she took for granted were revoked.

Seth had been a sunshine child. He lay contemplative, grinning, for hours in his crib or in the rocking chair Jude rigged for him, or on her lap. She was sure he understood things past her understanding as he suckled at her, blue eyes wide and huge. She had been drunk. She remembers that much. She has spent the intervening years forgetting, and there were many things about the night she never could remember. But she remembers some argument with Judah as to squatter's rights. She'd said the nation was built by squatters, and like as not his ancestors had got what they'd gotten by squatting, and the early bird catches the worm's a phrase for birds and worms. Therefore those who took land now had no less justice in the taking; more, seemed like, since the government made it a good deal harder to keep. He'd scoffed at her. He'd said how about the three hundred acres of bottom land; how about everything that abuts the river; we're not using it, now are we, so why not just give it away? Why not, she'd answered, and been serious, and he'd looked at her and seen that but said you can't be serious. Why not, she'd repeated; what are we holding it for? For our sons, that's who for, Judah said. For men who'll make the proper use of it in time. I'm glad of that, she'd said, of course (but thinking back on it thinks maybe that's when she thought she heard Seth; maybe that was pride's signal and the time that outrage settled in, suffocating and betraying and sucking every bit of air up from her infant's room; maybe that was the self-congratulatory shepherd penning the wolf in his fold, then ticking off his blessings as he heads back for the hut). I'm glad of that, Maggie said. I'm glad for them, and grateful, but it doesn't change the argument; it doesn't mean that those who need the land shouldn't get pasture rights. I've built this place, Judah said, with these two hands I've tilled it. Your great-grandfather built it, she said. You've tilled it for lack of anything better to do. There's been no necessity here—and thinks she hears it again, thinks as he looms above her, furious, passionate, the advance he makes upon her prelude to some sort of grappling, but whether to beat or embrace her she's never certain till joined; thinks later the susurrus she heard was the whistling, whimpering final breath Seth drew, and had she not taunted her husband so, had they not finished the bottle, had the night been less loud with cicada or had she not insisted on Chopin in the aftermath, bedded by him on the couch and therefore not even stumbling past Seth's bedroom to their own—had she only been less idle her son would somehow live. There's no real blame to attach. There's no way to prevent it, and nothing to have done. But Maggie takes the blame up anyhow and knows that otherwise nothing makes sense; if his death is wholly senseless then the world is wholly evil, and she'd rather think there's meaning she can't as yet grasp. Hattie said the same. Only Hattie said it, saying there was meaning in the soul's salvation and punishment for evil ways, and Maggie told her, never quite saying it, say that again and I'll pull out your tongue.

She washes herself. She is attentive. She uses the toilet and lifts her right hand for the chain. She hauls at air, then lifts her left hand and finds the chain and pulls. She washes again. They measured land in rods here, Maggie remembers, and remembers thinking it's a better word than acreage. She knows that millions die yearly. She knows that crib death is the sort of graceful gathering to God a theologian might use. She knows that, by comparison, death by starvation or cholera or bombing is a fate far worse than crib death—that the best thing of all is not to have been born. Next best, she knows, is to die young, and in untrammeled innocence surrounded by your loved ones in a world that they seem to control.

Yet that suspicion of a whisper was enough—that susurrus on the second floor while she strained against her husband underneath. It meant Seth suffered while she took her pleasure, meant the world was wholly evil and absurd. She hears it now more loudly than any scream of pain. Things are out of control, not controlled; innocence gets smothered in its crib. From that time, therefore, Maggie aged; from that fell turning she hacked her own way. Light changed in the afternoon, and woods that seemed benign enough were suddenly hurtful and threatening; birds fed on dead flesh. Owls that seem wise are ferocious; mourning doves are fierce. Leaves that seem blunt-edged are needle-sharp. From that time on her beauty was a weapon—shield and spear. She would endure, she said to Judah, no third child. They'd lost one altogether, and the firstborn, Ian, seemed independent already and would make his way, gain or loss, without them. Hostages to fortune, she says, that's what we are, wife and child. Whose talk is that, he asks her, feigning interest, and she says William Shakespeare's, and he says big talk, big talk. Don't feign illiteracy, Jude, she says, it's bad enough as is. What's bad enough, he asks her. Being a hostage to fortune, she says. Being on the top of fortune's wheel. It means you take a turn. For the worse? he asks her, and she tells him, For the worse.

She rose again, of course. Folks rise, he tells her, sententious; can't keep a good man down. That's a dirty joke, she wants to tell him, that's boasting. That's the sort of purblind optimism she's earlier embraced; all it is is turning; all it is is evil evil chance.

Maggie forces herself. She has to think of other things. She will not think of lust or Seth or any of his beauty accoutrements nor her vanished own. She will think about cats. She'll concentrate on cats and dogs and raining cats and dogs and dogdays and dogpounds and penny wise, pound foolish. But her association word for foolish is careless, and her association word for careless is careless love. She sings this to herself. And so she is word-trammeled, circling, caught in the vortex center or the web he'd spun that is this bed. She studies the brown leather chair by the bed and the three photos of her son. Judah lies like a vast spider next to her, at home in such intricate tangle— and all she, Maggie, manages are nonsense songs. Come into my parlor, said the spider to the fly, she sings; come fly with me, let's fly away; *away in yon valley, in a low lonesome place, where the wild birds do whistle, their notes do increase. . . .*

That had been Judah's song for her, she knew. That had been his courtier's tune, and he sang it with a plangent grace that never failed to move her. It overpraised his ear to call it tin. She didn't know if there were cheaper alloys even than tin; she could call his ear aluminum foil, she supposes, or plastic, or claim it was made out of mud. But he sang "Saro Jane" with emotion that beggared complaint— believing it, believing he was some rejected rancher and she, Maggie, had elected silks and comfort while he rode the range.

Range was home on; range was kitchen; kitchen was the place she came from when he called. Maggie sighs. The game is working. She is carried from this evil place to her apartment's kitchen, or memories of Judah with his caterwauling earnestness, or how she'd seen Gene Autry at the circus once, his belly all over his pants.

"That's better."

"Yes," she says.

"That's what I want from you," he says and turns to face her.

"Your servant, sir," she says.

"For better or for worse," he pronounces—only half in mockery. "In illness as in health."

(He had wanted, he told her, no nonsense speech. He had been straightforward in the taking, as in asking "Will you be my wife?" That was honorable discourse, and she had known it for Judah's plain speaking, without embroidery. He had gotten to his knees. Generations of Sherbrookes had gone to their knees and cracked their joints before generations of soon-to-be-Sherbrookes, he joked. He'd not get off his knees, he said, till she said yes.

"Is that a question?" she'd asked.
"Yes."
"A threat or promise?" Maggie asked.
"Promise," he said. "A promise to keep."
"You'll hurt yourself"—she bent above him—"down there on that hardwood floor."

He looked to see her swaying, not so composed as all that, not certain if he meant what he never would ask without meaning. He told her so. She shut her eyes. She breathed deeply, considering. He listened for her breath.

"It doesn't surprise you," he said.
"No."
"You've known it was coming," he said.
"I thought so, maybe." Maggie had opened her eyes.
"Well, what did you think"—he rocked back on his heels, adjusting—"when you thought it was coming?"
"I thought I'd tell you yes," she said.
"Is that what you're telling me?"
"Yes."

He put his hands on her knees. "That's settled then," he had wanted to say—pleased with the plain saying of it, and her precision of gesture. She stooped above him, then knelt where he was kneeling and smiled and said, "That's settled then." He kissed her, elated, proud she would repeat him and only realized afterward she'd taken the words from his mouth.)

It had happened offhand finally, after all his preparatory scheming, his traps and teasing preludes—happened as he knew it would now, looking back, coterminus with his not caring that it happened anymore, with his decision that the legacy was trivial and separation trivial and who cared how he handled it or fouled or let fall the reins: that suddenly Jude kept his seat, was graceful as he'd been when in his riding prime, was mastering that comic turn the world calls circumstance and gave his wife what she'd anyhow always possessed—his house, his lands, his body to dispose of in the way that she saw fit. "Thanks anyhow," she told him, "but no thanks. It's kind of you to offer but I'm otherwise engaged."

"You can't mean that," he said.

"I do."

"Be reasonable," Judah said—and recognized this too as comic, that he'd call on reason who was feeling's fool.

"It's just I've lost the words," she said. "My mind's a blank. There's so much I wanted to tell you."

"Try."

"I can't. I've told you that."

So he glided on past her and mocked the world's turning, playing his desire's dervish and a top with a slack string. He was his own caught creature in the garden's Havahart trap, and he'd bruised his foot.

Later still he tells her, "Take it," and she says, "All right." Take everything I have that's yours, which is anyhow everything I have and may it give you pleasure in this life. She takes it with the negligence she'd always shown to favor, as if it were a debt redeemed and long since overdue. "I've fixed it with Finney," he says. "I gave you the house and the barns."

She hates the past. She ignores it. It's a whipped pup come back to haunt its master, tail wagging under its legs. Hattie makes jellies for Christmas. She makes jams and marmalades and sometimes they spend slow hours together, stirring, adding pectin, melting the paraffin, labeling: the past, she says to Hattie, it's nothing to conserve. "That's a bad joke," Hattie says, and Maggie says "No worse." "No worse than what?" the woman asks, and she says, "Than others that I've heard."

"Tell me where you've been," he asks.
"New York mostly. San Francisco."
"New Orleans?" he asks.
She smiles at him. "A little."
"To visit your cousins?"
"To visit the queen."
"And Providence, Rhode Island?"
"No."
"Do you have an apartment," he asks. "A house? A hotel room?"

"Still the same apartment," she says. "In New York City. On the river. In just about the exact middle of town."

"You've said that before," Judah says.

"I know. Which is why I said it again."

"You've got a memory."

"No. It's you who used to quote it. I wouldn't remember," she says.

Now she knows herself once more. She is creature-comforts Maggie who knows her way around. She is mistress to the house and wife to the man in the bed. He holds her, vehement. She is fifty-one years old and, without much adjusting, a blond. She had, she tells herself, been asked for help by him who'd never asked before—though much of that begging seemed malice and some of it certainly fake. She thinks of the endless demands on devotion that devotion, once constituted, makes: it isn't a question of manners, or habit, isn't a question of not needing to hurt what seemed so vulnerable now; it is for Maggie simply that she doesn't know how to refuse him this night; what he asks of her she gives because for twenty-one years she gave or gave in or gave over.

"I don't need charity."

"This isn't charity," she says.

Yet she is startled by his near-divining of her thought. He always had been generous—with that offhand largesse of the rich who need no money since it all was earned before. She used to tell him he threw checks at foundations like scraps at the bluetick hound, only with less careful aim. He'd not even read the brochures.

"You're wasting it," she'd say. "These people use ninety percent of their funding for office space. None of it goes to the needy."

"They all of them are profligate," he said. "I give a tithe of the farm's take to the first takers; it's simpler first come and first serve."

"But unfair," she'd protested. "Immoral."

"Then slip your envelopes on top of the stack," Judah said. "It won't make any difference. But if it makes you glad . . ."

So she'd selected and directed his charity for years. He'd spent less for himself than anyone; she granted that. He wore the same old coats and boots till they were worn to patches, and then he had them patched. His car was always ten years old (though he'd flung that Packard at her, and tried for furs, and the Steinway concert grand). It wasn't self-denial or a planned austerity; just that he had no use for what she labeled useful. Somewhere Judah must have heard that men who loved their women gave their women gifts—that husbands who could manage it would manage a fur coat, or car, or diamond rings. So when he remembered he took her out shopping—rampaging through Georg Jensen's with pockets full of hundred dollar bills, and emptying those pockets out, floor by floor, as she trailed after him protesting. It was luxury, of course, but not her sort of luxury since he paid more attention to the cattle at an auction barn than to the silver service, or the goblets he bought her, or plate. His gift-giving was so dutiful it undermined desire—and he'd thank her, frowning, for her own few gifts to him, then fold and store them away. It was a frown more of puzzlement than reproof; he just didn't know what to do with a second overcoat, or a carryall with his stamped initials on the flap.

"I got no need of charity," he mutters at her now.

"No," Maggie says. "You don't. You're self-sufficient, darling. I know that."

"Correct. One hundred percent."

"I'm not dispensing charity. I hate that word. I'm glad to be here and glad you let me come." She wonders, is that true? "Truly," Maggie says. "And grateful for the house."

"You're not"—he twists his mouth—"the lying kind."

"No."

"One hundred percent," Judah says.

"Be quiet," she commands him. "You'll tire out with this talk."

And then he is obedient and she takes his flesh between her hands. She prods and rubs and massages his shoulders, feeling him quicken then ebb. He is a white-haired elder at her side, the muscularity gone flaccid now and limp. She is dispensing charity. She wonders, will his offer hold and is it some expensive trade-off; Finney knows, she tells herself, she'll talk to Samson in the morning and find out what's what. She soothes and strokes him, wishing there were rubbing oil. She makes circle motions on his lower back. Maggie rises above him, not mindful now of the sheets, warm with this familiar exertion, watching her breasts sway and dangle as she works.

"That feels fine," he says. His mouth is in the pillow.

"Hush," she repeats. "Don't talk."

She labors like this for some time. She finds herself caressing him and making for his buttocks like an alien, secret place, and knows herself aroused.

"It's good to be here," she whispers.

He makes no answer.

"Judah."

He shifts his head.

"J.P." She hears herself whispering, hoarse. He draws his hands down to his sides.

"Jude, are you listening?"

Ponderously, he draws up his knees.

"It's good to be back, do you hear?" She touches herself, expectant. "It is."

He pushes himself up on his hands. He is on all fours at her side and turns to face her, focusing. She watches him watching her. He licks his lips. He bulks above her.

"That's not polite," she says and smiles. "You shouldn't stare so"—and places his hand on her left breast and lets it settle.

"Touch me, Judah," she tells him.

He balances. She feels his hand veer.

"Please."

He falls upon her and is a great weight; she flattens herself and supports him.

"Talk to me," she says.

He does not move.

"Say something, Jude. Whisper sweet nothings," she teases.

Still he is silent. She listens for his breathing and does not hear but feels it, in concert with hers. She holds her breath. He does not breathe.

"Jude?"

She feels the panic's edge again and tries to force him off her; he does not move. She scissors her legs shut. His cold leg moves, in consonance, and he lies atop her two closed legs not moving.

"Are you asleep?" she asks him.

He does not answer.

"Sleepy, darling? That's all right. We've plenty of time in the world," Maggie says. "Rest."

His hair is lank. She reaches to brush it back from his forehead, then stays her hand. She holds it there suspended, shaking, and shuts her eyes again. Now panic enfolds her utterly and is out of all control. It mouths her mouth and pours itself into her ears. It stops her nose and fingers her and runs rough lover-hands along her body, squeezing. She drops her hand. It holds her hands. It plays upon her spine as though her spine were something like a xylophone, but with no sheathing for the hammers, with nothing to cushion her; there are no blankets; she shakes. Panic is efficient; it tongues her without haste. It licks its chops and tastes her and is not perfunctory; she vices her legs against it but it pries her easily apart. It has a throat and makes percussive noises in its throat. She weeps but keeps her eyes closed, screams but keeps her lips together and is dry-eyed, soundless. She screams, "Judah, Jude." She repeats this several times. She has a sudden memory of Ian, eight months old, with a flu and croup and fever that reached one hundred and five degrees in the first two hours; Judah took their son and plunged him in the bath, with ice and cold water, and Ian screamed and shivered while they brought the fever down. She remembers Jude's huge hands, the size of Ian easily, and how they held and tormented her son, but helpful, but healing, and she tries to marry panic and embrace it now. It enters her. It is practiced. It penetrates her with thick rigid members of ice. It scrapes her womb and fills her mouth and reams her asshole out. It ejaculates everywhere, grunting, spewing ice. Its sperm is like sea spume where even the tideline has frozen. Ian was blue in the face. He spat and had been mottled and outraged. Yet Ian healed. He sucked at her afterward with lips through which she saw his first three teeth. Panic assaults her, stiffening, where there is no pleasure left. It continues. She sprawls and kicks against it, but it is an avalanche and the problem is survival, is a snow pocket to breathe in while her breath goes rancid. Heat hurts. She lay with her ancient husband, and he knew her not.

BOOK

3

I

JUDAH WAKES, AS HE ALWAYS DOES, QUICKLY. HE IS ASLEEP, THEN wakeful, with no intervening space. He focuses on the pillow beneath him, then the sheet above his head. There is light in the room. He consults the dials of the clock. They are luminous, and therefore radioactive, and Hattie said that if you wore a wristwatch with radioactive dials you contracted cancer of the wrist. He shakes his head. He disagrees with her, disproving it by proving how many men wore how many wristwatches with dials like that for how many years. No cancer has ever been reported, to his certain knowledge, that they traced to radioactive dials.

It is like strychnine, he said. Swallow a small dose and you build up resistance; swallow a big one without any practice, and it's your final swallow. She had been adamant. What about sciatica, she asked; what about that? They thought they knew about it all the time, since the word was invented, and here they'd been using it wrong all along and now they'd swear on Bibles what they gainsaid just last week. She made him swear to wear only his uncle's gold vest watch, with its slipcase and chain. She'd made him send back Finney's Christmas gift, which illuminated the day and the date. He'd promised, to humor her, and had been out of the habit of timepieces anyhow. He raises himself to make some joke to Maggie about her sister-in-law's grim insistence, and how time flies if you throw your watch out the window. There is a janitor at Smith College, he jokes, who's worked for thirty years. When the girls ask him what he wants for a retirement present, he says, I wanna watch. So they let him.

He chortles and slaps at his side. He turns to see how Maggie takes the joke. She is not there. He swivels, scanning the room. There is a form beside him, bloated, its breath stertorous, and he shrinks from it because his wife was always whippet-lean and a light sleeper. He had not dreamed her, did not dream. He cannot remember his dreams. She has slipped away from him again, and that is once too often in this life.

Judah extends himself from the bed. He rises like smoke. It is no distance to the closet, nor any real accomplishment to stand. He acknowledges, departing, that the shape beside him was his wife. She owns the house now and will not leave. It is his turn to go. He will gather up his errant son and they will go together. He has Maggie in the bed but now he thinks of her as bait, not prize. His quarry will be Ian next, and the trap is Maggie in the middle of the house. He turns his attention to tracking his son; he attends to that. There are rings on Ian's fingers and bells on his toes. He will seek his lost son out and force him to return. Ian has a banjo, possibly, or a beer bottle to whistle in or guitar or jew's harp or piano; he makes music wherever he goes.

He selects his locust cane. The cane has a leather thong; he'd drilled through its head. The ends are silver-capped. Next Judah chooses his duck-hunting jacket to clothe his nakedness and stands there hefting it in the closet's warm oblivion; the oil lamp by his bedside gutters down. The shape on his bed rearranges itself. He fits his arms into sleeves. The sleeves are thick. He rests, standing as he used to stand in duck blinds in the darkness, a piece of the surrounding space, indeterminate. His coat has a health stench. He needs no boots. He has his cane and body-cunning and will track whoever lies with Maggie where they lie.

Judah makes his way into the hall. He pads down the center of it, secretive. It is a thing he'd noticed early on that men strode down the centers of streets, or skulked on the paving, or couldn't make their mind up and would cross the road at puddles or for the sake of sun. And early on he'd chosen to walk each walkway's center. He'd give way to cars of course, or a team and cart, but not concede dominion to some engineer's idea of who should walk in which direction when. It was a habit now he'd not break for the sake of stealth, though he walks on tiptoe, without shoes. And anyhow it is his hall, and anyhow they'd see him if they chanced to look.

"They're giving out tickets for that in New York City, Mr. Sherbrooke," Sam Burgess said. Sam Burgess lost the use of his left arm in a driving accident, so they made him stand outside the elementary school, whistling and waving at cars.

"What do they ticket you for?"

"Jaywalking," he said. "That's what they call it. It costs you fifteen dollars just to cross between the green."

"I call it freedom of movement," Judah said. "I call it my own skin."

"I wanted to warn you," Sam said.

"You've done that. But there's no car coming, and we got no traffic light."

"I just wanted to warn you, that's all. If you get down to New York City and they throw you in the clink."

"Not likely," Judah said. "But thanks all the same."

Sam's left arm withered with disuse; he wore a yellow slicker when it rained or snowed. There was a riddle Ian asked one morning, after school. "Hey, who's the strongest man in the world?" he had asked.

"I don't know," Judah said. "What's your opinion on that?"

"Superman," Ian said. "You're supposed to answer 'Superman.'"

"Superman," he said.

"Wrong again," his son had crowed. "A traffic cop. Know why?"

"No."

"Guess."

"I can't. I can't imagine."

"Just guess."

"Because he's got the law behind him—the force of the law."

"Because he holds a hundred cars up with just one hand. That's why."

"And that's all he has," said Judah. Ian veered off to the kitchen to try the riddle out on Mrs. Sattherswaite.

(Judah Sherbrooke lies, they whisper, on his deathbed now that was his marriage bed. He thinks that he hears them consulting. We could give him poultices, they say; we could perform open-heart surgery. We could make him take his morning constitutional and see whether yogurt would help. It's the mitral valve, they say, it's an infarction; it's all of that beefsteak for all of those lunches for years. He lies, he hears them say, in splendor, in great pain, in peace. They lie. He is merely husbanding his strength. Bears hibernate, and ducks go torpid in the wintertime, and many beasts are sluggish till heat quickens them. The bedsprings creak and complain. The frame's securely jointed, he knows about that, but the rails of the sleigh bed need sanding. There where he flings his legs to the floor, or sits at the bed's edge winding his watch, the inside of his legs has rubbed the edges smooth. There's grit on his flesh. There's nothing like the action of the flesh; it gives a sheen to the wood no varnish can accomplish. It's endocarditis, they say, it's angina pectoris, it's all his sins upon him at long and final last. What can't he shoulder by bearing; which trick or two remaining is the trick to play? He asks himself that. He asks himself who let the doctors in, the lawyers out, and where is Maggie, and why should they whisper if he hears them whispering anyhow. It's blockage on blockage, they say, it's enough to fell an ox. Nonsense, he winks, no such luck. Come here till I tell you: there's caterpillars coming out of moths. There's beasts in air and water that will walk upon this earth. It took him six shots through the head to kill one snapping turtle, and the jaws were moving even after that. He'd hunkered in the grass by the pond, sighting, waiting for the thing to surface, and it surfaced not six feet from him and was an easy shot.)

It lies there soiled. In his mind's eye he sees the letter to his son. Its edges curl because the envelope is larger than the paper it contains. Finney has a new secretary, and she insists on folding things twice, the letter turned in on itself, when a single fold would do. She has, Finney tells him, advantages. She can take shorthand faster than he talks, and her typing is acceptable, and she has many talents in the field. Hayfield, Judah says, and Finney winks. The letter has been postmarked March thirtieth. It is their only attempt. It says *Please Forward if Necessary* on it, but Ian leaves no forwarding address. It requests him to contact his father or his father's lawyer and be present at discussions of the terms of the estate. It suggests such presence would be vital to the nature of the settlement, and proposes a per diem allowance and, of course, that travel expenses would be furnished at his father's expense.

The envelope is cream white, of excellent stock. Finney's title and address are printed in dark green ink, on the upper lefthand corner. He employs an IBM Selectric typeface for Ian's address, but resists a postage meter as a mark of the impersonal. There's not that many letters, Finney says, that you can't lick and stamp them by hand. They've tried, Lord knows, says Judah, to haul him home before. It lies on a hall table, under magazines. In time the dust will form a diagonal consistent with the left upper edge of *Popular Mechanics* that lies athwart it, protective. The table, Judah imagines, is a plain pine table with walnut stain. Its two front legs are on the hall runner, its two back legs on the floor. There is therefore a slight downward tilt to the angle of the whole (though not above an eighth of an inch) and the consequent seven degrees, since the table weights sufficiently to mark the purple runner, and the runner's threadbare anyhow. Ian's off to sea, he thinks, and in this seaport town the mildew happens quickly. It's as if the envelope was sweated on, or steamed; it's as if the formal furtive language is a circular, and any lost son everywhere is always welcome home.

The stairwell is another matter, since it gives on the library door. He would be discovered surely, and his sham would be exploded and his illness turn to health. He thinks of the parapets and windows, and of the back servant stairs. But they lead past Hattie's room, and he knows her far more wakeful, even sleeping, even behind a shut door, than his careless wife. So he turns and sees the elevator shaft. He pads to the door and pulls it open carefully and peers within; the cage is there.

Judah shuts the door again; it is of solid oak, and squeaks. The door to the library, too, is windowless oak. If he opens it a crack, he tells himself, he might well hear and not be heard, see and not be seen. They are in the library, discussing him; he is certain of that. The elevator reeks; it is memory's confinement and a box for invalids. Still, it fits his spying purpose and will make no noise.

Pleased with his contrivance, he rests for the count of ten. Then he pulls the door open and steps inside and unscrews the elevator's lamp. Next he feels in the new darkness for the button, pushes, and feels himself fall. There is a soft whirring and complaint from the elevator cables, but he knows they would not hear him or distinguish this new noise from the surrounding house noise. The cabinet settles, and he settles himself for his vigil, breathing to ten.

("Count to a hundred," Ian had said, "before you start to look for me. And keep your eyes closed or it's cheating."

"I won't look," Judah said.

"But keep your eyes closed. OK?"

"OK."

"Now count to a hundred," he yelled, distancing.

"I'm counting," Judah said. "One one hundred, two one hundred, three"—and leaned his head against the wall and listened to his son. Ian hid in closets or would bang doors then shut them without running through, and early on he'd fitted underneath the couch.

"No fair peeking," he'd shout, and Judah gauged the echo.

"Oley, oley infree; ready or not here I come."

What, he wonders now, did "oley oley infree" mean; how had he clambered over furniture, shouting "Fee-fi-fo-fum, I smell the blood of an Englishmum," in pursuit of that elated son he could not locate now? Then they played "Thing in the Room," and Ian chose an object and Judah guessed which one it was by circling and pointing, while Ian cackled "Getting cold. Ice cold. A little bit warmer. Getting warm now getting hot, getting hot as a person can get." So Judah, nosing up to the vase, would know it was the vase and turn on his heels and point to the still life of oranges. "Cooling off now," his son would crow, delighted, "but still pretty warm." Then Judah stepped past the still life and across the mantelpiece and Ian would pretend to freeze and shiver, beating his elbows and saying, "Brr-r it's cold in here. So cold.")

"Though there be severall who think it improper," Peacock wrote, "we will not heed the world's scurrility but take our bounden pleasures in that almost-Eden whence my thoughts continually fly. Oh to be in Vermont where the first green things this week will testify to spring and to His ceaseless Husbandry Who watcheth over all. I seem to see the Easter lambs at their frolics, and freshening cows, and the season's wheel which here on this Pacific Coast seems not to turn, or grudgingly, though th'Inhabitants call it healthful and breathe this salt-slime down. Had they one taste of Mountain air, once filled their lungs as I have with the sweet pine-scent of our beloved pasture-land, they would choke with every inhalation or keep Cambric pressed to the nose. There is profit to be made here in the better class of lace. . . ."

There where he keeps his ladle the stream runs all summer long; the ladle is tin and large enough for two to drink from—not together, though they've tried that too, her head butting his, their noses opposed, hair in his eyes, but one after the other, his wife going first—and in April or June he just has to dip, not even bending, to fill the cup full, and later it tastes of metal, and later it tastes of leaves with a flavor not so much the residue as presage of decay, the maple and oak leaves thickening the streambed banks, and clogging the rock sluice he'd chosen. Nearby he built a salt lick and an apple stand, building it at Megan's urging and high enough to clear the snow so that the deer might have unimpeded winter access, and when they snowshoed in to see they saw that the apples were gone and the salt lick troughed hollow by tongues, so she laughed and held him and said, "There, we've helped that many at least," and he didn't answer, "For a week maybe.

For the dogs to kill a little later," but only pressed her where she held him and said, "You. You've eaten those apples. They're in your cheeks, Megan," and she answered, "Lordy. Lord, I married a romantic. The last of the red-hot romantics," and he scooped the snow's crust back and dug till he uncovered the stream and thrust through the crystalline surface to the sluggish trickle beneath—the ladle's cup was snow-stuffed and he knocked the powder back and filled the cup with icicles and chill white water and drank and made her drink: the tin adhered to her lips and, tearing the ladle free, he shredded her lips' flesh.

He has tried to reach Ian by phone. He called the last numbers he knew. There had been no answer or the phone was disconnected or the parties that he reached had never heard of Ian Sherbrooke and couldn't be bothered to look. He didn't blame them. It wasn't a question of blame. But he had known that Maggie knew where Ian could be reached, and tried the phone in Wellfleet once but hung up on her father when he heard the first: "Hello."

Nor was this all. He formulated telegrams; he thought of taking out ads. He tried to send a letter but the words evaded him. He was tonguetied in the phraseology of need. Maggie had been fluent, and she would have found the language, but his own stock phrases stuck. He could not bring himself, he knew, to beg for what was his by right and what each man could anyhow expect: a son beside him in his house. He imagined there were protestations that would haul his son back, hat in hand, protesting that he too had left for love. He imagined Ian reconciled and by his bed, saying, "Why didn't you tell me? Why didn't I understand sooner? What a fool I must have been!"

"Not foolish," Judah would say. "Just a bit stubborn, that's all."

"A willful piggish fool," Ian would accuse himself, and the tears would blind him while he spoke. "How can you ever forgive me; how can I best make it up?"

"No need," Judah told him. "Just stay here. That's all I ask."

"Done," Ian said. "You didn't have to ask for that. My stuff is at the station. All of it; I'm here to stay."

"That's good," he said, and closed his eyes and smiled.

When Judah comes to, there is silence. He does not know the space; it reeks of lemon oil. The air is bad. He breathes and stretches and opens his eyes but is in blackness nonetheless. Stretching, he touches two walls. He remembers, then, his place and purpose and gathers himself to his feet. The furnace ignites beneath him; things collapse. He builds them back again but they collapse. He reaches for the light switch and finds it and presses and then remembers that he has unscrewed the bulb. "These are letters I've lived by," he says aloud. "Peacock built the place and never got to live in it; I ain't leaving now. I've read them out so often I can tell them off by heart."

The effort of this wearies him, and he gathers himself up again to breathe. He takes mincing, sideways steps around the floor's perimeter and toes the bulb in the last corner and leans to retrieve it, then rests again. There is silence in the library; he feels for matches in his hunting pockets. Patting at the pockets, he drops the bulb and hears it bounce and shatter. He curses himself for a loose-fingered fool, and continues. There are empty shotgun shells and a handkerchief and sand grit and a penknife in his pockets, but nothing like light. He sighs. He hears his breathing echo. He decides to ascend and presses the button for the second floor but does not move. He thinks perhaps he's pressed the wrong button and fingers each button beside him, then presses his palms against the instrument panel entirely. There is silence. There is not even a boiler below him, or any sort of clanking in the elevator chains. Hattie had been claustrophobic. She had feared just such a breakdown, she told him, just such a short in the lines. What if I'm riding, she asked him, between one floor and another, and lightning comes and knocks the power out, what then? You pays your money and you takes your choice, Judah said, not sympathetic, not wanting to coddle her fears. For every fire, he maintained, there's twenty false alarms.

So he collects himself and breathes again—the air denser this time, acrid—and counts to ten. He shrugs himself out of his coat. The insides of his arms are wet; his right foot itches. He wants to sneeze. He holds his nose and sneezes three times but hears no alarm outside. He can always, he tells himself, open the door. He tries the door. It does not give. He tries again, leaning his weight on the slab. He knows enough of circuitry to know the circuit holds. It clicks and does not give. He had known, somehow, in the dream from which there is never escape, that the door too would be locked. There is air and space and time in abundance, he tells himself; there are people in the house to find him when he calls.

He blames himself, at times. A man should stand up and take

blame. It wasn't a question of whether he deserved it so much as whether he was willing to admit the possibility. Judah admits the possibility. He could have bent a little who had been unbending, could have guessed the way the wind would blow and made his own adjustments. He'd stuck to his last, while his marriage and life came unstuck. He should have checked on Seth that night and should have checked on Maggie on a hundred nights. But he'd thought that not reacting was a reaction also, that a man of his stamp sits and takes it till there's nothing left to take. Lately he's decided that his *nothing* done or doing was to blame; he'd thought of it as *something* for the prideful, but had been undone. "You can't take it with you" was a fool's compliance. He would take it with him since there was nothing to take.

(They stand there attentive, awaiting him, eyes left, though what they see he can only question, seeing in their stance the marines at Iwo Jima, scaling the rock face to plant a bronze flag—or perhaps the imitation of a statue that he barely remembers, the Laocoon, an old man muscled as is he, Judah, surrounded by sons and a snake that surrounds them. His eyes are blood-engorged and blind with possibility—mottled with effort, the rock-veins bulging—and so they clasp each other and embrace with a concentrated fury that proves this combat mortal, proves the opposition absolute of arm to arm, knee-knee. His right knee has fused with his opponent's left, the fulcrum there where one must surely topple, go flailing full length out over that rockbed as base. Once spread-eagled, Judah asks himself, once felled and pinioned and made to cry mercy, what variety of mercy might be his to beg—since he had asked no quarter nor offered any ever—mercy not his strong suit, never his strong suit, he knows, and not the kind of quality to outrank justice—not in his ranking, at least. Put them in a scale and he'd put his thumb on for punishment, weighting it with probity and willing to accept and pay whatever was assessed as his fault's due—and at the door's unyielding handle sees collapse almost as a kind of comfort, as the promise not threat of thirst finally slaked. Perhaps "The Kiss" is the statue he sees, or one of those headless, handless statues that Maggie made him study while she enthused about proportion and he waggled his toes in sequence, trying to see what she saw. Or some time-blunted frieze of centaurs raging, drunk with undiluted wine, through courtyards where the women cower, shriek, yet—does he imagine it?—exult. He is exultant surely in the knowledge of completion, and finality inhering, *whatever it is this is it,* come to the invasion of some long-resisted adversary, men in the streets with naked swords, the swords aloft and wavering, seeking that unguarded entrance to some palpitant flesh sheath, or ambushed, upended in wells, the well throats stuffed with this clot of carrion. Nor will the lazy circling birds bother to investigate who surfeit on the easy scavenge and are heavy-bellied by noon, those legs that were so pliant once now rigor-stiff, unbending. And he shifts his stance just slightly, imperceptibly rocking on his toes and heels to make minute adjustments, the motion imperceptible to those who watch, except only perhaps as the witnessing eye's nictation, or the sun glinting off some new flesh facet, or a sudden breath drawn, and offers and acknowledges and yields up his arrogant shame. . . .)

Then there is light. Then he sees himself naked, holding to his duck-hunting jacket, and there is blood on his foot. There is no light in the elevator, but there is light in the room, and he is in the room since the latch had released. He has fallen forward as the door gave way. It has opened without warning, since his weight was on the door. He has not harmed himself. He stands. There is no one in the room. There are fire remnants. There is cigarette smoke, and he wondered has she blown smoke rings and did Finney admire her pursed-lip dexterity. It is—he considers the grandfather clock—two twenty-three. The minute hand moves slightly backward, always, before it moves the minute forward; Judah thinks of springs uncoiling to advance.

The blood is dry. It has been the itching of his foot. He broke the bulb; he recollects that. He turns into the elevator once again, but propping the door back, and retrieves his locust stick. The mess is negligible. The door should be oiled, he reminds himself, and the lock system changed. He hears house noise above him, but they have not opened his door. He has not been found. Fleetingly he wishes that he had been discovered—here, sprawled on the landing, bleeding, blinded by the sudden light burst, a hero spat back. She would have bent above him and been solicitous. She would cradle his head in her arms. She would ask if he were hurt, and he would answer not too badly, and then she'd say, in a low voice to Finney: "Run. Fetch the doctor. Quick."

Finney, less solicitous, would pause. "Do as I say," Maggie would order. The man would scuttle off and she would bend above him once again, protective, smelling of her cigarettes and scent. Now Judah stands half naked in the room he fears she's fled forever. He breathes. He walks, without disguise or limping and precaution, to the mud room. He takes three rights and one left. He has not been found. He pulls on pants and a shirt there, and his walking boots. He replaces his hunting jacket, stuffing himself through the sleeves, but leaves his cane.

"We none of us," Peacock had written his daughters, "should forego the Pleasure and Profit of Travel. There is instruction in the Temples and the Pagan mosques where no man has a pew to call his own, nor can he keep his shoes on in the sight of God. For whatsoever they name Him He is immanent, as if Allah or Buddah or Thor be the nick-name childishly put on by youthful Pleasantry, until we learn that nick himself is but the Devil's label, and there prove one proper appelative only. Just so with methods of Food preparation and marriage and ornament and all the Customary appurtenances of this life. First custom seems peculiar then it seems but quaint then regular then normal then the rule, and by these slow succeeding ventures we who were Parochial become what now they call Cosmopolites. It is a stage, as any Other, to endure."

II

FIRST HE WALKED WITH IAN OR TOOK HIM PICKABACK. HIS SON WAS long-legged even then, and Judah made him stretch his legs. He tried to teach him pace. But Ian would bustle and dart and get tangled in the grapevines or make a game of puddles, jumping, stomping flat-footed into the deep center to see how much water it sprayed.

"Don't do that," Judah said.

"Why not?"

"Because it gets your pants all wet."

"They're not all wet," said Ian.

"OK. Because it gets me wet."

"You're not either. It doesn't."

"Because your mother would be angry."

"It'll dry. I promise." Ian jumped three feet across the flagstone and landed like a geyser in the mud.

"Because I tell you to," said Judah.

Ian turned.

"That's all the reason you need."

"That's not a reason."

Judah leaned and lifted him and held him up, spread-eagled, eight feet above the ground. "This'll dry you off," he said.

"Carry me, daddy."

"Not wet like this."

"I'll dry. I promise. Please."

So Judah eased his son's soaked legs around his neck; he held to Ian's ankles and they continued. "Giddyap," yelled Ian. "I'll get you to a canter, daddy-horse."

"Not now. Let's walk."

"Let's canter. Let's jump that old fence."

"What do you weigh now?"

"A lot," said Ian. "Forty-seven pounds."

"Well, that's too much for this old horse to jump a fence with."

"No it isn't."

"Yes."

"We did it yesterday."

"But yesterday you weren't all wet. That makes it heavier. You've got to add the water," Judah said.

"Giddyap."

He pressed his son's knees to his ears. He heard only Ian's burbling instructions, felt only the self-willed warm extension of his flesh. He jogged and bucked and pivoted across the woven wire, and they were in the pasture, stalking sheep.

"That one," yelled Ian. "Get the buck!"

"We'll let them eat," said Judah.

"No. Up close! Up close!"

"Horned Dorsets," Judah instructed him. "That's what they are. Those bigger one are Suffolk. The most of them is culls."

"We'll get them at the pass."

"What pass?"

"The gate," said Ian. "Up ahead. That's where we'll head them off."

"Not this horse."

"Giddyap."

"Not this horse."

"Why not?"

"You tell me."

"Daddy, *please*."

"You're not checkreining. You haven't given signals."

Ian pummeled at him and he veered left. For all his gruff disclaiming, Judah felt the victor when he lost.

Now he sits in the kitchen's deep dark, having placed himself precisely in the center of the space between the sink and table. He knows the room's coordinates. He is at the apex of a triangle with the cutting board and faucet forming the base; Judah makes himself a tangent to the pantry door. This has not been simple, since the body postulates no single dimension, but three. He tucks in his arms. He leaves his legs askew but tries to point them in the tangent's line. He follows his nose. He is someone sitting, he assures himself, in the middle of the kitchen that is the middle of the downstairs wing in the middle of the house.

His chair is painted white. It has three slats in the back. It has a solid seat, and the legs are squared off. There are three more chairs drawn up to the table's three sides; Judah bisects the chair that had been opposite his. He then draws the line from that apex (where Harriet had used to sit, and he splits her down the center from her mouth to fork, imagining her intestines and esophagus coiled around the bisector that makes of man a mirror) and connects those two legs across the table's plane, and has an isosceles triangle similar to that which his chair makes, bisected, with the far legs of the flanking chairs. Only he has moved. The room will not stay vacant. No matter how hard Judah stares at the wall as though it were Euclidean, he sees his parents backed against it, wearing evening clothes. They are gesturing and fretful in the middle of some argument he cannot hear, but feels himself central to also. It is summer since the screens are up, and he hears the June bugs clattering against them. His father had his arms upraised; his mother was not cowering but shrinks from him, is wearing silk, and the rustle of her dress is like the rustle of the June bugs on the screens. Then Judah sees himself with Maggie on the cutting counter, watching her reflection in the kitchen window as she bounces and jiggles. He balances on his toes. "We'd best not wake the boy," he says. She makes appreciative noises although he covers her mouth.

Therefore he does his roots. The square root of four is two, and the square root of two hundred and fifty-six is sixteen. The square root of one is one, but the square root of minus one is an imaginary number, i.

Yet Judah and Maggie had multiplied out. Ian was a real result and Seth an imagined result; they multiplied an *"i"* by *"i"* and got minus one. "Don't talk square roots to me," said Hattie when he tried to tell her. "There's no such thing as making a mistake with roots. Or children, matter of that. You water them and feed and love them and they grow; you got a taproot, Judah, long as anybody's in America. Down and up. Don't ever be ashamed of that."

"I'm not," he said. "I'm not."

"There's glory in it," she would say. "It's not a disadvantage to know that you've got roots."

The root of nine was three, and three had a fractional root; the root of eighty-one was nine, and nine squared was eighty-one; things fit. He could imagine apples doubling and contracting and being bushel after bushel and then stacked crates. The world was a warehouse of numbers, and if you kept close enough track you'd know where everything was stored and when it had been put there and labeled and how it stood with reference to everything about it. There are no memories, no panting wives or generations scrabbling at the edges of composure like June bugs at screens. Maggie played cat's cradle for him, and he was elated at the intricate interlocked twining; there were patterns she could twist and fatten or reverse and then she'd flick her fingers at him and there'd be, only, string.

"Do it again," he'd beg her.

"Why?" she asked.

"Just once."

"You know the trick. You've seen how it works."

"It isn't that," he said. "It's that I love to watch you being such a spider. With that web."

"Judah," she scolded him. "You keep a civil tongue."

"I mean it. It's wonderful to watch."

So he could get around her as she got around Hattie, cajoling; she'd pick the limp lengths up again and turn her back to him and work her arms and then turn back with magic entanglements, fanning out and in. He wanted her to try with tinsel, but it wasn't long or strong enough. So he fashioned her, one Christmas, a tinsel necklace and bracelet and earrings and said, "They'll hold. You wear them," and she was his glitter-creature in the blue and green Christmas tree lights. They made daisy chains from Reynolds Wrap, and Maggie said, "Imagine. There's country where it's warm enough so you can find real daisies in December." He imagined that.

As the years went on, however, Ian lost his interest in farm games. The boy was studious. Judah read him Peacock's letters and he liked them well enough but said that history had passed the old man by.

"What's that mean?" Judah asked.

"You know the frontier thesis," Ian said.

Judah waited.

"Frederick Jackson Turner says you have to keep on going if there's wilderness in front of you."

"What of it?" Judah asked.

"That's what makes America. That's why we're so busy moving all the time."

They were in the study. Ian had his Hammond Atlas and a sheet of copy paper and was making maps.

"I follow," Judah said.

"Well, the way that Mom sees it Peacock got to the Pacific but he had to turn around. He should have stayed there, maybe."

"Is that how she sees it?"

"Yes. Then we could all be California people instead. It's an improvement, Mom says, it's the Gateway to the Orient. It's warm."

"Your mother talks that way to you?"

Ian drew the Mississippi, using blue. He made the delta just above the gulf and put a big black spot at Hannibal, the birthplace of Mark Twain.

"She says that Peacock's partner, Colonel Frémont, was a brave man with men's lives as long as they weren't his own. She says that General is just another word for coward, and we won the west by genocide."

"By what?"

"By genocide. What's that mean?" Ian asked.

"It's when you kill off everyone. But there's some California people left."

"That's decimate."

"No. Decimate is one in ten."

"Well, anyway," said Ian. He crosshatched the Texas panhandle in red.

"That's where Davy Crockett went. It's Kit Carson country."

"We stole it from the Indians."

"The Mexicans."

"It's a history of pillage," Ian said. "That's what Mom says. And Frederick Jackson Turner, if you stop to think."

So his son curried favor, not horses; he cultivated books. Judah took some pride in this but could not help suspecting that he did it for spite. When Ian learned to love to paint, he bought him easels and sketch pads and a box full of oil tubes and brushes. Then he set a five-gallon can of Barn Red beside them and asked which was likely to last. "That's not the question, is it?" said Maggie. "Look at this sunset, darling. See the way he handles clouds."

"Look at this barn," Judah said.

He set out on his walks alone. He took the pickup or a tractor to the bottom land and saw his fields splay out around him, untenanted. He watched his son, come back from school, practice lay-ups at the basket he had rigged behind the sugarhouse for twenty minutes only, then practice at the piano for two hours every afternoon. It grew dark while he played.

"Aren't you proud of him, Jude?" Maggie asked.

"Why, surely."

"Listen to that. Grieg. It took me years to get just the opening chords. He'll play it in the school recital Thursday."

"What time is that?"

"What time will that be, Ian?" she asked.

He looked up at her from where he sat on the piano bench. He used no music.

"Three o'clock," said Ian and commenced the phrase again. Maggie bent above him, nodding, tapping her foot and wiggling her fingers in time, and Judah—watching from his leather chair beside the fireplace—saw that his son's eyes were closed.

"It's beautiful," said Maggie. "It's just right."

Ian continued.

"Sixteenth notes," she explained to Judah. "And every one of them clear as a bell."

"They're muddy," Ian said.

At two o'clock that Thursday, Judah got stuck in the Shed field. He had been seeding alfalfa, and turning on the western slope he sunk his right rear wheel. He tried rocking. He took his length of chain and led it around a locust tree and pulled. The tractor stalled. It settled. He had only one pass left to make and took his work coat off and tied the sleeves around his neck. He filled this sack with alfalfa and completed the field by hand.

"Let the buildings be laid out," Peacock had commanded, "in the Shape and Memory of our Savior's ransom, with the four points of the compass being the four of the Cross. Let the barns be due west of the house, pointing as His strong arm pointed to where I scribe these lines. Let the Carriages and suchlike be stored on the easterly Axis. South at a suitable distance, where his feet were nailed, you may build in whatsoever fashion but not above one story's heighth, the farmer's house. Thus even to the eagle's eye, and surely to him who stands on the Cupola, will we furnish instruction. Somehow I seem to see the Holy Spirit hovering, in the bird-guise he assumes wherewith in safety he may visit this nether pit, and to avoid a suchlike crucifixion—for what are the yearly migrations but testimonial also to the Flock's disgust, and do not greylag geese even example this search, scanning the Compass-points for some clear sign that our Redeemer prospereth—

espying the Reverent arrangement of our Severall buildings, and knowing and reporting to the august Captain that in this township at the least there thrives one Honest man!"

The order in the house evades him. He knows what each closet contains. He knows the way the servants' stairwell curls around the dumbwaiter and laundry chute, and how the elevator shaft takes the southeast corner of what had been the ballroom once. He knows the hall's dimensions, and that it takes him seventy-two steps descending from the room she used to sleep in to the door. He knows that Bierstadt painted "Yosemite Valley," and that Frederic Arthur Bridgman painted the oil painting of "The Donkey." He knows the man who painted "The Portrait of a Girl" was Spanish, but that the man who painted the "Lady in a Fashionable Dress" was the Frenchman, Edward Boutibonne. There are plaster ornaments he can trace, eyes shut, and he knows the feel of the oak fireplace from those that are sided in walnut; he knows who bought the billiard table for the billiard room.

He knows there must be patterning throughout. He knows the plaster dining hall ornaments are pineapples and grapes and that it is a fat-armed imitation of Cupid who draws the bow back on the bedroom ceilings. He knows the greenhouse stands empty, though Maggie once had it replete. Her Christmas cactus bloomed for months, and then the poinsettias commenced.

The difference between four and fourteen, Judah knows, can be ten or the first integer or he can multiply by three and then add two. They are all of them codes to be cracked. They are patterns to copy out and, therefore, predict. And it had been the same with steamer trunks or women's protestations and the jobs he held then quit and the houses he entered and left. Within the seeming random sets there was always this arcane rigidity—always his own sense of system and logic and the exact opposition of change to growth. From one to two, Judah knows, you either add one or double the original; you also multiply by seven and then subtract five.

Yet these rooms had no series he could plumb. Nor did his age and illness seem sequential to the block-hard rock-thick middle age he'd known. Nor is Maggie's disappearance and return and disappearance a series; you go from one to four to one to six to one to eight to one, and someone on a contrapuntal series thinks you've never left at all. He was running home, mud-crusted, with the taste of metal in his throat. He was hiding in the laundry room behind the wicker baskets, staring at the shapeless, starched gray uniforms of maids. He was chewing on a syrup stick, and his hands are full of beet sugar, and he added water to it till it was a paste. He shuts his eyes and focuses and creates color: red and yellow and the sun's orange arrangement. He wills it, this one dawn, to turn as he turns, motionless, and slip around the world the way a sleeve might on a scrawny pointing arm. He opens his eyes and is gratified: flame comes from the west.

Fire: he sees her also as flame, though this is more his element, and of the four he'd qualify for earth and fire, she for air and water (he knows that; they have worked it out in the game that she called "Essences": "What animal is Jo-jo," she would ask. "What time of day?" And he'd answer "Skunk," or "Three o'clock in the morning," and she'd swat at him and grin and say "Raccoon. Early evening." Then he'd ask, "What color is Hattie? What scent?" And she'd answer, "Mauve. The smell of pressed lilacs," and he'd interpret "Green. Because you ate my second piece of apple pie. . . ."), but still he sees her firelit, her face become a kind of screen with shadowplay, that hair of hers alight ("Enclosed air spaces," he would say, "it's the secret of flame. And build it back up tepee style, and far enough back there to catch the draft." "Why are you telling me this?" she would ask. "Because," he'd say, "although I hope not, there may come a time when you need one without me. Or when I'm just not here to build it. Check the flues." "You're always here to build it," Maggie said. She mock-shivered, then stretched. "You're my heat source. You're nice. . . .") —so flame was domesticated for her, and a comfort not terror, and he thinks of her always as "toasty," which also was her word, or bending to the match flare that she'd light her cigarette with, or standing by the chunk stove with her hands out, fingers spread. He gave her a rotisserie one Christmas, and she used it often then, so he'd stand in the kitchen watching while she trussed the chickens up, or ducks, and pricked them with her long-handled fork and added seasoning, then skewered them with what he could only call relish, ramming through. While the bird was turning they would watch it sweat and pucker and his wife would say, "That's it. That's heaven. Name every pleasure and the chicken has or is it now"—the fat igniting underneath the broiler coils, and liquid sizzling that would later coalesce. Yet there are ways he sees her also as a kind of parody, the temperature rising when she closed her hand upon his thermometer, and squeezed or, what was the popular song, "My Old Flame; I can't even remember her name" —or in steamy, hellish posturing, an abandoned woman whose bed is smoke and deviltry, hot coals. If they had an argument it was how she hated winter (and it was true, he came to acknowledge, that their first three meetings had all been summertime meetings, that she maybe had thought of Vermont as a place of green abundance, not mud and granite and ice): fire her servitor somehow, so that she'd have only to breathe on the last white ash heap of the last set of embers on some abandoned hearth to kindle the household again, to set the stewpot bubbling and the ice-stiff clothes to dry. . . .

"We'll walk the lines."
"No."
"Yes. You ought to know them."
"Why?"
"Because it's important. Men should know what they live on."
"I'm hungry," Ian said.
"We'll take something. We'll bring yogurt with us."
"I hate yogurt."
"Pretzels then."
"And soda?"
"Yes."
"Why can't we just have them here?" Ian aked. "Why do they have to get all soggy?"
"Come on. We're wasting time."
"My ankle hurts."
"Come on, I said."
"It hurts me. Mom said I shouldn't stand on it."
"I'll take you part way pickaback."
"I know the lines already," Ian said.
"Not the part we're going to. Not north."
"I do so."
"OK," Judah bent to him. "No more discussions. Not another word from you, hear?"
"But I've got to go to the bathroom."
"Go ahead then. I'll get the pretzels and Coke."

"Can we check traps?"
"Yes."
"Can I take my .22?"
"We'll see."
"Can I? Promise?"
"Yes. I thought we said no more discussions."
"Promise double-promise?"
"Yes."
"It's muddy out there," Ian said. "I hate those boots."
"The hell with it. You stay."

"Well you might ask," wrote Peacock, "why I promote this Residence and why purport its Excellence of size. As well ask the midge in the evening wherefore he Elects to bite. As well inquire of the Salmon here why it should scale Rock!"

When Ian sprained his ankle jumping from the Toy House roof, Judah had been jumping with him and he took the blame. "Thirty-two feet per second," he said. "It's true all right. We timed it."

"Are you hurt bad?" Maggie asked.

"Of course not," Judah said. "The shingles just broke loose is all."

"Tell me where it hurts you."

"He's all right."

"Let the boy answer, Judah. Let him say so for himself."

He had carried Ian to the house. He laid him on the daybed by the porch and put a blanket over him and then called Maggie. She had come running; she knelt. "Are you frightened?" she asked.

"Don't baby him. He's fine."

"I'd like to hear *him* say it."

"We were doing roofing. Look, his toes move. Ian, wiggle them at your mother so she'll know there's nothing broke."

Ian spread his toes. Then he raised and lowered them while the face he built for Judah came undone: his lips jutted out, the skin around his eyes bunched up and wrinkled and his nose went white.

"Don't cry," she said.

"He isn't crying."

"He can if he wants to," she said.

"Who's stopping him?"

"I want some chocolate," Ian instructed his mother. "I want a whole big box."

"I'll get that," Judah said.

In the pantry, accumulating chocolate, he could hear his son's high wailing two rooms over and across the porch. There was a row of soup cans and chick-peas and tuna fish in front of him; the soup was stacked two high, and the tuna four. He put his hand at the edge of the shelf and swept it, right to left.

Wind: he thinks of her also in that, and airy; always there are breezes where she walks, and he thinks she could float if she stretched her arms out far enough and let her hair billow on the updraft, a flaxen parachute to let her down securely wherever she might land. Judah thinks her the wind's consort, easy with airplanes and landing and what they call the sickness of jet lag. It was always windy when they played at badminton, and though he said it was stupid, a grown man batting at a bit of air with feathers on it, swatting at nothing with wood and catgut that weighed next to nothing, no heft to it or solidity, she made him play and skipped happy circles around his aggrieved opposition, contesting his service and forehand assault, not ever sweating though she jig-stepped all over the court while he stood planted, immobile, in the court's dead center, stamping the grass into mud. Using wrist flicks that he barely saw and a scampering grace that caused him to teeter from frustration to envy to lust, winning always, she won with the wind at her back or in her face or coming at them sideways, gusting. There was the created wind they rode or drove in, with the windows open, and the winter's continual probing, ice fingers fisting down chimneys or where they hadn't caulked or through the storm window sash, under doors. He cannot remember her out of the wind, now that he comes to think of it, or ever less than airy light for all the years' stiffening additions—and he remembers now the nursery rhyme about the oak tree near the ocean, and reeds: how everything is leveled in the last big wind but bending reeds, how roots and all mean nothing when the hurricane and thunder come. So he's been her protection till the storm outlasted him, and that willowy thing at his feet is hovering above him, span-waisted still, protective. Air is what you can't do without; air is what you needn't notice till it goes bad or stale. Next he remembers fire drills with Maggie and Ian, so that they'd know how to blanket flame and close off all air sources and where he stored the plywood to cover up the fireplace if there were chimney fires, and how to keep low under the heat and, more important, the smoke, how to crawl not for the nearest exit necessarily but for the smartest, how to take short breaths and hold them, how to follow his two golden rules, Keep your head, and Keep your head down. So Judah now follows those habit-instructions, keeping his head and keeping it down and exits where he entered through the kitchen door. Air is something that you watch at sunset maybe, or when it's coming on rain and there's a field to load yet (reminding him of when he'd burned the bottom land by accident, and how it smelled then: they had a brush fire going, trusting to the windless March wetness, and there were only embers when he broke for lunch—returning to the Big House and taking his ease, sitting in the kitchen's warmth and washing with relish and putting so much sugar in his coffee that the spoon got sluggish, going back at noon to see the smoke and run to it and hear the whole field crackling and the ground already crepitant, but there were marshy spots and snow at the field's edge and what wind there was stayed southerly, herding the small flames to water. So he'd not been overworried and stood watching the bottom land gutter, smelling what he smells again now, and the field indeed sprouted greenly in April and gave a thick first cutting by June, and they took three cuttings off it that summer and by September he started claiming to have set the blaze on purpose, that it was controlled). Air's inconsequential till you need it for fire or to let the liquid out of cans or just to put some sort of God above this earth.

III

"You'll want to make your peace, Jude."
"Yes."
"You'll want to set your house in order."
"And lands."
"And lands."
"How do you prefer it, then?"
"The way I always did," he says. "No nonsense. Straight up and down."
"How do you mean?" Finney asks.
"You know the one about the millworker. Who's so dumb his cronies convince him he's pregnant. He says that isn't possible, and they bring a doctor into the joke and the doctor examines him and says, yes, Sven, you're pregnant all right. So he goes home and wags his fingers at his wife and says, from now on none of that fancy who's-on-top stuff. From now on it's straight up and down."
Finney laughs.
"That's how I want to make my piece," he finishes.
Finney stops laughing.
"Next question," Judah says.
"That isn't what I meant," his lawyer says.
"I know. I know what you meant, what I mean."
"What *do* you mean, Jude?"
"Nothing. There's no peace to make," he says. "There's not any bargaining table. You got me those three testaments and I gave one to Maggie. There's nothing to sit down around and nothing to draw up or change."

Light: the gradual accretion of it, sift in an hourglass weighting the time scale, first the seckel pear tree, then the tamarack then elms ignited, their twig-tips silver in the moon that is diffuse then fused from the east through that cloud bank, there, then suffusing everything. And Judah sees lean yellow leaves on the willow, and deadwood that he's notched but not had time to cut, saw the rooster distending to crow, saw cockfights in the silo they'd cut down to head height and covered over with chicken wire and used for a testing arena, but not with razors on the spurs. Then they moved the better cocks to Hamilton's old barn and bet on them and tied the razors on. Judah saw blood on the sawdust and cock's wings and on the sheets they soiled together, sees dishtowels he had used as tourniquets that time he hemorrhaged, and stumps that had been rooster spurs, the sinew and gristle gone black. The blackness swarms as Judah nears and rises and settles, buzzing, attentive, so what he took as guarantee was only the promise, at eight-to-five odds, and with men milling about him impeding the view, that this false dawn is light. . . .

He sets out for the barn. The path is familiar. He has been robbed of his youth. He feels in his shirt pocket for the peanut brittle. He crumbles it with his right hand and pulls a fragment out and licks at his fingers. There is earth on his fingertips also. He coughs and hears the sound as if it were a stranger's—dim, tinny, high in the throat. He wonders is that what they mean by a death's-head, death rattle? Ian, holding rattles, had been fierce. He pounded on the highchair's tray with a sounding delight. Ian is left-handed, and no Sherbrooke was left-handed that Hattie can recall.

So Judah gauges his steps. Once he ran the mile circuit for kicks. For the joy of it he'd spot Maggie a third of the distance and try to catch her and half the time succeed. She'd be a wheat-colored blur by the sugarhouse, then resolve into component parts at the corncrib, then become all legs and jostling laughter as they shared the finish stretch. She could outrun him, nearly, for the sprint. He was slow and steady and had the better wind. So he'd catch her as she lay back for him, laughing, head over her shoulder, feet dragging, elbows out. Then she'd spurt in front of him, hair in the breeze like a banner unfurled, her jackrabbit skittishness gone suddenly intent. He ran by the paving's edge and gauged it took three flagstones for her single stride.

The house is behind him. He steps from its shadow. There is a ring around the moon; it's two days off from full. He studies his shadow. It moves. He lifts his hand, and the shadow's elongated hand entices him, and he thinks, *Well, look, I'm a rabbit, look a giraffe without a flashlight, look at the antelope horns.*

"Make me a rhino, daddy," Ian said.

He made a rhinoceros head, and horn.

"It's got a little one too, daddy."

He let a knuckle protrude.

"Make me a unicorn."

He rearranged his middle finger.

"Now make a rabbit again!"
He had kept the light behind him and his hands seemed huge. When he brought his fingers close to the light—close enough so that the blood within was luminous—their shadow wavered and grew indistinct. He would prepare the rabbit shadow and know, by Ian's breathing, that Ian was asleep.
His breath is plumes. His feet take root where he stands. At the tideline, standing in sand that the current subtracts then adds to his ankles, watching the water's pitch and yaw and sure he heaves within it, sinking where he weights shore while she, Maggie, is a quick glimmer in the surf beyond him, Judah has known just such stasis in the middle of giddying motion. He was a rock who footed sand, but the sand was shifty. The world is a careening thing; the moon and sun are its outriders, and he hunts connection since his balance had gone bad. Time was he'd walk the barn beams, quickest way to cross to the hayloft without even seeing the forty-foot drop; time was he'd top the pines by climbing them, right hand holding the saw.

"A morning's constitutional," Peacock wrote, "should not exceed one mile. That is a sufficient distance for the soul's repose and the body's repast to settle and assert itself. The gentleman avoids excessive exercise before and after meals. Provide a one-mile path. In His eyes there can be no distinction twixt the camel and the rich man mounted on the camel's back, in terms of distance travelled they are of course coequal. For the camel bears the passenger as burden, whereas the Passenger is burdened with the spirit's apprehension, and the task of guiding his insensient chattel through the endless sands. Lo how elusive proves that promised fount where each might slake his thirst, where the Weary Traveller might bathe. How myriad are the Phantoms and False Lures. How often do we think ourselves within the Grace Oasis. We stoop to drink of lambent and sparkling elixirs, werewith the Soul might cleanse itself and raise the liquid Illusion to our parched and avid lips but find it dust. Dust the dream of surcease, Dust the hope of Merit that it might earn mete reward, Dust the ardor that enkindled this proud pilgrimage, all ashes and dry husks and dust. So might we not need Compasses; might it not be Useful to have the Path marked as with Flagstones and not, as in the fairy tale, breadcrumbs for the vulture to swallow. There are those who go before and should they not leave signposts for the Quick?"

* * *

"Hey, Ian, what about this baler?
"What about it?"
"What are you doing now?"
"Nothing."
"Give me a hand," Judah said.
"What's wrong?"
"Just hold this."
"I need gloves."
"You don't need gloves."
"I do. I've got to practice after."
"Christ," said Judah. "Hold the twine then. Only hold it while I fix the goddam feeder."
"You said you fixed it yesterday."
"It didn't work. It cuts off short."
"It's snarled." His son's voice cracked.
"You're telling me?"
"Why don't you get it fixed? Why don't you get Harry or someone from Allis-Chalmers to fix it?"
"Screwdriver."
"Yes, doctor. Scalpel at your service, doctor."
"Not that one." Judah shook his hair back. "The one with the Phillips head."
"Sorry."
"The big one. Look at this screw."
"Well how was I to see it?" Ian asked. "Under all that grease?"
"All right."
"All you had to say was Phillips head."
"All right."
"Anyhow it's raining." His voice slid an octave again.
"Hand me them pliers."
"Sutures, doctor."
"The socket wrench. You don't know your ass from your elbow."
And holding, forcing with his left hand, Judah overpressured with his right and came down hard on his wrist. The Phillips cut a star shape just between his palm and wristwatch; Judah stood there, bleeding, letting the blood spout and clean itself out, watching his son go white-faced with his white hands full of string and said, "Now look what we've done. Look what you made me do, boy."

* * *

So he shuffles forward and attains the sugarhouse. There he gathers his things—the newspaper, the match tin and the can of kerosene. There is a law now against burning leaves. For years he has made leaf piles and has burned them and inhaled the smoke, and there'd been nothing wrong with that until they called it dangerous; then men burned leaves on the quiet, coughing, tying handkerchiefs across both mouth and nose. He'd loved the smell of maple and oak leaves, and the smoke's whorling progress. The smoke was the color of mother-of-pearl, and it had dimension against the blue sky-shell. But you saw that less and less often lately and the smell was strange—boys raked leaves into bags and twisted them and stacked them on the paving now for trucks. It was a waste of compost, and Judah figures they burn the leaves in some landfill anyhow. Somewhere he hasn't been to there's a leaf-burning pit, and men stand by with asbestos boots and gloves, but there isn't any danger and they break open bourbon at three; at four they'd sniff and drink their fill and watch the sky go cloudy with its own opaque sweet-smelling sunset; at five the smoke would be lighter, not darker than the night air it eddies through, and at six o'clock they'd huddle to the many-layered embers, taking comfort in the color and the perfumed heat.

("Judah."

He sits. There are upturned sugaring buckets.

"Consideration, Ellie."

He shifts his weight, settling in.

"The Preacher calls it vainglory," Peacock wrote. "And vanity indeed, of all the Large or Venial sins, seems dangerous to him who builds. For Foundations are quicksand, not stone."

He wants to be by that landfill. He wants to be where everything is buried, with a group of friends, not talking except with the no-talk that beats back silence, not needing to claim or reclaim or apportion leavings. He'd sniff the acrid sour flame and drink the acrid sweet bourbon from a bottle that is everybody's bottle. Men would pass and raise the liquor and tilt and swallow and pour the final cupful on the flames. Hal Boudreau would bend to drink it, if he could.

"Judah. J. P. Sherbrooke. My wild one. The Lion of Judah."

Somewhere off in Africa, he's heard, they have embalmed Haile Selassie. The little emperor he's named like, half his weight and half his height—he pictures the flayed, dead old man. Maggie always said

it helped your feet to walk in sand; like emery board it took the dried skin off.
"What I mean is, what I meant . . ."
He stands. You can tell the town line in winter by the sand. His own town sprinkles the stuff on with a saltshaker, but next township over they'd drop a load on either side until it humped. He's taken his ease now, foregathered himself, and he leaves.
Outside it is colder. He hurries to the center of his woodpile and drops down the paper and matches and kerosene can. There is gray light now, and the kerosene sloshes lightly out of the air hole. The smell assails him, making him wakeful.
"Judah, man of names."
He breathes.
"Show me the color . . .")
He breathes. His inhalations are willful, since his throat is a streambed in August, with the springs dried out. He brings air in like water, sluicing it across his teeth like rock. They salvaged everything these days, so why not salvage teeth? There are landfill operations and operations for hearts and lungs and kidneys and blood and eyeglasses; a woman could go to a sperm bank and sleep with some pure stranger in a tube.
"And therefore," Peacock prophesied, "there will be stately progress in the Park. I seem to see my grandchildren's grandchildren curtsy, see them laugh at some Bright pleasantry or knit their brows with concentration at some sportive Feat. We shall build a brown Pagoda in the Chinese vein."
His cheeks would flush; her throat, too, flushed; she could run barefoot, often as not, on ground he'd have to pick his way through, even wearing boots.
"Let the park be Glade and Bower for the gladding of the wakeful Mind; let there be Enticements such as Benches by the Grotto, and japanese maples in profusion, since they teach us scale."
He continues. Peacock's grandchild's grandchildren are Ian and Seth. Ian has been gone forever, and Seth is dead in the house.

"Don't go," he'd said the final time.
"We're leaving," Ian said.
"You're making a mistake."

"I'll make my own from now on," Maggie said. "With your permission, Jude."
"And what if I don't give it?"
"That's why we're leaving," she said.
He looked them over, locked them in the chambers of his heart.
"I'll miss you."
"Come and visit, father."
"We'll miss you too," she said.
"So stay. So save us the trouble."
"I'm eighteen," Ian said. "I can make my own mind up."
"Is that what they taught you in school?"
"I'll get the car," Ian said.
They had had what Maggie called a *pied-à-terre* in New York City for years. He'd lost them both already, had refused to select or visit or pay for the apartment. It was on Sutton Place South. She saw the river, she told him, and if he came they could take walks and go to concerts and she'd arrange for parking so it would be only four hours, door to door. It was a point of principle, he told her, and not practicality; he never again went south.

When Ian began at Exeter, Maggie moved and left him, Judah, alone in the house. They both came back for Christmas and part of the summer and maybe a birthday or Thanksgiving to make a show of unity. But it had been sham unity and nothing to anticipate or, looking back on, remember as fun. So he had been nearly relieved when Ian left for college in their final summer and came to take his leave by taking Maggie to New York.

"So this is it," she'd said.
"Yes."
"We'll meet again."
"I suppose so."
"You're welcome in New York. Whenever."
"You don't mean that."
"I do."
"I'd give you warning," Judah said. "So you could clear whoever's in there out."
"I wouldn't require it."
"One thing I hate"—he tried to shift his feet but they were rooted, stuck with gum-sap to the Persian carpet. He looked down and saw what seemed a pineapple design; he stood in the pineapple's center.

"What's that one thing?"
"Is other men's coats in my closet," he said. "You know."
"Yes. I do know about that."
"So there's not a whole lot left to say," said Judah. She made a motion toward him but his shoes were stuck.
"No. I suppose not."
"Be seeing you," he said.
"You've got the address," Maggie said. "And the number. You've got Ian's address and his number. Keep in touch."
"Be seeing you."
"It's not fair, Judah, just to let the boy go off like that. Without a word of luck or love or anything."
"He's welcome back. I don't want to talk about it."
"Labor Day," she said. "We'll have a lot of traffic on the road. We'd better be going."
"Good-bye."
And so she spiraled, making her advance-retreat, and was off down the steps and into the car and that was all he heard or saw of her for seven years. He sent them checks, through Finney, for schooling and clothes and vacations, but never for the rent.

Now he walks into the hay barn. Judah selects bales. Time was he'd walk with one in either hand or lend a hand at stacking and not notice when the lunch break came; now a single light-packed bale is overmuch to manage, so he cuts the twine and takes the hay in sections, clump by clump. He spreads it assiduously under the locust wood and uses it as chinking where the logs let too much wind in; he spreads himself a pallet in the center of the square. There are burrs and thistles in the hay; there is too much weed for use as anything but bedding, and he is glad for that. He wouldn't have wanted, he tells himself, to use feed hay for his pallet; it would have been a waste.

What is pure grass is timothy, and he calculates which field this cutting comes from. The field they called the Shed field had been planted in timothy three years before, and Judah decides it is time, this spring, to turn it over into corn. He coughs; there is chaff in his throat. He comes across a garter snake, crushed by the baler, and what has likely been a chipmunk that is pressed now and extended like a carpet of itself. He hawks and spits.

("Judah," they told him. "We got enough now."
"It's coming on rain."
"No. Maybe just a little bit. No more than a wetting."
"Not enough to mention. To say so."
"Dinnertime."
"Suppertime."
"Smoke time. I need me a cigarette."
"Jimmy Slocum's cousin said he seen a camel. Like that old workhorse, Clyde, they called him, only he was humpacked and not swaybacked and maybe three times as big."
"Judah. J. P. Sherbrooke. Mr. Jude."
"You got a name to match each name they give your wife."
"Except maybe Missie. Except maybe vixen and harlot and Abishag the Shunnamite.")

His sleep was troubled, and his digestion troubles him, and everywhere he aches. "Flesh of my flesh," he intones. "Betrayal on betrayal." He likes repeating words for the sense of solidity it gives him, and balance; he feels himself a tightrope walker using words now to ward off collapse. He extends his arms. There are spotlights trained on him, and he squints so as not to lose his focus on the necessary end; ears, however, are the root of balance and he prays that his hearing will hold. "Flesh of my flesh," means sons, though what he'd planted in her was more a seed than flesh. He pictures it clinging to her womb wall like a cockleburr, or swimming, and then it was not "it" but Ian, and then not "it" but Seth, and Seth reverted.

"Of the various infirmities," Peacock wrote, "I hold with those sages who hold loss of Faith the Gravest, since belief in Wrongs is tantamount to the belief that Wrongs shall be redressed. Yet without the latterly conviction, Man is but cast ashore as if he were a Castaway upon this Life's grim Strand, nor can sumptuous food or welcome or a bed of goosedown and Satin be the jot and tittle of True Comfort by Compare. Therefore for every Inward Arch I wish an outward Pillar, and for each circle a square or rectangular Shape. It is necessary in this monotonal Era to provide Relief. When tired with a long day's wrangling in the dusty offices or glittr'ing Courts of Law, I sometimes for an hour at work's End seek diversion with fencing; then do I see on the target before me not some dancing bobbin or Image of th'Adversary, but rather Delirium's Fancy: my house in

Female Shape, its outline dark yet definite, and with one single window lit there on the Second Story's left-hand passage where resides the Heart. I lunge at it and pierce it through repeatedly. It does not extinguish. It burns on. There is an Awful Glory in the sight. Long past what we Inheritors have come to Know as the Expulsion, past the point of Eden's incorruptibility, the light in the Garden glowed on—and as I lay my foil to rest I seem to see it beckon me, the Devil's very handiwork tricked up as foxfire. Gleaming . . ."

When Judah finishes he pulls the barn door to. It squeaks and complains, and he remembers that the rollers should be oiled. The struts in the barn rainbow out. There are springs beneath it, and he'd cursed the siting often. They should have built above. There are springs that fill the gutter every time he cleaned it, and one of them is strong and pure enough to bubble up above the rim; he's lost more lambs to water than disease. They'd cleared the barn of stock when he quit his serious sham farming, and now it just holds hay.

So he imagines himself in the gloom in the hay barn, with Maggie beneath. He would have baled and stacked three hundred bales that afternoon, and they would fill the top loft full, leaving only the chute uncovered. There are tree trunks shoring up the barn with the bark still on them, and the braces and crossties are two foot across. The men would leave but his wife would be waiting, expectant, with wine and soft words and balm that beat horse liniment to stir the fire in him.

That afternoon the sun would angle through the barn boards, roseate. She would fall on her back in the third rank of hay, in a level space he'd made when stacking, and where the sun illuminated air motes and her hair's wheat sheen. He, Judah, lowered himself. She spread and murmured "Husband," to the rhythm of his strokes, and there was pain and pleasure intermingled past the separating, their particles fused, or more like cream and milk suspended in one rich solution, and as his battering concluded he bent his head to kiss her and kissed the hay chaff instead and sneezed ("Apologies," he said. "I didn't mean it."

"No apology needed," she said.

"It won't happen this way again."

"It's not your fault," Maggie said) and subsided. There were dragonflies. There was a profusion of barn swallows; he counted six, then ceased.

He wads up the newspaper and spreads it from his pallet to the wall. Hattie made what she called *Rutland Herald* logs. She twisted the paper tightly and tied it in three places and soaked it in the bath, then let the whole thing dry. She piled her paper logs in the corner of her closet, saying this will always burn and what else is it used for once you eat the headlines up. She accused him of gobbling the paper for news. He should read in a more mannerly fashion, and let the news digest.

He bends to his work; he had been shucking feed corn. The barn cats splayed about him, and the pigeons settled back. Chaff danced in the light; the air was wet but warm. He inhales it lazily. Maggie slept. She is his dream of consummation, light in the heart of the house. He threw his head back to study the vaulting and heard himself half-singing, making noise in his throat. This is it, he tells himself. This is as close as man need ever get to where he's going, and still call it worth it, and still have a handhold on joy. This is more than most.

"Let there be chestnut and butternut wood; let the mantel be oaken, and every door be walnut of the House. Let there be Chinese Porcelains and statuary abounding, and fluted columns of the Doric Mode. I wish Lamps to be ceaselessly burning, in Continual Remembrance of the wakeful Husband that is Christ. Let there be four large rings and additional Cross Braces; let there be protective Skyworks to harbor the design from weather and Wind. . . ."

He unscrews the kerosene cap and sluices slows circles around his pallet, standing again. Then Judah walks—the kerosene not racing out but not just trickling either, a stream he can control with his thumb on the air hole, a rivulet corkscrewing over the hay, a reservoir he dams and then, swinging, releases. He likes the smell. He likes the smell of all wood extracts, resin and syrup and creosote—and the patterned wetness of the hay. He splashes his initials, then hers. He splashes a cross, then triangle, then circle, then paces his dark perimeter until the can is dry. He wipes his hands.

("J. P. Hiya, how's my girl."

"Darling. Son of a son of a son of a bitch."

"They's dead in the ditches of France. Come here till I tell you. Count to one one hundred. Two one hundred. Three.")

Voices natter at him, dying, like casement flies in the window in winter: a black swarm falling even as they rise. It wouldn't be so bad, he tells himself, if there were instruction in the prattle; he sits. They breed in the corners by the thousands. They live in his refracted heat and cannot be expunged. He works his toes in the boots. He loosens the laces, then removes them from the top eyelets and lets the ends hang free.

"Hiding in the pine lot. Hiding in the tack room. Hiding up under the roof."

"Ready or not," she repeated—and he was tender-footed, naked, picking his way through underbrush again. The leaves were wet. She hung her skirt and sweater on a low extended birch branch, so as not to soil them. She wore a yellow skirt. She was the color of autumn, he told her; the leaves were her flesh tint, and the moss they lay on had her body's smell. Yet he has been with her this night and shaken off the fleshly envelope. There is no luxury remaining; he has put back childish things.

So lying there he thinks the straw shape beside him is hers, the cold indistinguishable from that pervasive chill they'd known by the Walloomsack in their second marriage-winter, sleeping out. Wild nights, wild nights, he tells himself and remembers how he wrestled with "Bear" Starkey, not losing. He tries his memory trick. It was April seventh, and he remembers that day a decade previous, then a score, then thirty years. He remembers forty years previous but loses the exactitude; he knows, of course, that he was living in the Big House even then, that there were hard times because Roosevelt knew nothing about orchards, and what he did know he forgot in order to build roads.

He remembers running from his mother's sickbed-side. Nose clamped against the smell of it, mouth full with air gone rancid, unable to swallow, Jude left the elevator's stench and bounded down the steps; there on the portico breathing, there across the trellis with his lungs commencing to clear, there quicker than it takes to tell it in the tack room, taking his saddle and bridle and breathing in the horse smell, out of this barn and already at a canter as he passed the gate. . . .

Judah moves. He sees old men on streetcorners, gauging the traffic. He sees them step down gingerly, like swimmers toeing water in the swimming hole. The curb is a perilous height. There is mud on the road. Cars menace him, screaming. He wears his walking boots. He would shave that afternoon. The cars that idle at the light send smoke at him and at the mountain ash trees in the traffic island. There are, in that one engine, three hundred fifty horses shitting smoke.

It had been him, of course, who found his mother there—hands crossed as though to save them the trouble, eyes shut, with only her tongue hanging out to instruct him, and nothing moving in the room except the long-fluked fan.

He tries the fifty states. He tries their capitals. Once he knew all the states and capitals and state flowers and could fit them lickety-split together for Ian's jigsaw puzzle. He knew the boundaries of Arkansas the way he knows the Shed field's perimeter, and the way it butted, north and east. He remembers North and South Dakota now, and North and South Carolina, but has the nagging sense that there are other pairings, that New Mexico, New Jersey and New Hampshire and New York aren't the only states, for instance, with the label "New."

There are other games to play. There is ticktacktoe. He'd played leap-frog and Scramble and football in his time. Later he played hide-and-seek and Fuck your Neighbor's Wife. My Lord, Judah thinks, there was gaming. Cards and horses and baseball and dogs and fighting cocks and you name it, he'd bet; given odds enough, he'd have bet against the dawn. Or at least that it was visible, or at least that it was visible past ten o'clock, and to a blind or sleeping man. He'd have bet his bottom dollar things would bottom out, that Roosevelt would get us into war and guns and profit and he, Judah, would do best by letting well enough alone. He'd accumulated land, therefore, at each foreclosure auction, but let the land sit still.

"Let there be fifteen-hundred and forty component parts in the Stain Glass design. It was in the year Fifteen-hundred and forty that the descendants of Canute, the lineal cadet inheritors of that Excellent King Alfred, first considered travel from the Sherbrooke Seat. The actuall Pilgrim entrusts himself to ill-favored or favoring winds. The actual Voyager will think of his body as Boat and entrust it to the Isthmus as I myself have done, for what was lost is always found in Christ's pocket, and the accounting kept Completely in his ledger-book, if one might write of a pocket and ledger-book in this Connection. Then let us think of Him as a clerk of all souls, as an Adding Instrument that never makes mistakes."

Judah strikes a match. He does so negligently, not cupping his hands. The matchbook is damp, and the flame sputters out. He tries again. This time the match fails to take; he watches the sulphur head disintegrate. His third match takes, however, and he protects it and tries to kneel. His body has gone clumsy, and as he shifts position the match is extinguished. He wonders, does that signify reprieve? He wonders, does it mean she seeks and yearns for him still in their shared bed? His fourth match fails; his hands are shaking; he is an idiot, he tells himself, to have brought no lighter. The fifth match breaks in his fingers and the sixth one shreds; the last has no sulphurhead.

Therefore he tells himself again that he must ferret Ian out; he'll follows his son west. He turns. He stands again and sets out from the barn. He follows the track from sugarhouse to garage and stealthily past the Big House porch and past the Toy House to the entrance gate. The moon is gone. He knows the path so well, however, he could walk it blind. He steps out unburdened, his bootlaces flapping. The iron gate is open; he closes it behind him. This takes force at first; he puts his shoulder in it, and the thing clatters clangingly shut. There are stone entrance pillars; they recede. The road is tarmac now; he sees the night lights of the village beneath him and starts down the hill. His neighbor, Reed, sold farm-fresh eggs but never kept a chicken. He had a fifteen-foot-high elm sprouting in front of the house; nobody planted elms these days, but Reed's kept right on growing. He kept his hat on, always, and Judah knew the man was bald as billiards—Hattie said he wasn't human, had no eyebrow hair.

The slope is considerable. Judah picks up speed but steps in a pothole and buckles, nearly falls. There is no pain but he continues slowly now, favoring his ankle. The brick bulk of the Library is to his left and Morrisey's ahead of him, and as he hits the crossroads he sees cars.

Judah stops. He considers how to head west. Hattie thought that west was always a left turn and north was straight ahead, since that's the way the map looked. He had tried to show her that west changed. He had turned the map around, then showed her how the compass north was changeable. "Nonsense," Hattie said. "The needle's broken. Every time you walk ahead you're walking straight ahead."

"What about south?" Judah asked. "Does that mean you have to go backwards?"

"How should I know?" she had countered. "You've never taken me south."

"It wouldn't be backwards."

"Turn right," she said, "and straight ahead you'll find New Hampshire and then Massachusetts and the sea. I know that much; it's east."

So he elects Route 7 where there's traffic. Ian might be in the bar, or driving past, or paying a courtesy call to Lucy Gregory and Elvirah Hayes. He holds out his hand to slow down the cars, and the first car slows for him. He remembers that you make a fist and put your thumb up for thumbing a ride. He wonders, should he hitch? West is New York State, then maybe he'd dip south and go through Pennsylvania, Ohio, Indiana, Illinois. A white car corners on two wheels and speeds off, blatting its horn. He wishes that he had a bicycle, at least.

And now he asks himself why ever he let Ian leave. The boy went off to college, and Judah could have driven there, could have shown up for the football games or plays or weekends Ian mentioned in his first few postcards home. You could fetch him for vacations, Hattie urged. You fetch a dog, said Judah; a son comes home if he wants to and shouldn't be begged. It isn't a question of begging, Hattie said, and Judah agreed that that wasn't the question and let's not discuss it anymore. All right? he asked. All right, she said, but started in at dinner till he laid it down as final that he'd neither fetch or visit unless Ian asked.

The boy was headstrong; he'd not deny that. Judah'd figured to outlast him and that Ian would come running back for his first college summer—or the second when the first went by with only a postcard from Boston and then one from a place called Elk in what the postmark showed was California. Then he instructed Finney not to forward college bills, but simply to pay and not tell. So by the third year Judah'd scarcely known if Ian was in college, or what he studied there, and then his son was twenty-one and on his own in legal terms also and time was not on Judah's side; he'd been outlasted, shelved.

Some months later—four years back, he figures now—Judah got a bottle in the mail. He knew it on the instant for a liquor bottle, since it had the heft and shape. He unwrapped it carelessly, tearing at the thick brown paper that had been torn in the sending already, then tossing the cardboard and paper both into the fire behind him. It flamed. Only when he'd read the bottle's lable, Sherbrook Whiskey, and broken the seal and tasted it right then and there, laughing, not liking it much, telling Finney who'd been there for supper that the family improved with "e," that the bottom of the silo tasted a sight

226

better and was twice as strong—only then, as the carton adhered to itself in its own ash shape behind him did he recognize what he had burned, or think the clumsy fold and printing (in block letters, underlined, with blue-black ink and no return address he'd noticed) had been Ian's hand. He put his own in the fire to find it, but the form collapsed.

So he imagines his son. He tracks him to some nightly revel, where redheaded women are dancing. They are drinking, wearing only sequins and anointed with bath oil or perfumes. He imagines Ian in prison or board meetings or the Blueridge Mountains that he'd sent a card from, once. He imagines him in concert halls, with his mother applauding from the second row. He gives Ian a moustache. Then Ian shaves it and he gives him shoulder-length hair and a beard and shaves it all off finally and has him in a raincoat, army coat, denim work coat, sports coat and then what Sherman Adams got, vicuña, and sporting a cigar. He takes his hand; he takes his money and takes a kidney out of him for transplants and accords it again; he has him dead in Vietnam and Memphis and then, miraculously, as he had done once a quarter of a century before, gives Ian life. They hold conversations. They laugh. Bygones are bygones, and spilt milk is under the bridge. He will not, can he help it, die a wheezing, slack-mouthed fool. He will break his life off when the time comes like a piece of brittle, and the edges will be trim. "Let's neaten up the edge," Hattie says. "Just before we put it back"—and would take her knife and pare through pie or brittle or cake—"Just one more bite." He tracks Ian to his mother's, Maggie's, on the edge of the East River where the sun rises and ignites them and they are drinking coffee on the balcony together, steam rising out of their cups. He gives them matched silk dressing gowns then shoots them from across the river, using his deer rifle and needing just one shot for each. They do not cry or fall, however, and he is glad about that.

A second car avoids him, honking. A mail truck speeds past. Judah has no money and no matches and not enough clothes. His ankle aches; his boots are loose. His estate is settled; it looms behind him and he turns to see the cupola and wonders is that backwards, is it south? He lifts his hands in front of him and opens and closes his fists. The palms are white. He peers at them. With a queer final fluttering, he drops his hands and puts them in his pockets and climbs back up the hill. The elms are black. The gate is too heavy; he skirts it and follows the wall. He clambers across where the rocks seem to dip and, negotiating purchase, jumps and tumbles back inside. He lies there for some time.